# BOLD WATER

# BOLD WATER

DAVIDA McCASLIN

**CUTTING EDGE**

ISBN-13: 978-1-957868-64-6

Published by
Cutting Edge Books
PO Box 8212
Calabasas, CA 91372
www.cuttingedgebooks.com

The term, bold water, does not mean, as one might think, wild white spray against thirty feet of rock and thunder that never ceases. It indicates depth so great that large vessels can sail in—watchfully of course but surely. There is no dashing, no wild pounding, no threat. The water is navigable right up to the shore and from the shore right out to sea.

"Little" Jessy once asked Sinbad, "Could the 'Titanic' have sailed in?"

"I believe she could have," he answered her. "Safely."

Bold Water, the village, was founded by eighteenth century settlers: Paxtons, Heatherings, Maxwells, Greenleafs, and Hardys have been there a hundred and eighty some years. That strong stock persists in many ways, in English customs now grown quaint; in traditional English names: Colin, Celia, Ethelbert, Rosamond; in old idioms: a little boy hails an old man in a boat, "Grandsir!"

They do not all say grandsir—only those back on the coves, wresting a living from thin hay and lobsters and scallops. Now, there are electric refrigerators and an excellent little library. A plane whose tail-light children watch going right through the "Dipper" lands twenty miles away. The Sparkses, who still own the pink granite quarries, have lived with a degree of state for four generations, and Isabel Sparks was the first Bold Water girl to go to college. The Smithpeters family also had the dignity of independent income and of land. Back in 1793, the pioneers gave security to their pastor and his heirs and assigns forever by endowing him with a house, a hundred acres of land, and a hundred pounds a year. Thereafter, from the day of a distant old Thomas, there was always a Smithpeters as pastor—by a zigzagging sort of primogeniture, sometimes a son, sometimes nephew—until Edward broke the sequence. And the land was continuously Smithpeters land, though not always was the house the manse.

From the days of the first pastor onward, persons on board any craft making her way toward Bold Water saw a Smithpeters house—the little one for its hundred years and then Isabel's big one—from a long way out. For they were in turn set high above the village in a great circle of meadow as though the woods had been cut out "with a giant's wife's cookie-cutter," as Edward's salty old grandmother used to put it. That circle Isabel and her architect landscaped formally and handsomely—a subtly designed drive sweeping up through ingeniously cleared woods. And before the windows of each house, there spread a grand semi-circle of mainland, islands, and the wide channel that led to Merchants' Reach, and so to the end of the world. That view never ceased to lead the old lady's wistful but lively imagination to far lands which her captain and other captains and some of their wives had seen. Isabel loved it too. She sailed for her tours abroad from New York on a big Cunarder.

Soon after she married Edward, Isabel swept away the low roomy old house—shipshape and snug in spite of its wavy roof and uneven wide floor boards—and all its furnishings except the study equipment, incongruous in her paneled library, which had belonged to Edward's father. It was moved up two flights where, after her early death, Edward carried on his studies at the walnut desk on which his father had written out his dour theology.

Isabel would have removed the grave-yard too, except that Edward with the old law behind him would not consent. It was a spot too serenely lovely for the strife that fouled it more than once—a little opening on the wooded hill, surrounded by spruce-spires. Within the circle was a neat rectangle of iron fence through whose gate time after time a procession on foot had made its sad and dignified way—up from the house through the almost hidden opening in the trees. On sunny days, one sat as though at the bottom of a great pool of warmth and light, dreaming memories. Grandmother Smithpeters had loved to stop there at noon of a day when she had been picking blueberries on the hill, as the women buried there had picked them before her, she used to reflect. She liked it on foggy days—mysterious and solitary; and, even though the stones barely showed above the snow, she floundered vigorously up there each Christmas to lay a nice branch from a favorite spruce on the most recent grave. On exceptionally clear days she liked to sit on a mossy piece of granite at the entrance to enjoy the sweep of the view.

When she had buried her husband safely, she set over him a stone on which was carved a full-rigged schooner.

Two years later, she set out at seventy-two on a voyage of her own.

"I may never get back," she said to herself, "but I am going to sail out over that water as far as I can go."

She was like a figure-head on a vessel—leaning out ahead, pressing into the wind—but not like the one in the Mariners' Museum, with the woman in the buttoned basque carrying her umbrella and hymnbook.

"I've always been sorry for the master of that ship. He had a wife like Martha and he couldn't get away from her," she thought.

She did not say so, but she left for another reason: she did not like her son Thomas since Martha had married him, nor did she like living in the house that was now theirs.

"They are too righteous," she thought, "but I am sorry for 'em. They don't have any fun. Funny, when Thomas is a minister, that he doesn't know which sins Jesus was down on most. That woman taken in the very act he said to 'Neither do I condemn thee.' "

She often considered telling Thomas what she had thought about him and about that Scripture, but she never did.

3

"Afraid I'll be like 'em if I do. The ones Jesus was hardest on were the righteous that took pride in their righteousness."

She was irritated by the two years of daily life with them—by casual remarks.

Her daughter-in-law was given to saying, "I've lived on the water all my life—born and brought up here, but I don't like it."

She never took the boat that went directly to the mainland port where they went shopping two or three times a year. She waited for low water and boarded the stage that took her round-about to the rackety railroad.

"I always take the cars," she always said.

"And good bold water a half mile away," her mother-in-law sometimes could not forbear retorting. She liked bold water and she liked the term. Her grandfather had named the place.

She and little Edward were congenial. Secretly she longed to take him on the voyage, but since she knew she could not weather the parental disapproval the suggestion would bring, she sailed away watching his little figure on the dock through the late Captain's binoculars.

She never came back. She had never actually lived at sea, but she died there of the good quick "shock" she had always prayed for, and was buried according to nautical tradition and the directions sewed to her corsets. She left the place in trust for Edward, to be his when he should marry, and with cheerful spite she stipulated that his parents should not live with him after his marriage.

# CHAPTER ONE

The first Jessy owned only one book—besides her *Key of Heaven*. It was *Andersen's Fairy Tales,* and her favorite story was "The Dancer in the Red Shoes." Jessy was like Karen and she knew it. Her red shoes could not help dancing either, even if the people at Holy Communion and all the portraits of dead and gone priests looked sternly at her. She, too, danced right around the church; she couldn't stop.

Jessy was like that, and Edward brought her to Bold Water to ask if he might marry her.

They came early on a summer morning when the water was brilliant and the sky deep blue and the air spicy with spruce odor brought over salt water from the islands. They stood on deck at the rail—first port and then starboard side. Jessy was eager and happy. After all, she was a country girl.

"I'd like to dance across that water," she said. "I believe I could if I went fast enough. And I'd go right toward that island and have a costume like the shallow water there—blue and purple—with sparkles on it. And that mustard color on those rocks. What is that mustard color?"

"Rockweed. Low tide." Edward said. His high spirits were gone—so far that they seemed never to have existed. He had come back to the anxiety which even in his incredible interlude he had known was there—suddenly aware of the impossibility.

She turned around.

"Your feet don't dance, do they? Not really. Just on ballroom floors. Not very well there!"

Edward did not laugh as usual at her jibes, nor did he reply. He was looking backward at the storm blowing up. No, his feet did not dance.

When the boat had gone far enough into Bold Water harbor, he pointed out the house in its circle above the village.

"It will be mine some day," and he told her about his grandmother and her last voyage and what bold water is—how they could sail right in at every hour of the day. No mud flats.

"And you can sail right out," Jessy commented. "I like to sail out. I like it all," she went on. "It's nice to look at and nice to feel under you and nice to breathe and nice to smell. There's a lovely smell coming from those trees across the water. I guess the sun likes them and they like the sun. ... Trees are wise, aren't they?"

Still nearer the dock, she said, "I think I see your mother. Is she the one with the umbrella?"

Edward took off his hat and waved it stiffly.

"Yes," he said, "that's mother."

"She wouldn't know how to teach your feet, would she? ... I could have taught you."

Then with that detachment from immediate surroundings, and the shrewdness which had surprised and charmed him, she talked on while the boat was making her slow way to her berth.

"You could learn. I don't care how awkward you are. You've been brought up with those trees. They're marching down the hill. ... And the tops of those others against the sky have a pattern. Sawtooth. You could play it on a fiddle. ... And you've been brought up with waves. They are beating time, and tides beat it all around the world and from the world to the moon and back. You've watched the sun come up out of that water and drop behind those hills. And your body is full of the rhythms of life."

"How do you know so much?"

"Oh, I'm Irish. ... Everything's rhythmic—trees, waves, music, dancing. Life. Love."

"Even my mathematics," he said. But Jessy did not understand that. "You are Irish and you are an artist." She did not understand *that* either. She had never painted anything, she said.

Behind them, the wind was bringing in the storm. It came fast—caught them before they landed.

Mrs. Smithpeters had little to say at that first breakfast. She suggested that her husband give Edward two codfish balls and asked Jessy about cream for coffee, but her inflexible manner and face and back were disapproving. Jessy knew. Edward and his father talked stiffly about weather and the commencement just past and the coming election.

Jessy watched the storm. It was an odd one. The strong south wind seemed to be blowing the whole sky straight north—all the clouds over the heavens moving at once and the downpour slanting northward, too. The sea was green and black. A bell was ringing out in the channel. The sound came in gusts. She ventured a comment on that bell in one of the heavy pauses.

Mrs. Smithpeters made no reply. After a moment, her husband said, "It is a warning. There is a great rock there." His voice was deep and quiet—with solemnity in its vibrations.

Jessy looked at him. His face was different from his voice. It looked as stern as his wife's. Thin narrow faces they had, curiously alike.

Edward smiled across the table. So she knew she was doing just right, and he found her conscientious demureness enchanting. Her round little figure was as erect as his mother's, but it was a springing straightness. She went on with her breakfast. Once she asked another question of Edward's father and listened to his reply without looking at him. She knew now: his voice was like the priest's at the altar—the priest at home. She liked that altar voice.

Suddenly, the storm was done and sun warmed the unfriendly table. By the time breakfast was over, vivid blue clarity had come back, and every drenched leaf and blade and stem was glittering. It was too much for Jessy.

She rose swiftly and smoothly—like a bird—Edward thought, and she stood poised like one at the window.

"Isn't it glorious? It's as beautiful as Killarney and music and heaven!"

She was oblivious of the censorious silence behind her. Even Edward had a distaste for exuberant expression—at least, here he had.

"I think we will all be excused," Mrs. Smithpeters finally said, and added, "Yes, it is sightly."

"Look at that!"

A spray of elderberry crossed one corner of the window. Each of its green-white blossoms in their symmetrical flat group had a crystal drop on it.

"It's like the great stars a king wears on his coat! It's a decoration for the breast of beauty!"

She whirled around.

"Edward! Darling! Look at it!"

Another silence fell—a silence that even Jessy sensed.

In the sitting room, she sat down on the hassock at Edward's feet, and after a glance around jumped up and sat in a straight chair beside him. She listened uncomprehendingly to a chapter from the *Old Testament* but knelt nimbly when the others did so, facing the seats of their chairs. There was not much help in the prayer. Mr. Smithpeters seemed to be praying for people he hated, asking God to rebuke their wickedness and save them before it was too late. But his voice was the altar voice: it spoke to her even though the words meant nothing. So she crossed herself as she rose. Mrs. Smithpeters saw the swift movement.

Back at the window, Jessy watched the waves the wind was sweeping across the meadow grasses, while Mrs. Smithpeters washed up the breakfast dishes. The right girl would have wiped them for her. Not that she wanted that Irish girl in her kitchen.

She would not permit idleness, however, and took the string beans into the dining-room, with a paper for the strings and ends, and a kettle.

"You may help me, if you wish, Jessy."

Jessy obediently set to work.

"You remind me of my Aunt Maggie," she remarked sociably. "She's a good housekeeper, too." I'm not she thought, but did not say. She was learning.

"Where do your people live?" Mrs. Smithpeters sounded like the catechism.

Jessy explained that she hadn't any people.

"Mother died when I was only thirteen. Father skipped out long before that. ... I didn't know where he was." She added casually, "We lived in Ireland, you know. Aunt Maggie's still in County Kerry, I suppose. *I* skipped out from *her.*"

Her hands with a pod in them dropped into her lap. Her eyes were watching the meadow again. There were dots of yellow and orange in the waving stems.

"And how did you come here?"

"Well, I got a chance to dance in London. They said I learned fast. We came to America, and then the troupe broke up. So I was a waitress."

Mrs. Smithpeters' austerity was compelling. Jessy hurried on.

"I managed. The college boys were kind and gave me lots of tips. Some of them had known me when I was dancing, you see."

There was no further conversation over the beans.

At the appointed time Edward sat down in the sitting-room—by the only window, where he watched Jessy moving down the meadow toward the shore. The evening light flushed the stems of birches ranked against dark spruces—flushed them just a little. Her slenderness in a white dress was another young birch at sunset he thought—not rooted. He tried to summon the strength he would need to meet the planned control already in the room. If only he could announce—not request! He hated his submissive timidity before them.

Edward's parents were like those two in "American Gothic." Mrs. Smithpeters looked as rigorous as that spare figure in the apron trimmed with rick-rack braid, and as narrow as those pointed windows. If there were mitigating qualities about her, if she too was pitiable somewhere down under, no one saw. Her husband looked like the man in the clean collarless white shirt, and he was formidable like that pitchfork. He preached a flesh-less gospel, literal in conception and rigid in terms. He hated and feared and fought Roman Catholics and Unitarians and pagans. But he did not know how deeply and purely akin he was to St. Francis and Emerson and even to Buddha; how simply his horny doctrines were a set of symbols for their wisdom, too.

Edward's mother spoke first. She would never consent, she said. What kind of woman would go traipsing to a young man's house? What kind of woman would dance on a stage?

"What kind of clothes did she wear? Tights?"

Edward only said briefly that she wore a ballet costume—the kind that was always worn. The facts were all against Jessy. She had been incredible in that vulgarity.

"The garment of the scarlet woman! … And she couldn't hold even that kind of work."

His father's voice came from the corner chair. He sat in judgment and pronounced sentence by a question.

"Why did the college boys give her money in the restaurant?"

"That is customary."

"I know that, but I know also what the lusts of the flesh are."

Edward did not try to explain how he felt. The old dumbness before his parents had come back as soon as he stepped into the bleak rooms. He had known it would. That was why he had brought Jessy. It had seemed as if they must see her charm, her sweetness—yes, her goodness. But the disapproval of even that first day was too strong. He saw it already. There would be no convincing. If only he could stand his ground!

The discussion went on. In the end, the severity changed direction. Jessy was Catholic. Even if she were not, what kind of wife would she make for a minister?

"Would such a woman be able to learn anything from your mother?"

"I think she would." Edward spoke with sudden vigor. "And mother could learn from her. I have."

Mrs. Smithpeters rose and lighted the lamp and seated herself again beside it. With its light on her face, she turned toward her husband. Then he pronounced the ultimatum. If Edward did not give up this woman, he would receive no further support from home. His father would not help to educate a man with such a wife for the sacred ministry. His education would stop with three years of college.

A decision crystallized in Edward's mind at that moment which circumstances had held in solution a long while.

"I have decided that I do not want to go into the ministry." He stated it flatly. Then, without stopping for reply, he poured it out with more detail than he needed, to say that his interest had turned to mathematics and to philosophy and to the relation between them. He wanted to go far in that field—study in Germany after college—go into academic life as a vocation.

One sharp remark of his father's he caught and attacked. It was not mere figures he wanted to study. It was the higher—the highest mathematics—the mathematics of philosophy that leads into infinity. Some day, he might learn from a new mathematics and a new physics more about eternity and religion than he ever could from theology. He was not shallow-minded or careless! He was not abandoning religion—only seeking it from a new angle—the enigmas of time and space and human existence.

After his eloquence he was trembling as he always did in strife. He hated and dreaded it...his big hands...and his lips.

But he had made his declaration. He held out his right hand and stiffened it to steadiness.

There was no reply. Suddenly the father said, "Let us pray." The three again on their knees by their chairs, he poured out his condemnation. He prayed sternly that his son might be delivered from the great dangers toward which he was drifting: the pride of life; the lust of the eye; atheism. He demanded pity for those without God and without hope in the world, and rebuke for all wickedness.

To Edward, the words were only words echoing from a barren church service—from twenty-one years of such services.

The flow of sentences ceased. There was no Amen. After a pause, Edward looked up. His father was still kneeling, his face raised, its hard planes distorted.

He began to speak again, but this time there was no pulpit sonority—he spoke the words not as though memorized but as his own utterance.

"Out of the depths have I cried unto thee, O Lord!"

From those depths he could not raise himself: and God was so far away that he shouted as one shouts to an unheeding rescuer: "Lord, hear my voice: let thine ears be attentive to the voice of my supplication. If thou, Lord, shouldst mark iniquities, O Lord, who should stand? There is mercy with thee, that thou mayest be feared. ... I wait for the Lord. My soul doth wait, and in his word do I hope. My soul waiteth for the Lord more than they that watch for the morning."

He was praying more quietly. The cry had been heard; and the flash of answer revived patience—the long patience that brings the mystic's transfiguration.

Mrs. Smithpeters rose first. Back in their chairs, the three found nothing to say. The whole matter was on a different level, but no one of them knew how to use that level. For Edward it meant something vaguely new—though not altogether so.

His mother said suddenly, "What will the Sparkses say? They have to know. I wish Isabel's mother was alive."

The evening light was still clear when Edward started down the slope to the shore. But he was afraid the tide was too high to sit with Jessy where he wanted to sit. It was high; between shore and his grandmother's "evening rock" water was wide and deep.

"I am afraid you can't make it," he said regretfully, "and I can't jump it with you in my arms."

And then Jessy was on the rock smiling back at him—all the beauty he had perceived on a tawdry stage made an abundant reality—the pink eastern sky of sunset and the flat silvered blue of water a theatrical back-drop—three-dimensional. Westward, vividness strove in after-glow, but eastward was exaltation. She held out her right hand toward him—its oddly long index finger beckoning.

In the deep, high-backed seat beside him Jessy spoke for the first time.

"Darling, what are we going to do?"

There was no need for reply. Here the problem was solved—difficulties unimportant. The closeness which the eagerness of her body could always achieve brought content.

For her, love was not something to talk about; yet in such moments she was voluble—sometimes gay, sometimes not—her perceptions sharpened and responses quickened. Edward was quiet.

The water close to the rock was black and clear—rockweed standing up straight in the almost high but falling water—its top spreading on the surface in bunches of little amber grapes. It looked like black and old gold brocade. Jessy liked it and the pointed top of a big rock near them with a wreath of green floating around it. She laughed at a prematurely yellow leaf shaped like a duckling with a dot for an eye and a twig for a bill. A gull went by—flying home.

"What has that bird got in his beak? ... it's a fish!"
"Flounder," Edward said.
The flounder's tail was fanning in the flight.
They left soon. Chill had begun to come.

# CHAPTER TWO

The Sparks family usually carried out its plans, just as the workmen in the quarries year after year brought out the pink granite that had built their prestige. That was part of the reason for the outrageous course of action Isabel started at the wedding.

Once when they were children, she said to Edward, "Now if you do everything exactly as I say, you'll get on just fine."

They were going to the fair—a dainty little girl and a gangling but strong boy.

She was both executive and royal, even then. At the children's parties she gave she was always gracious and courteous but inflexible: the games ran off like classes in school, though with increasing grace as the years went on. She could never participate in anything as an equal, but she was not petty in her domination. She simply wanted to be on a throne, a step or two above others, and in competition she wanted to win. In games, she was good because she worked until she could excel, and would not play with those she knew were her equals; recognized defeat she could not bear. She was small and blond, sunny in temperament, pretty in manners; and ruthless in determination—imperious as the young girl Victoria. Only her family connections were not the fabric of international relations, and she was not a princess who would become an empress. She should have had a kingdom or a task or an adventure whose success and welfare depended upon firm and brilliant direction. As it was, she commanded for the sake of commanding.

In school she was always ahead of Edward. He studied hard partly because he was docile but mainly for the love of knowledge and thinking. She simply wanted to be the head and known to be so, though she was not at all conceited about her high abilities. They were companionable children in spite of her aggressiveness, for Edward would not quarrel. If she infringed too much upon his liberties, he went off by himself. He liked solitude—to play his flute—to work on his successive collections—shells, birds' eggs, butterflies; and later to watch mushrooms and lichens and wild berries grow in form and change in color. He learned a little about geology and liked to prowl along the shore with his hammer. His father helped him with that and with the constellations and planets.

It was ironic that Isabel prepared him for Jessy—Isabel and the rigor of his home. She made him see color and form and line and light out of doors and in. He liked to hear her play the piano. She played well—with a singing tone which he learned to prefer to the brisk thumping of the other village girls. Sometimes, remembering, he would whistle under his breath, "On wings of song I'll bear thee." He could whistle in tune.

But his eyes were veiled and his hands muffled. Always there was a beauty and a freedom he could not savor. In a later stage, he tried to tell Isabel about that, but she was carelessly scornful.

"Don't be that way," she said. "Everything is here for everybody except the stupid."

She liked best those brilliant days when the last island was etched with clear sharpness on the horizon—as obvious as an easy melody or a naive lad. But there was nothing to look for, Edward felt. She saw and heard the tones but not the overtones. Some of his books she borrowed but not his favorites. Hers he did not care for.

They were good friends, however; there was fun and gayety to share. In due time the good times drifted into love-making. It came to be understood by both families and guessed by others that they would eventually be married.

Isabel dealt with Jessy through Mr. Atwood, the lawyer who handled the business of the pink granite, and with Edward through her brother—though her father and Eugene—her father especially—thought they had initiated the proceedings.

Jessy was bewildered by the complicated formality. She did not "decide" things any more than a bird would set a date to leave New York for Nicaragua. His inner rhythms start him off. So did hers, and impulses were little more a matter of right or wrong to her than to him. The red shoes told her where to dance.

Mr. Atwood was clever in appraisal. He did not present arguments nor did he make the mistake of offering her money.

Eugene had made that mistake in an advance activity of his own, based on a sophistication of which he was youthfully proud. He offered her the money to let Edward off and hinted that there would be more if he and she could meet again sometime. He said with a smirk that he'd seen her show. He was repulsed with such a fury of scorn and abhorrence that he never forgot it. Eugene was a dictator like Isabel and vindictive besides—but much duller.

The lawyer, however, recognized her kind of balance and tried to upset it—gently and subtly. He did not mention Isabel, and Eugene had not. He realized, he said, how deeply she cared for Edward and how unselfish her love was.

That last meant little to Jessy, but she listened, gray eyes watchful.

He went on to explain what marrying her might mean to Edward. Quietly and delicately he pictured what his life was to be like and what the duties of his wife would be. That did not seem important to Jessy.

Then he said what he had come to say. She must be sure, he hinted carefully, that Edward really wanted to go on with the plan as much as she did. Young men do change sometimes, he pointed out, and he developed the idea. Jessy laughed at that, and Mr. Atwood did too. He departed with some justifiable satisfaction—and with some compunction.

Eugene, who was a stout young man, slightly bald, could, like Isabel, make himself precociously impressive to Edward. This time he happened on a tone which eventually complicated the first Sparks plan into a long-distance plot. He talked seriously, though insincerely, about the sacredness of a promise. He used the words honor and gentleman a number of times. He dwelt with rising voice on the indignity that embittered heartbreak when a girl was jilted, the gossip that followed, the possibility of blighting the girl's life. And for Isabel such an experience was not to be borne. He called attention to her photograph on the bureau in Edward's room where they sat.

Eugene was right, too. Edward recognized that. What he had planned would be abominable for Isabel. But he had not done much planning. In that interlude he had been oblivious of his past and his future, absorbed in the flowing happiness of the present. Only when the boat pulled in at Bold Water did the idea of inevitable continuity overtake him, and with it the feeling of responsibility. But the latter was divided: the responsibility of love and the responsibility of duty. With one there was happiness and honor, with the other only honor—urgent and bitter honor. Around that circle of anxiety, back and forth in that dilemma he went. Conscience had always made a coward of him.

There was one phase of the matter that had not yet been brought to light. Edward, in his confusion, spoke of it to his father as though it were already known.

"You mean," said his father in his Old Testament tone, "you mean that you have to marry her?" For an instant or two Edward's dumbness before him was gone.

"I mean that I want to so much that nothing else in my life at college or in my past here or in my future has meant anything to me for all these months. I mean that knowing her has given me the first free living I have ever had. I mean that she has wisdom that I need. She is as wise as a—a—tree! She—"

"You mean," the voice went on undeflected, "you mean that unless you do so your child will be born out of wedlock?"

"Without a legal ceremony, yes! But not out of holy wedlock!"

"Then it must be. I will marry you myself. It is your duty. To your family. To the woman. You must expiate your sin. You must marry her."

"But I want to! I want to! That is what I came to say to you!"

And he did. Every fiber of him longed to.

But the constant "you musts," the old ordered rectitude, the broken promise to Isabel started him backward into repentance, and as the wedding approached, his feeling was faintly clouded with a sense of sacrifice to duty.

Isabel did not know how craftily conceived her procedure was. Her technique came from that paradoxical depth which is the source of both wisdom and viciousness—hidden like the eight-ninths of the iceberg in the schoolbook diagram. And she did not know it was fear that she fought.

Her father told her in circumlocutions what Edward's father had told him. To his relief, she agreed, in the end, that there was nothing to be done. After all, there was no formally announced engagement.

She waited just long enough. Then on a brisk and brilliant morning—so clear that the world of land and sea was contracted—she drove up the hill. As she made the last turn, she was busy with the antics of her horse, Mischief, who pretended fright at a sheet flapping on the line and took the curve in a sportive mood. But she was able for a second to wave her whip at Mrs. Smithpeters and Jessy. Jessy turned to see who had come, with her hand still on the clothespin and her full skirt blowing in the high wind. The clever right hand on the reins brought Mischief to a dancing stop; he looked over his shoulder with friendly malice, ready for more fun.

Isabel, with as much gayety, called to Edward in the vegetable garden—by the old name of fifteen years before.

"Come and hold him, Neddie! He thinks he's Pegasus!"

And when Edward had snapped the hasp of the hitching post chain on Mischief's bridle, she waited for him to hand her out though the phaeton was low slung with a long broad step. Calling gay greeting and swinging Edward's hand like a little girl, she walked over to Mrs. Smithpeters and Jessy, still silent by the clothes-line. She looked even prettier than usual in a frock of a royal blue that made the golden hair vivid.

"I hear there is exciting news in our little circle! So I had to come up and bring good wishes."

She was able to put them at ease; Isabel's social gift was real. When most of the washing was hung, as she insisted it must be (she did not help, of course), she walked into the house with Mrs. Smithpeters, leaving Edward and Jessy to finish and follow behind.

Mrs. Smithpeters was relieved. Isabel, she supposed, did not know all there was to be known. Perhaps anyway she had misjudged the feelings of Edward and Isabel for each other. It was good to have one source of anxiety removed. The humiliation was bad enough without a quarrel with old friends. Her manner became freer than usual.

Isabel was talkative and interested in Mrs. Smithpeters' ideas about the wedding. Indirectly, she managed to convey the idea that too sudden and too private a wedding would be undesirable. She accepted charmingly the invitation for herself and her brother and father which she had come to obtain.

When Edward came in he was less responsive than his mother. He knew Isabel. Once when memory failed her at the piano in the middle of her performance, she had fooled three hundred people by her graceful collapse over the keyboard, but she had not fooled him and the other boy who supported her faltering exit. That episode was in the back of his mind. So was the time when, after he had defeated her for junior honors, she gave him the costly butterfly book he longed for but could not think of buying. She won senior honors.

Jessy had little to say. She had lived in a secret world ever since Edward had told her. He had simply said, "It's going to be all right." She asked no details about plans. Until later, when she came to realize who Eugene was, Isabel was not important to her; but she watched her, even now. Isabel ignored her, but without marked rudeness.

On the morning of the wedding day the Sparks' surrey brought Isabel and Lyddy—Lyddy bearing a handsome cake. She spent the day—though not with her usual affability—lending a hand where Mrs. Smithpeters needed it. Later "Sinbad," her husband, arrived with the big freezer and a block of ice in the cart, ready for the caterer's job he loved. They had been Isabel's faithful retainers from her babyhood.

Edward's mother did not think much of Isabel's plans for decorating. There were roses in the garden to fill the three vases she had set out. The peach-blow pair would have been fine on the organ, she thought, each with a nice large bunch of the pink roses in it, and the white glass vase with six red roses would do nicely on the dining table. Sinbad carried in all sorts of kitchen containers, too. But Isabel made an airy background with the kitchen containers and the asparagus plumes cut in the vegetable garden. She banked it against and above the narrow fireplace and mantel, the top line of it irregular and lacy against the gray wall. There were two niches on the shelf for the tall peach-blow vases. She would put the roses in them later. It was lovely, they all agreed. Jessy was not there at the moment, though she had been watching Isabel earlier. The question now was where to place the long-stemmed pink peonies—too lavishly long, in Mrs. Smithpeters' opinion. They would not fit into any vase she had. She hated to have them in the old brown crock. Cut about six inches in length, they would fit into any one of several nicer vases.

Just then, Jessy came in, her arms full of green and white.

"Watch me," she said, "and see if you like it . . . hold them for me," she directed Edward.

From his armful she took the long sprays of Queen Anne's lace, one at a time, and thrust their stems down into the water, not too many nor too regularly spaced, and in uneven lengths. Against the fluffy green they were as lovely as snow crystals. In the vases she put the few tall stalks of white larkspur, slender like candles on an altar. She had done it all deftly and quickly, with her little audience absorbed in her motions.

There was a silence when she turned from her work, her face eager like a child's, anxious to please. Mrs. Smithpeters said nothing. All this was being done for Edward's sake. Toward Jessy she had shown no relenting.

Isabel's remark was kind, but that did not mean that she was fundamentally kind nor that she knew why she made it.

"Why, Jessy," she said, "that is perfectly lovely. And you will look lovely against it. Is your wedding dress white?"

It was. Jessy had made it herself before they came, when even Edward felt no misgivings. She told Isabel about it. She ought to have a veil, Isabel said. She thought there must be one at her house. She would send Lyddy to look. And they would put the jar of pink peonies in the hall.

Edward said nothing, and he could see nothing but the radiance Isabel had brought to Jessy's face.

Jessy did not wear a Sparks veil, however. Lyddy saw to that. She found it wrapped carefully in dark blue tissue paper, ready for use but, for once in her life, Lyddy handled a fragile thing roughly. Its filmy length was split by an angry hand.

Jessy looked odd, Mrs. Smithpeters thought. The plain tight-buttoned basque and the full-gathered long skirt had neither puffs, furbelows nor panniers, and her hair was hanging down to her shoulders in ringlets, like a child's. She looked indecent too. Mrs. Smithpeters took occasion to touch her under the pretext of adjusting the basque: she had no corset on and her basque was not lined or boned.

Isabel, with her father and Eugene, arrived. Her manner was irreproachable—just gay enough and just careless enough. She commented on the lovely surprise Edward had given them all, on the prettiness of Jessy; but she did not overdo it. Eugene contributed his kind of aplomb.

One prying question she handled superbly. Mrs. Smithpeters' sister put it. . . . Isabel did not appear to hear, and instantaneously she remarked, "It is time for me to begin."

She seated herself at the organ, looked around like an artist at a concert waiting for silence, and began to play a prelude. When the time came she played a wedding march and then—during the ceremony, very softly and very beautifully, "On Wings of Song." No music had been planned.

Jessy was conscious of no one but Edward and herself standing together, and the cadence of the voice of Edward's father lifting them to the holiness of beauty. In those moments, Edward perceived it for the first time in his muffled life, the past gone like cloud-shadows from a hill.

"And whom God hath joined together let not man put asunder. . . . The grace of our Lord Jesus Christ be with us all evermore. Amen."

Then Edward's father stepped forward and kissed Jessy and called her "my child" and said "God bless you."

Isabel played triumphantly, and there was much gayety because Edward had had no chance to kiss the bride. The others gathered round, and Mrs. Smithpeters slipped into the kitchen where Lyddy was waiting. The little company was happily at ease for the rest of the evening. As someone remarked, all was as merry as a marriage-bell. Isabel had won—so far.

Perhaps that triumph released those few outbroken sentences with a crafty wisdom of action.

She seized the moment when Jessy was alone.

"Jessy, I don't believe you know my brother—my twin brother," she began.

Jessy looked up, steadily, into Eugene's face, and then at Isabel's.

"Yes, I have met him," she replied. "But I did not know he was your brother. I see now that you are alike."

"Why, no! He's taller and dark!"

"Yes, he is." Jessy faced the situation undaunted, but she knew already what she was facing. "You are just alike, all the same." She turned her erect little back upon them.

Then Isabel struck. She spoke over Jessy's shoulder—smiling at someone beyond her.

"If you are married to Edward for fifty years, you will always have me to cope with. I will never give him up. Don't forget it." She said it with a brilliant hardness.

It was Edward that she smiled at. He came across the room. With his arm around Jessy, he said, "Isabel, you've been a brick!"

Jessy knew then she could not tell him. Isabel knew it, too.

To Edward the wedding brought a new heaven and a new earth, but in his exalted images, curiously, he did not include himself. He saw only Jessy—and his father as once, several years earlier, he had seen him. It was the year that the comet, on precise cosmic schedule, was swinging nearer and nearer. After it became visible, the two had watched its waxing light, evening after evening (once until daylight), the boy somehow aware of incredible wheeling distance and the mighty timelessness of time. He had no words, not even boyish expletives.

Presently, his father had said, "It is the music of the spheres."

The old phrase was new and full of revelations to Edward. It gave him the sharp accent of expression, and the first glimpse of a poet and a seer behind the austerity which he had known all his life. He felt again the music of the spheres when his father kissed Jessy, and again the comforting clarity of kinship in the presence of the ineffable—a kinship now tinged with remorse.

# CHAPTER THREE

But those moments did not mean that rigor would be relaxed. He knew that. The morning after the long vigil, his father had relentlessly roused him at seven-thirty to stumble off to a useless morning at high school, not content with the rich and permanent wisdom that had come with the night. The kiss did not mean that the ultimatum about Edward's future would be mitigated. There would be no money to educate him for his "godless" rebellion against orthodoxy, nor even to prepare him—now Jessy's husband—for the ministry.

"We will decide what is to be done after the wedding," his father had said, and Edward and Jessy, still confusedly triumphant, were acquiescent.

So there had been another family conference—Jessy included this time. She had insisted without argument, only saying, "It is for me to come."

His father's first remark had been unexpected.

"This house, by the terms of your grandmother's will, now belongs to you. We must first take the legal steps to carry out her instructions."

Edward was as astonished as though he had never heard of the legacy. The "some day," about which he had told Jessy so short a time before, had come without his knowing it. He had no reply to make.

Indeed, he had no chance. His mother's tight-lipped restraint had broken.

"This house was to be his on his marriage. Yes," she said. "Not legalized adultery! Unchastity cannot be cleansed by formality."

"But marriage is a sacrament," Jessy struck in.

"It made an honest woman of you!" She was stitching a scarlet A on Jessy's frock with a ruthless needle.

Jessy's head was erect and her color high. Mr. Smithpeters had given her one glance, and then he had spoken with abrupt authority.

"Martha," he said, "you are talking like a shrew. What you are saying, moreover, is beside the point. It is the law that the will be executed. A duty. The property is Edward's and must be transferred to him." He looked toward his son.

"Father and Mother ... "

Jessy struck in again, dramatically.

"I don't know what Edward is going to say, but I know what deep down in his heart he wants to say. Let me say it. Father and Mother, the house may be legally Edward's, but we will never live in it as long as you feel as you do about us. The walls would not protect our happiness. The darkness of hate would keep the sun from shining in our windows. The curse of condemnation would blight our baby."

In a slow discussion, the impasse (now curiously between Jessy and her father-in-law) had finally been solved by a monetary sense of fairness. The will would be executed and title transferred; Edward's parents were to live on in the manse since he and Jessy would not. In lieu of rental, it was insisted, and so drawn later in contract, that they were to live rent-free in a little house which was not Edward's but a part of his father's inheritance.

Jessy was charmed with it from the first glimpse as they paused on the hill-crest above. It stood on "the street" which curved around the harbor. The lobster-pound and the steamboat wharf were at one end and the church at the other, with the shops and the postoffice, the town pump, and some of the older houses in between. And it was built close on the water side, firmly based on the rocks, which dropped off so sharply to a cove below that the piazza had been built out on piles. On the top was a square railed area in which no captain could ever have walked however, since it was too tiny.

"My grandmother liked it though," Edward said. "I can remember her telling how she used to sit up there and knit on days when she expected Grandpa's vessel to come in. And when she sighted her around the near point, she'd stand up and wave a big handkerchief in a circle as wide as her whole arm could make it, until she could see somebody else circling a handkerchief on board. She made a game of it for me. She was a dandy! She lived here until her captain inherited the old manse."

Jessy gave him a wicked dig with her elbow.

"*He* got it when he inherited it, didn't he?" and she laughed so infectiously that Edward joined in. "I'll race you down the hill!"

"No, you don't! We're going down in dignity. This is a solemn occasion. Take my arm!"

Down they marched, Jessy circumspectly hanging on his arm—"like a reticule," she said, his long stride and her airy gait thrown hopelessly out of rhythm by the steepness and the rowdy fun of relief.

"And now we will live happily ever after," she concluded dramatically at the door.

"If we don't it won't be our fault!"

His key opened the front door on the street directly into a square room. Jessy walked straight through it and the other one behind, slipped the bolt on the back door, and stepped out on the piazza, Edward following.

"Why, we're right out over the harbor," she said, "with the masts and the winds and the tide, everything moving quietly and strongly. All the meanness is behind us. Everything is as beautiful as the day we came."

She liked the blue cone of mountain beyond the harbor islands, beyond the reach.

"There's a story about blue mountains. Beyond each one a wise man lives. He knows all we want to know. You can't ever see him, but he gives you glimpses if you watch."

She loved to talk in symbols. This one he caught.

"That is just what I should like to do," he responded, almost solemnly, "all my life—with you to help me."

Jessy moved over to stand formally beside him, both still by the seaward window, facing out.

"Now we are married." She held out her hand with the wide ring upon it. "Feel of my ring—how strong it is. And see how it shines."

Holding her firm hand, he looked out steadily to the blue cone. The wise man was not far off just then. She repeated, "Now we are married. This is our great day and the great moment of our day. I promise to remember it always. And you must."

He promised and he kept the vow—and once on a day of blue mist, he told Little Jessy about the wise man on the other side of the mountain—told her to watch for him—seek him.

Back in the street room, Jessy said, "See what your Grandma left for us on her parlor wall."

It was a cross-stitched motto in blue and red and purple, "God Bless Our Home," framed in four walnut sticks which passed each other to make an outward angle in each corner. Jessy took her rosary from her pocket and hung it on one of the little cross-pieces.

She did not allow the poignancy to dwindle: she broke it off to keep it safe. There were practical matters to think of. For one thing, it seemed a pity to have the kitchen looking out to the end of the world and the sitting-room looking in. Why not reverse the plan? "So that when we are quiet we can watch people who are going far—not up and down a narrow street."

Edward objected. "It's never been that way. People never do have their kitchens in front, do they?"

"It isn't the front," Jessy was insisting, just as Isabel knocked on the door, calling gaily, "Your door's ajar! So company must be welcome."

She took friendly sides once the issue was presented. "Why, that is a wonderful idea, Jessy. Everybody ought to do it that way."

Jessy said nothing then nor to Edward when he surrendered. "Well, if both of you are against me, I am overpowered."

"And the carpet in the parlor would fit perfectly in the harbor room," Isabel went on. "One of Edward's great-grandmothers raised the sheep, Jessy, spun the wool, dyed it, and wove that carpet on her loom. Did you know that, Edward? It is really famous in this village, and it is good for a long time to come."

So the plan was adopted and the argument strengthened by the fact that there was an opening to the chimney in each room so that the cooking stove could be in the front room just as well, and the reply to Jessy's question, "Where do we get water?" clinched it. For since the pail must be carried to and from the town pump twenty feet from the door, that room was the place for the kitchen.

Edward apologized for the inconvenience but Jessy scorned his apology.

"At home, I had to climb the hill with two pails to a spring, summer and winter! My regular job!"

"Gracious!" said Isabel delicately. "Well, you won't have to do it always, Edward."

"I'm the man that can!"

When she was gone, Edward swung Jessy off her feet in a surge of happiness, and her arms clung tightly around his neck even though he was holding her up so firmly. She kissed his neck just above his collar.

"I can't reach any other place," she said a little tremulously.

"That is a nice place. . . . Oh, Jessy, here we are! Together! It's going to be all right."

Jessy made an appealing little home. Mrs. Smithpeters had said that it was only right that his parents should furnish Edward's house. So necessities like the two stoves and the bedding had been grimly purchased—with some little joking later by the store-keeper and his cronies about Edward's dowry. Furniture came from the Smithpeters shed attic—discarded from time to time for the heavy dark pieces now in the manse rooms. Jessy liked the "old stuff" better: the clean beauty of the slender spindles, the hard satiny surfaces, the clear color that came with years of use.

There was a study for Edward. It had a dormer where he could read and write, and there was a straight ladder nailed to the wall which led to the lookout.

"So you can escape," Jessy pointed out. "You won't be shut up ever."

He carried up a writing table and chair, and built himself a bookcase by putting up shelves between two solid upright timbers.

"We've got a good house, a solid house," he told Jessy as he worked on it. "It's been here a long time and will be for a long time more."

And he showed her how the uprights were mortised to a crosspiece by stout pegs—a good inch in diameter and sharpened at the end by five broad cuts—thrust through the heavy beam, the angle still true.

"And lots of people have drunk tea out of the blue teapot and rested in the spindle bed," she responded. "Everything is full of old happiness left over and put away for us."

The bedroom was beautiful, she thought, when the spindle bed was first made up high with the snowy Marseilles quilt and pillow shams, ruffled and stiff, and the mirror over the chest of drawers was polished. She liked the "feathers" on the front of those drawers and the toilet crockery with the squatty pitcher, each piece decorated with green landscapes, castle and forest, cottage and stream.

The harbor room gave a surprise on their second inspection. One of the windows on either side of the door was of ordinary size, but the other was larger, both wider and higher.

"That is why I thought we were going to live in the harbor," Jessy commented and explained. "We didn't see the window because we were so busy looking through it. It wasn't built that way first," she added, "and I know who had it made over. I like your Grandmother."

Edward did too, and affection made the old things all the more delightful. On the shelves of the open cupboard Jessy placed a teapot with a big sugar bowl and cream pitcher, a generous platter, and an amber glass caster. Opposite, she hung a picture found in the shed—face to the wall—a full-rigged clipper in color, "outward bound," as the title explained. The round table with its solid spread legs stood in the middle of the room with a red cloth on it where they would have their meals—sunshine at breakfast and quiet lamplight at supper. Beside it, between meals, the Boston rocker faced the big window. The firm fabric of the honest old carpet had become both mellow and bright by careful washing.

# CHAPTER FOUR

sabel had seen to that—she had insisted upon having Sinbad do that job—insisted with such pleasant consideration that Jessy could not refuse. Sinbad also stretched and tacked it expertly on the harbor room floor.

Lyddy had helped too. Several times during the settling she had brought provisions from the Sparks larder and the big Sparks garden. One rainy day, she put a husk doormat down by the street entrance and went away only stopping to turn and bow stiffly at Edward's shouted thanks. She came to give her help—or Sinbad's—in window washing—an offer that Jessy was able to refuse with dignity, for the wavy glass of the big window was already shining. So she said with thanks that the windows were done. Lyddy noticed with disapproval, both of shiftlessness and of untruthfulness, the grimy street windows. All her kind acts were done without kindness to either Jessy or Edward, though with decent mannerliness; for she steadily resented the slight to the Sparkses and the gossip that emphasized it. But she also disapproved of Isabel's procedures; she knew very well the motive of the attentions given to the harbor house. She carried out the practical details of Isabel's many plans doggedly and with misgiving.

Isabel was gay and friendly, in and out of the house as the settling went on—always when Edward was in the house, Jessy noticed she would come with a bunch of sea-lavender from the beach, a bright cushion for the Boston rocker, or a book for the new shelves. Once she brought a picture of Edward photographed at the age of eight, standing beside a round table which was covered with a long fringed cloth. Beside his little hand carefully placed on the table was a neat pile of books and behind them a globe.

She gave it to Jessy, her pretty face made lovelier by genuine gentleness, and laughed at the solemn little figure and its philosophical background.

"But he was not always so serious," she said, "nor so dressed up."

Jessy did not laugh. The sober little face brought sudden tears and resolve. She was not deceived by Isabel's sweetness. At every visit she was watchful even while she expressed gratitude for gifts which, like this one, she could not refuse without rudeness. Rudeness she would not permit herself; it would grieve and annoy Edward and put her in the wrong. She was too shrewd to make that mistake if she could help it.

Edward was not fooled either, but he was not alarmed. Jessy was perhaps not alarmed either, but shaken, more particularly as he grew more grateful for the pleasant things Isabel did.

Once she ventured to say that she wished Isabel would not come so much, that she would not do so much for them. "It worries me," she said with careful vagueness.

"Oh, that's all right," he assured her. "That's just the way Isabel is. She likes to be prominent in things. She'll be on something else soon. And she loves to be a Lady Bountiful."

"Lady Bountiful," Jessy repeated slowly. "Yes, I guess you're right."

The words made her again a bare-footed little gray-eyed girl by an Irish cottage watching the great lady roll by in her carriage—and turning an impudent cartwheel in its wake. Only now the cartwheel was harder to turn.

Once she rebelled, and then only because Edward was not at home. Isabel and Lyddy came together, bringing two pairs of curtains for the harbor room. Lyddy climbed on a chair, efficient hammer and nails in hand, to set the fixtures, Isabel chatting pleasantly amidst the tapping, apparently oblivious of Jessy's face, dark with resentment.

"She knows how I love that window, and she likes it herself! She wouldn't put up curtains in her sea room! She's too smart! She is doing a mean thing and she pretends it is a kind thing!"

She said "Thank you" (and little more) when the stiff whiteness had duly obscured the view, but as soon as the two had gone, she mounted the chair still in position, slid the curtains off into an angular heap on the floor, tumbled down the poles, pried the nails out of the fixtures, and got everything out of sight before Edward came.

She repented for a moment that evening, temporarily, when the "surprise party" came trooping in to pile their gifts on the round table with jolly exclamations of congratulations. Maybe Isabel had really been kind after all, trying to make things nice for the party which no doubt she had planned. Maybe she really thought the curtains made the room prettier. But the window itself in the late clear twilight was refutation. Isabel must have recognized the loveliness of that eastern sky flushed at evening and of water quiet in the sunset lull after a breezy day. And by and by the big moon would come up behind the notched sky-line of Little Horse Island.

Isabel made no comment, but later when Jessy thanked her for her gift—with Edward's hearty echo—the two girls looked steadily at each other for a moment. Isabel was made more determined by opposition, and Jessy was strengthened by the shedding of subterfuge. The situation was advanced but not improved.

It was a lively party. It was fun to see what everyone had brought, as Edward with many flourishes unwrapped the packages; jars of fruit, a scarf for the chest of drawers, a pair of red glass vases. Isabel's, of course, was the handsomest gift. It was a clock—not a new one—she hastened to explain. She thought they needed a certain kind to stand on that carved shelf which had hung on the wall so long. So she had searched until she had found it—an old Seth Thomas with a picture of Independence Hall on its door and pink roses wreathed on its square dial. It was running accurately and, as she was prettily saying so, it struck eight in such a surprising soprano tone and with so rapid a tempo that everybody laughed except Jessy and Isabel.

There was a set of teaspoons from the group, presented with some formality by David Blake. After he handed them to Jessy with a bow, he shook hands with Edward, and the others clapped and called "Speech!" Edward made the speech of his life, sincere and gay—with Jessy tucked under his arm. He mellowed the liveliness into a warmth of friendliness.

Then they sang on the piazza all the songs that are sung in the moonlight—"Juanita," "Seeing Nellie Home," "Sweet and Low," "Stars of the Summer Night," as Edward's tuneless voice took a soaring lead which was not at all sweet and low but supremely happy. Everyone saw everything in the house and, two or three at a time, climbed to the lookout with much squealing on the ladder by the girls. They went down the flight of steps to the beach and watched for the moon—with more squeals when the bright edge appeared.

At that moment, David Blake and his plump wife and Jessy and Edward were standing by the big window, David, surprisingly, with his arm around Edward's shoulder. The chatter of the others was forgotten. David tried to tell Edward and Jessy how much happiness he and Polly wished for them and how they would always be their friends as he had always been Edward's— all very haltingly but movingly spoken—and Polly chimed in "We certainly do," and "We certainly will!"

Up in Edward's study, when the others—even Polly—had gone home, David made his offer practical. He brought up the subject which Edward had been wanting to bring up: how he could support his home and Jessy. Not a great deal of money would be needed, Edward thought. He regarded the house and its furnishings as honorably his. His father would pay the taxes—rightly, David agreed—and taxes on Edward's own property. But clothing and food and other expenses he must provide himself.

"Doctor bills," David pointed out. His daughter was eighteen months old then.

There were not many opportunities for employment. Bold Water men sailed on yachts—none better in the races. They fished and lobstered and scalloped and farmed and kept store. But none of these pursuits—though Edward stoutly maintained that he could do what other Bold Water men could do—could do more than provide a living and that poor and hard. None of them would lead in the direction he wanted to go. He tried to explain to David about his ambition—without much success (David was in the hardware business), but he made it clear that he wanted to be a scholar—perhaps teach in a college—later write books that would discuss important problems—be a writer who had something vital to tell.

"Of course you are not ready to do it yet," David observed. "You don't know enough."

"That's it," Edward agreed. "But I never want to forget the hope. If I can do something that has some slight connection with it or something that gives me a chance to study, I can hold on until I can see ahead further. Professor Burcham encourages me."

"If I understand what you mean by those basic problems of human life," David replied, "any job will have some connection with them. There's lots of human life at sea and in the coves and the fields. I see what you mean, though."

He had practical suggestions, moreover. Very likely there was going to be a new assistant at the post office pretty soon—not very hard work nor long hours—not very philosophical, but it would give him time. Edward had better take the examination at the courthouse—coming in a few days. Better perhaps was a job in the academy six miles away. The fellow who had been teaching arithmetic, algebra, and geometry was going back to college. It would be easy for Edward and keep him thinking about things. Of course, he would have to drive back and forth, but David's horse, Molly, didn't have much to do in the winter and Edward was welcome to her. There was a buggy out at the manse which was not being used; Edward knew his father would lend it to him.

"All sounds good to me! I bet I can make a go of it."

"School begins on August 20," David went, "and I guess there'd be no salary until October. I could fix you up, though, or maybe we could find you a summer job."

That conversation accomplished a good deal in those few minutes—not merely in planning. Edward had not been sure what the Blakes would think. When David left he said, "Good night, Jonathan," as he used to do sometimes, and the slap on Edward's back was heartening. Happiness was in sight. The little house was becoming a home with hope of security and pride. Jessy was inexpressibly dearer, his delight in her enhanced with new color. His earlier anxiety about Isabel apparently had been crossing a bridge to which he did not need to come. And the world stretched before him now full of happiness and pulsing quiet.

Jessy could hear their voices as she waited downstairs—and the slap of water on the rocks. It had been almost a perfect evening. The simple courtesies had been gratefully received after all her years of neglect, and the very primness of provincial sociability brought gracious relief from shoddy frivolities. Edward's happiness and content she had shared with some sense of triumph. But now, the gayety cooled, she was frightened, as she used to be frightened with the children in the fairy book—by an evil power which could bewitch or destroy; and the guardian angel which had always soothed her childhood did not that night hover over the spindle bed.

# CHAPTER FIVE

Jessy's idea about the harbor room was a good one in some ways, but it was not the thing to do in Bold Water—for her to do, that is. There was talk. Even Grandmother Smithpeters would have disapproved of having to go through the kitchen to the parlor, though her friends went right through the parlor to the kitchen—to sit down beside her big window. She spent leisure there just as Jessy did. But she also spent many vigorous hours at the stove and the ironing board and with the mending basket. Perhaps Jessy would have been a better housekeeper if her kitchen had faced out.

Her house plan was different, and the difference called attention to other differences. She was Catholic in a village where only a few shanty Irish families and two or three "Portygees" were Catholic. She went dutifully with Edward to the ugly new church, which was referred to on formal occasions as a "commodious edifice," but its colored windows hurt Jessy's eyes and its service, though (or maybe because) in her own tongue, was meaningless to her. The little wooden Catholic church had a pretty name, "St. Teresa's Star of the Sea," and the red lamp burned brightly in its sanctuary. So on the Sundays when the priest came to Bold Water she went to Mass, confident in the power of its mystery, and then to church with Edward because it was Edward's church and because his father's voice had dedicated her to him. This solution of the religious problem was queer. Single-hearted bigotry would have provoked less criticism, as Edward realized uneasily. Her Irish speech which he found so fascinating was laughed at with provincial condescension, and a short full red skirt which she wore with a white blouse and white stockings was an outrage to matrons like her mother-in-law.

Mrs. Smithpeters, however, entered into no gossip. She protected her pride with an aloofness proper to the pastor's wife but also in humiliating realization of the undercurrent of scandal. She knew that the hasty wedding had not been overlooked.

"And you can't blame her," Polly Blake said to David. "It is hard for both of Edward's parents. He did do wrong."

"That is what makes—or will make it hard for him, I'm afraid." David was soberly anxious. "Not that I condemn him or Jessy. Seems as if there was more to it somehow."

Jessy, however, was happy as the days went toward high summer. She did not know how great was the disapproving interest in her, nor how rapid its growth. And Isabel had, as Edward predicted, become less assiduous in their behalf. The house gave a satisfaction which she had never known before—waif that she was—in its shelter, in the dignity of housewifery. It was fun to seek flowers for the round bouquets which she liked in the red vases; and field daisies and paint brush and feathery grasses to sway in the firkin on the piazza; or a dark spruce branch with bright new tips to put behind the frame of the ship picture. It was fun, too, at first, to have dinner ready when her husband came home from work at the grocery store (which was filling in the time till other plans matured)—a meal which was discussed and admired.

"One thing I do like is good meals," Edward declared loyally, "especially when they are set out with a bouquet in the middle of the table."

But her new dependence gave a sense of security, and security a sense of unchecked leisure, and leisure a zest for beauty—a mood which in Bold Water was sheer indolence. There was much to see in the cove below the house—the red jelly-fish and the kelp and the thin little geysers which clams make at low tide;

what the water did and looked like at rising tide as it crept nearer and nearer the rock on which she perched as long as she could, drawing up her feet—bare to make a run when the time came; how the color would creep into shallow water in the morning light—patches or streaks sometimes purple, sometimes green as St. Patrick's Day: how, on a bright afternoon, lines of light in a nearer pool were so crinkled by ripples that they looked like gilt wire unwound but not straightened out, sometimes in loops around lavender spots, constantly varying in shape and tint. The reflection of seven little trees was crinkled by the ripples, too— birches gathered in an intimate knot like girls telling secrets. She listened—to the gurgling, tinkling, slapping of quiet water, gulls' cries, the straining of oarlocks—and she liked to sniff the salt fishiness of the damp beach.

She lingered so long sometimes that she would run guilt-ily up the steps to look at the clock but, before she got the door opened, sit down on the top step to see the sparkle and the color from there, or to watch a kingfisher in momentary tenseness, poise before his plunge, and then, in triumphant flight to a limb, with a fish in his beak. Then she would perhaps stay a little longer because a tiny moth which looked exactly like two petals of flax was fluttering around the steps. When it alighted, that unmis-takable blue was folded between the little wings, their outside surface hardly more than a dull white—only faintly bluish. Or a fast boat, cutting its wide circle, would show a peacock fantail of foam in the brilliant water. Then the morning really would be gone, and what a wonderful morning it had been!

Once when she had gone down to dig clams, which she had learned to do because Edward liked chowder so well, the whistle at the quarry blew when there were only six clams in her pail. She put them back in the water because they were too few to make their sacrifice necessary and concocted a clamless chowder from the rest of the ingredients, at which Edward laughed hilariously but found appetizing with some new beets which his father had sent and the peaches which had come in someone's jar to the party.

Jessy had made it a pretty little house, but she could not keep it tidy and running smoothly. The bouquets which sometimes took a whole morning to gather and arrange often were standing in their vases a week later dried and dusty—faded petals scattered on shelf or table. Somehow there were always dishes waiting to be washed, and the bed which had been carefully "put to air" often was still airing when it was time to get into it again. So after some weeks of scanty dinners eked out by canned fruit Edward did not laugh so much. He remarked once that she ought to think ahead and watch the clock and, in trying to lighten his serious tone, added that such a pretty clock was not hard to look at. He went ahead to say that canned fruit was for winter—not for now, right in the height of the blueberry season with raspberries coming on. His mother was probably picking enough berries not only for pies and dumplings but for "putting up."

"Just remember that I'm always hungry," he concluded with conscientious humor. "Takes a good deal to fill me up."

Edward's justifiable criticisms were no more than almost any bride may hear, and Jessy herself, had it not been for Isabel's threat, no doubt would have been tart or tearful or gaily careless, and then, repentant, resolved to try harder. But, as it was, his mild words brought back her fright. That man—the lawyer—had asked if she thought she was "fitted to perform the duties of his wife." Perhaps, she thought fearfully, he had the evil eye. Fleeting shadows on her face Edward saw only vaguely and without inquiry.

If his wife had been a Bold Water girl he would not have been critical at all, for there would have been nothing that had to be proved. One of the episodes would have tried any young housekeeper's reputation, however. He had met Polly Blake and Mrs. Caldwell on "the street" as he came home in the late afternoon and at the same time spied Jessy in the lookout. He greeted the ladies and invited them to go home with him. Jessy met them at the door and delightedly ushered them into the kitchen—where naturally they paused a moment—a kitchen in which dinner dishes and kettles stood about, fragments of food adhering. In the "spider" still on the stove was a leftover fried egg, its yellow eye soggily collapsed. Jessy's kitchen plan seemed less than desirable at the moment. Polly was their good friend, but Mrs. Caldwell was Isabel's formidable aunt. Jessy, in the short red skirt and white blouse, was too cordial, Edward noticed. She was bloomingly pretty, however. She had been in swimming, she said, and the water was wonderful, just cold enough. It had made her red cheeks redder and her dark hair darker and curlier. Edward wondered with some concern what she had worn for a bathing-suit. He felt he ought to remonstrate when the ladies had gone, even though Jessy was repentantly clearing up the kitchen.

He had something else on his mind, however: his job. The grocery work would be over in September when the summer boarders went home. They were not many; the populous resorts farther down attracted more—to the big wooden hotels with rocking chairs on long piazzas. But there were enough guests in the two or three big boarding houses to boom the grocery business, for city products as well as local fare were desired. In winter, too much buying of "store" food was considered shiftless. The shop was one man's easy job then.

The civil service examination he had passed with a grade of 97½%, the admiring official had announced, but appointments had not been made. The interview with the principal of the academy had gone well, Edward thought, uncompromising though the procedure was. He was able to pass muster on his intellectual equipment; he had studied the right subjects and received the essential good marks. The principal requested, however, that the college send an official report. He was able to answer truthfully that he did not drink nor "use tobacco in any form," a remark which had brought a slight curve to the straight thin mouth.

"Of course, I scarcely need ask your father's son those questions."

He must, however, present the matter to the directors at the August meeting for ratification. He would see Edward on the sixth.

Not much time had passed, but enough to allow uneasiness, though the word *ratification* encouraged him. The principal had "the say," he thought. That job was, of course, the kind he wanted. He had not found it easy—even possible—to turn from weighing sugar and measuring vinegar to his ambitious though inexpert studies. But the post-office place would be a welcome second choice. The waiting was hard, but hopeful.

Jessy's sewing grew absorbingly important, and she did it well though not very practically. Her basket was newly fitted out with fine needles and fine white thread, crochet cotton and hook, and lengths of nainsook. Her silver thimble she showed Edward with much pride—the nicest present she had ever received—from her godmother when the sisters had added sewing to her scanty studies. She liked to work in the lookout and she liked to stop work to look at the busy harbor and the quiet distance behind it, unaware of a frequent pair of binoculars in a window higher up the hill behind her—binoculars equally shocked at busyness on a Sunday and at weekday idleness. The purest idleness the binoculars did not see, however—on foggy days when she sat there hidden in the soft grayness, watching outlines of masts and of islands appearing and reappearing, as the fog blew along; and listening to the rhythms of unseen water and creaking tackle. There was a bell she listened for early on Sundays. She could hear it only if the wind was right to bring the sound over the bold water.

"There's another church over there," she told Edward, but he did not know what kind it was nor where. "Maybe it is the sound of the church bell at home. Maybe it is always in the air, and sometimes I can catch it. Right now I hear many things."

He did not understand her clearly, but he was wordlessly aware of a ripening loveliness in these summer days, a shy assumption of dignity, a withdrawal. Once he found himself kneeling beside the bed in which she was lying, quiet and mystical, only saying brokenly, "You're so lovely, so lovely."

Without moving except to put a hand on his head, she said gently, "I know what you want to say and nobody must think it is not right to say—Hail, Jessy, full of grace. Blessed art thou..."

# CHAPTER SIX

She was glad she had her crocheting when Polly explained that the Kensington to which they were both invited was a tea party where one took her work. Or should she take one of the little dresses?

"The crocheting," Polly replied with hasty emphasis—too hasty, she realized later.

Jessy was particularly pleased to be invited by kind and comfortable Mrs. Bryant, for not many people had come to see the bride and groom. She did not know about calling etiquette, but she did miss friendliness and jollity, and besides she had the wisdom to realize that Edward must keep his Bold Water friends. Older ladies as well as younger would be at Mrs. Bryant's; she must take care to do just right.

"I'm a married lady now," she thought hopefully.

So she put on her Sunday blue organdy and the white hat she had bought for the journey to Bold Water. The bag with the crocheting in it looked very ladylike dangling from her white lace mitts.

The cheerful chatter heard from the piazza and from the bedroom where they laid their hats died down as she followed Polly into the group that circled the walls of the big room. In that awkward silence, Mrs. Bryant led Jessy around to introduce her to each woman.

Jessy smiled and tried to say something gay and curtseyed to the older ladies. A few of the guests were pleasant and kindly.

Some said stiffly, "Pleased to meet you." Others, including her mother-in-law, said nothing.

Isabel was there—back from a visit, very pretty in her new frock. She had kept her smart hat on, thus preserving her air of being somebody special. Some of the ladies were ill at ease with her, but most of them had an unbeautiful respect for the Sparks money.

Jessy sat down in hot relief between Polly and Mrs. Bryant and drew out the crocheting. The rhythm of the hook was a refuge of steadiness and calm. Gradually conversation got under way again. She answered a few polite questions about how she liked Bold Water and housekeeping and whether she minded the muggy weather. She volunteered a few remarks, but they sounded like interruptions.

They stayed through the long summer afternoon; two or three minutes of it were decisive. Isabel came to sit beside her, gracious and apparently unaware of the sudden focus of attention. She chatted deftly. Jessy was almost grateful—until one apparently innocent remark.

"I saw you coming out of the church last Saturday," Isabel remarked. "I suppose you feel the need of confession, don't you?" she said clearly in a pause in the general talk.

Jessy did not know what she was going to say nor how incisively. "Yes, I do. Don't you?"

Then her natural courtesy and her particular desire to "be a lady" that afternoon hurried her on to say that of course we all have our faults and it is good to acknowledge them, and then rather wildly she made remarks that sounded very "Catholic" in that stiff-necked silence.

Some good soul rescued her with the remark, "What are you crocheting?"

Her reply was a climax of ineptness. She recognized it at once. She wanted to tell Edward at supper, but she could not, and he was too busy revolving his own anxiety to notice her distress.

That day the post-office chance had petered out. The appropriation had been postponed—"maybe a year or so," the postmaster had added cheerfully. "Washington is awful slow."

David Blake told him later, though, at Polly's instigation.

Jessy did not know some things, he said … brought up differently … did it innocently enough. Edward ought to tell her.

"What things?"

"Things about the way ladies do in Bold Water. Like this afternoon. Polly says it was dreadful for Jessy. I guess she didn't tell you."

"No."

"Well, somebody asked her what she was crocheting, and she said right out, 'Some lace for my baby's dress,' and the ladies were terribly shocked. They don't do that way here. They conceal it as long as they can. I guess they don't really. They pretend to. Don't talk about it. Except maybe to one woman—or one woman at a time, I guess. You know how women are. They never speak of it in a group, Polly says. Even though every one of them knows it. Especially under these circumstances."

He paused a moment before he said,

"I guess I ought to know, Edward. There are—special circumstances, aren't they, gossip or no gossip?"

"Yes."

"Well, that's your business and Jessy's, and I guess it isn't just the way the old ladies see it—not nearly so simple—and I'd like to help you get a good start. That's why Polly told me I'd better tell you so that you could tell Jessy. She just doesn't know. I like Jessy," he added suddenly. "She's got good steady eyes. She will grow into a good wife for you with half a chance. There are other ways of judging a wife than by housekeeping—especially to begin with."

It was David's last remarks that moved Edward. Speechless, he put out his hand and shook David's gratefully.

To break that moment of unaccustomed bare emotion, David went on with equally unaccustomed volubility to say that Polly was worried about other things. She didn't think Jessy ought to climb up that ladder or go into the cold water or sit out in the sun so much. She was afraid Jessy was not making the first things first … flannel things … diapers (Polly's baby had had five dozen). Only fine dresses with lace on them.

The advice about taking care of herself was not hard for Edward to give and easy for Jessy to spurn. Polly had told her all that, she said. She thought it was silly. It probably would be bad for a woman who had always worn a tight corset to climb that ladder, and these silly girls that had never done more than paddle on the edge of the beach couldn't very well jump into deep water and swim when they were going to have babies. It relieved her a little to say something—even something inconsequential.

"I'm more like the animals than like these trussed-up women. They don't make such a fuss. I don't want to be so anxious and so careful that I miss all the glory!"

He could not bear to say that the glory was being dimmed. She had borne a good deal since she landed in Bold Water.

So he only said, rather feebly, "Well, just don't talk about it to the ladies—except maybe to Polly when you think she can help you."

She made no comment, but she thought she understood him perfectly. That last sentence was all he wanted to say. The rest was just talk. He was being kind, but he was ashamed of her and so was Polly.

August sixth came the next week. Edward asked for a part of the afternoon off and David drove him over, saying with careful lightness that they'd better see how Molly liked the trip. She did it briskly, and they drew up at the school a minute head of time— a good omen, Edward thought. "That principal is a stickler," he said.

The interview opened abruptly after a stiff greeting and was over as quickly as an execution. Edward broke it off as courtesy collapsed into incredible rudeness; he left the room and walked out to the buggy. David knew without being told that what might have been an episode had become epoch-making.

That afternoon the fog came in. It had lurked outside the harbor for several days—a white fluffy band beyond the farthest island ever visible. There was perfect clarity up to that line—clarity like a polished lamp chimney over a trimmed wick. Every day they had expected the wind to haul around to the east and bring it in, but storms gathered in the west and slewed around indeterminately, so that on each of the mornings clarity was holding and all day the skies were high and blue. Jessy had watched it from the Boston rocker before her one shining window; the lookout did not seem the place to go now. While the sun was still brilliant the fog began moving, and as it moved it grew higher and whiter, coming slowing—a stretch of sparkling water ahead of it—obliterating the islands and most of the shipping, leaving only a few shadowy masts and trees faintly seen.

She envied those trees in a comforting fancifulness—so straight, so free, meeting winds and sometimes rough water with quiet resistance. Some day they would fall, of course, but the stouter trunks would lie a long while, still beautiful, and new little birches would spring up around them. She thought she would like to stand with them in the grayness, but she stayed in her rocker till Edward came in.

He had not mentioned his errand previously, thinking to save her an afternoon of anxious waiting; and he did not now. He could not sit down and tell her factually what the situation was and why, and seek and find the companionship she knew so well how to give. As it was each was banished from the other. The distraught silence into which he was flung she interpreted in her own mood, though it came partly from his instinct to protect, hidden though it was in the distress.

They managed, however, to talk a little as they ate their supper—about the fog—a stray kitten which had settled down after a charitable meal—the chances for a fair day—whatever Jessy, chiefly, could seize for a moment's remark—anything unrelated to the thoughts tightening in her mind. Edward replied when he could. Sometimes her harmless comments were irritating. He could not leave her, however, though he had an impulse to do so. When she suggested that they sit on the piazza steps, he followed her out—irked even then by a wandering worry that she ought to clear the table and wash the dishes.

He sat on the top step with his long legs extended over three others, his back humped, only vaguely aware of Jessy on the second step. It was cooler and not so stifling as the house had seemed, and as the dusk came to thicken the fog there was a curtained isolation.

She moved closer to him—against his thigh, but his arm did not go around her. After a pause, which seemed to her full of effort, he put his inert hand on hers but it created no response. He was only being kind again. But he was not merely being kind. The shame came in waves—turbulent with contradiction.

"We seem sort of enchanted," Jessy said. Her voice had a high thinness like a child's.

As the hours dragged on her warmth against his flesh brought a slow faint solace. The dimness was shelter. Moonrise was only a glow, but it was quieting to watch it as it moved in true direction, dimmed out occasionally. Later, an upper breeze showed the moon riding high. Her clarity widened the space around them; and in that space was an island of intimacy. They were moving back to the sharpest reality he had ever known. The first time they sat side by side, he had had an almost literal sense of magnetic lines from her face to his—arrowed lines like those in a scientific chart. That force had held him. And she had loved him with the exquisiteness of youth and the fervor of maturity. Her natural happiness released his. On the step in the fog it was coming clear again. He turned his head; hers was already turned, waiting. He bent clumsily to lift her, but with a half-turn like flight she was in his arms.

After a little he was aware that she had left him—in a sense—had slipped from his arms and was moving around in the moonlit grayness on the beach. It was a way she had—straying off without putting distance between them. He remembered a day when she had risen and run down the hill on which they were sitting—high in the air as she ran as a fawn is when it races away, and even in his static awkwardness he was with her. The fog was thickening up down at the edge of the water now, twisting around the group of trees. He could almost see movement where he thought she was—a movement parallel to the water's edge. She had taken off her shoes and stockings perhaps and was wading along the edge. Then she went out of sight completely, but the arrowed lines still reached through the mist. They were drawing him into the suspension of a devotee.

A rift of moonlight showed her vaguely, standing among the trees. As she came toward him in the dimness, it was as though a tree with a wreath of fog—freed—was dancing up the beach in long smooth leaps, slender boughs moving in repetitive rhythm. She was bringing back the deliverance, flowing from her body in curves of soundlessness. She was unclothed like a goddess, veiled in modesty and grace.

The clatter of horse-shoes on the stony street and noisy singing flung him from exaltation to appalling realization: she was naked and the street above had an angle view of the beach. He was down the steps at a bound. Jessy, hearing, ran off through the fog. High gay laughter floating behind let him catch her in the group of trees.

"It was fun—fun!" she cried. "I feel so much better about everything!"

"Jessy, how could you? You mustn't do such things!"

"Why not? I just wanted to make something beautiful for you to see. To make you happy! And it did! Didn't it?"

But he could not know then that it had. He could only say, "Where are your clothes? Why did you take them off?"

"Right here! The trees watched them for me while I was swimming, and when I came out I ran up to you with the present I had for you!"

"But suppose someone on the street had seen you?"

Her gayety was undiminished.

"Oh, the fog was thick, man! They'd a thought it was the fairies, sure!"

"*Don't* talk about fairies now! Suppose the moon had come clearer. One glimpse would have been enough." His voice was tense and harsh—like his mother's.

The dancing gayety was gone. She put on her "shift" and her dress, full of shame that Edward turned away as she did so, and she went miserably up the sand beside him, her shoes and stockings in her hand.

Edward could not sit down on the steps again. She followed him into the house, and they sat down there in hazy darkness. The lamp on the table between them would have been unendurable.

He burst out.

"You can't do such things in Bold Water. Nor any place! It is indecent!"

"Oh, no!" Her voice was sudden as when a sharp knife slips from the loaf to the hand that holds it.

"If it is not it seems so! It will be misunderstood."

Sentence was returned for sentence—like a ball over a net.

But she could not retort. Retort means zest, and she had none then.

"It will be misunderstood," he reiterated stupidly. "You don't know."

You don't know! How she had learned to fend off misunderstanding with a shield of firmness and apparent insouciance! Somehow he never remembered the sordid surroundings he had found her in once she had left with him. "You don't know" was a stabbing tribute.

She made a faint reply. She must not seem sulky.

He went on—incoherently seeking words to say it over again. She did not hear much of it lucidly. She had thought she was escaping—for a few moments—getting free of the evil that pursued her. But it was not so. She was being swiftly overtaken while Edward was talking excitedly about Bold Water people and how set they were in their ways.

One sentence he chanced upon came clear to her mind.

"There is such a thing as protective privacy."

The stool was by his chair. She went around and sat down and reached for his hand.

"Why, yes, Edward darling. That is it. You are right. That is what the trouble was tonight and other times. I just wasn't private enough. I guess I am like the birds. They sit up in the top of the trees and tell the world how beautiful love and life are."

"Only you are not a bird." He tried to speak as quietly and as reasonably as she did.

"That's it. You are right. I was thinking only of you, and there might have been another audience that we didn't want. I just need thicker fogs."

There was healing in the hint of a laugh that ended the last sentence—for both of them.

But Edward was pushed into a moment's moralizing.

"Of course, we have to be more careful than other people."

"Why?" Her tone was defensive, but she was speaking responsibly, too.

"Why, Jessy, we did do wrong." He brought it out desperately.

"What is wrong? How are we so different from David and Polly? Just a few words said over them a little sooner—not even by a priest. You were my husband from the first day I saw you and you will be to the end."

Her defense was active fighting now, and in the heat of it she had said the wrong thing. The rationalization he had used himself was unbearable now, though for her it was not rationalizing; and so was the extravagance of her speech.

"Don't you know about the commandments? You are a Catholic! Didn't you feel the need of confession?" He asked what Isabel had asked.

"Of course I did! And I went to confession the day before our wedding while you were at the courthouse. I had to confess before a sacrament, and I was forgiven."

"Then you admit we did wrong." He could not help insisting.

Her burst of indignation died down. Her voice came through the darkness softened by her change of mood.

"There's a book, Edward. I guess you know what it is. I don't remember its name if he ever told me. ... After that confession—I was the last one—the priest talked with me for a while on the church steps. It was a nice day and the sea was blue from up there. He said he hoped we would be happy and that I would be a good wife. And I said I would. And then he told about the book. It was all about hell, he said, and how deep down in hell some of the sinners were. You'd be surprised which ones. But the people who did what we did were in the second circle from the top! He thought God would let them into purgatory and then into paradise. And us too. ... Have you ever read that book, Edward?"

He knew what book it was, he said briefly, but he had never read it. He did not hear her say, "Why don't you, Edward? He said it was a wise man's book."

His insistence could not see how much ground of understanding they had gained, and his own need of confession drove him on.

"It is the law of God and man! Society does not tolerate the breaking of it. There must be a punishment!"

"But there is forgiveness!"

Then he poured out his story.

"I cannot have the position at the academy because of what we did! The principal told me this afternoon! He wondered that I ever asked it. There is gossip everywhere! All the women are talking to each other and telling their husbands and *they* are talking.

It is spreading over the countryside already! Wherever we go people will be looking at us and whispering! ... But he asked my father, he said. He couldn't believe the scandalous talk. My father had to tell the truth! ... If only he had asked me! Had let me face it!"

His hand clenched itself on her strong hand and then dropped it. ... It was no use. She went back to the chair she had left.

His voice had ceased, but its utterance still pounded across the room. She could see his figure, strained upright, facing the window—blank now in the thickening. She could hear his breathing—like a spent runner's. Her hands gripping the arms of her chair, she lifted herself, heavy, to her feet. But she could not move to help him. Her chair, rocking diminishingly behind her, made a sound. He turned. Then he rose, too, but neither could move around the table.

"We seem sort of enchanted," she had said.

# CHAPTER SEVEN

Isabel's plan was not worked out in advance like a series of chess moves. It went on its ugly way through improvisings impelled by obscure drives. She had a daemon of timing which told her what deliberate actions to take and when. She had told her brother, for instance, that Edward was seeking the position at the academy and that she was "afraid for him" because of the scandal that was so incessantly discussed. Eugene saw through her, but he was willing to help. He had gossiped with the right person to get talk started among the teachers—adding that there was probably nothing to it.

With friendly concern, only partly simulated, she found out from Edward what day he was to have his final appointment and managed to be on "the street" and near—not too near—the hardware shop when David pulled Molly up. She merely waved her hand from that distance, but the swift return and the demeanor of the two young men told her even there what she wanted to know. She waited just long enough for the disappointment to get its full effect and not enough for steps to be taken, and then made a suggestion to her father.

He thought he might be able to help, and he would be glad to, he said. He considered, but did not say so then, that Isabel had behaved very well in a difficult situation.

Edward took the job he offered. He was to be bookkeeper at the quarry. He had no specific training for the work, he acknowledged, but he thought he could pick it up—with some instruction—if the books were not too complicated. They were not, Mr.

Sparks said. He himself had kept them as a young man and had grown up with them; he could and would start Edward off. "We both have a head for figures," he said companionably.

Edward accepted with relief. The salary would take care of the household for the present and the near future, and he could probably have it as long as he wanted or needed it. And the connection with the Sparks firm gave him a sort of spurious respectability. The thought was meanness, but he found himself strengthened by it. Going on would be bearable. The tenth day after a nine-days' wonder must come.

It was a good plan for Isabel's purposes, too—a climactic kindness in the series that had already strengthened old sentimental ties. She may not have been shrewd enough to realize her results in detail and in advance, but her daemon knew. Jessy knew, too, though not analytically either. When Edward told her that the livelihood problem was solved, he tried to suggest that all their troubles were over, and she tried to play up to him with gayety, a little too theatrical. The gayety was short-lived: it died at the mention of the Sparks name.

"You can't! You can't! It is dangerous! We will go away! We can make a living by ourselves!"

He was astonished, and his bewildered denial brought stronger protest, her nice sense of impulse thrown off balance.

"She is doing it to separate us! She wants to take you away from me! She will do anything to get you away! She is cruel! And her wicked brother helps her. She ... "

There was much more. Her outburst carried her too far and too long. He could not cope with her just then. He was too weary of anxiety and too relaxed by a little relief to muster the strength; the turbulence of voice and manner, the crude baldness of her accusations repelled him. He made no effort to quiet her or to comfort her.

At length, the turmoil began to diminish; she broke down in weeping. That he could not bear, and he gathered her into his lap and arms in the Boston rocker and held her snugly to his big body and rocked a little—waited … and then began a careful remonstrance.

"You mustn't let yourself get into such a rage, darling. It isn't good for you and it isn't ladylike and there isn't any sense in it."

She could make no reply. It was not good for her, and it was not ladylike, but there was tragic sense in it. She had known that, this long while, but she could not make him know it. She should not have tried. Sobbing brought a sigh—a long deep one.

He took it for the beginning of quiet.

"And do you know what you are talking about? I don't." He went on though there was still no reply. "Isabel had nothing to do with my getting this job. Her father asked me if I'd be interested. He is my father's old friend—has known me ever since I was born. Just wanted to help me get started. I take it very kindly of him; he is giving me a better salary than the last fellow had, just out of friendliness."

He thought that his reasonable voice was steadying her.

"You are acting like a naughty little girl—won't play with another little girl. You've got some silly idea out of a silly novel about her. Real people aren't like that. She has no more than friendly interest in me—the interest of an old playmate."

"She has! She has! She told me so! It doesn't make any difference how long we are married, she will never give you up! She said so."

Edward laughed.

"Why, Jessy, you're crazy! You dreamed it. Or maybe you're all wrought up the way women get sometime. Don't they? I can't believe it is anything else. I've known her all my life. You don't act like my good little Jessy."

And he was not quite the same Edward. That was the great bitterness of it. There was nothing to say. He had laughed off her consuming fear as though it were a momentary alarm. And he was ashamed of her, she thought. He was—in a way—but only in a minor way. That was what she did not know.

If her outcry had aroused any suspicion in him, he did not know it; he was fending off the inevitability of further scandal. Isabel's adroitness continually helped him to do so—not particularly to avert gossip, for she wanted it known in the end that she had dominated. She was careful not to let him see what others saw, but Jessy saw. Though she talked to him about books that Jessy had not read and music she had never heard of and laughed with him about jokes she could not see the point of, it was done only in separated snatches. Always she charmingly turned to include Jessy.

One Saturday she drove up in a two-seated surrey with a pleasant plan to drive out the mill road where the gold and scarlet was already gorgeous overhead. Jessy said she was busy, but Isabel would accept no excuse.

She echoed with too clever kindness a favorite remark of Jessy's, "Why, you don't deserve such a day if you stay home and do housework."

Edward handed Jessy into the easy back seat while Isabel gathered her skirts to mount by the high step in front. As she nimbly did so, she said, "I guess you had better do the driving in town, Edward, today. This horse is skittish."

Her timidity was credible; just outside the village a circus with a few shabby animals and shrilling music was doing business: a country horse might very well shy at such foreign sounds, sights, and smells. Edward could not, of course, refuse, but he was embarrassed as he drove through the length of the town, crowded by usual shopping and unusual entertainment, Isabel vivid and handsome beside him—and Jessy behind. It was not the thing to do, he thought, as he had often thought when she had maneuvered him into a position to her advantage.

But when they were rolling down the mill road, she disarmed him by insisting that he give her the reins and go back with Jessy.

"Stop here," she said, "until that ox-cart turns off. We don't want to follow its pace."

He gave Jessy's hand a squeeze as he sat down beside her to let her know that he wanted to be with her and that Isabel wanted him to be. She squeezed his hand in return but not in agreement. The subject was closed for her. As they went on, she watched the ox with its blue bow and the cart turning slowly and apparently happily down the home road, for there was strong laughter—young man's and young woman's laughter. Beyond them, seen through the wooded lane was a sunny clearing with a dormered house in it and a blue cove beyond. She and Edward could have been happy with that little house and its few acres of shore front and the ox. They could all have worked together to make time for Edward to study—he and she and the ox raking hay. And such a plan could have been carried out if the Sparkses had not caught him.

She was right. The quarry job was Isabel's master stroke. It contrived against Edward with the relief it brought and afterwards with a blight of futility. Bookkeeping, at first, was an interesting problem. He gave sharp attention to the instruction Mr. Sparks was so friendly about; he bought a textbook with which he studied the system used in the office, observing the entries of several years back and following them through. His first daily work was a series of careful exercises, and because of his knack at figures and his training in study, he learned quickly. Mr. Sparks commended him for the smoothness of operation which he so soon established and assured him that he could stay on as long as he wanted to—and rise in the company.

That very assurance, friendly though it was, dismayed him. Stay as long as he wanted to! The phrase opened a dreary vista. Lives become formed by casual events, and temporary arrangements have a way of solidifying. David never had meant to spend his life with hardware, he recalled, but he might have to because he had taken over the store in an emergency. Now he never would get back to engineering school.

The unimaginative and narrow limits of the work were increasingly uncongenial—as mechanical as laying brick and no more promising. Through the window over the high desk, he could see on clear days the blue mountain where Jessy's wise man lived—distant and high and formidable. He could not imagine the wise man keeping books in a quarry and smiled grimly at himself for such literal borrowing of Jessy's fancifulness. Who was it that said something about a wise man picking up shells on a beach? He had to find the beaches—many of them—before he could even begin to look for the shells. On foggy days he could not see the blue cone at all.

The depression that overtook him more and more often made him moody and silent at home. Whether Jessy understood that silence or misunderstood it, the effect upon her was the same. The evil eye that cursed her had cursed him too, and the double curse was forcing them apart—on opposite sides of a chasm. That was all there was to it. She knew what she must do.

Some weeks later, Lyddy, bound on shopping, left Isabel at the harbor house where she would wait while errands were done. There was no waiting. She did not notice the complex expression on Jessy's face nor the fact that she was not invited in. She went no farther than the kitchen, moreover, for Jessy said without apparent emphasis, "We will stay here." She pulled forward a chair for Isabel but remained standing during the few minutes of the interview.

There was no pretext even in Isabel's first remark, for the words of praise were full of retroactive scorn.

"How neat your house is!"

Jessy waited for what she knew was coming—in whatever form it might take.

"I understand you do a very pretty dance in the fog on the beach. My brother has been telling his friends about it. He says, too, that he knew you—very well—before Edward did. Only he did not get caught."

Then your brother is a sneak. And he is a liar. She did not utter the hot retort; her temper cooled and hardened too quickly.

"I suppose you remember what I said to you the night he married you. I repeat it."

Jessy moved toward her and stood so close that Isabel could not rise without scrambling backward from the little figure above her. She maintained her dignity as well as she could sitting.

"You think you are driving me out," Jessy said slowly. "I am the beggar girl and he is the prince. That's it, isn't it? Or you think you can chop off my feet because my red shoes dance to the left—and stop the dancing. You can chop my feet off, but my shoes will still dance on. You don't know about my red shoes. You can't stop them. Neither can I."

The suave and dominating Isabel for once was silenced.

"I am going, though, but not because you want me to."

She turned and went swiftly into the harbor room and came back with a shabby valise.

"See here," she said. She put it on the floor, released its fastenings, and laid it flat and open. "It was all packed with my things before you came."

Again she went in and out of the inner room.

"And here are my cloak and hat and umbrella. Look through the door. The supper is ready for Edward on the table under those napkins. I am going on today's boat, and I was all ready before you came. You are not driving me out. My red shoes are taking me."

She walked to the street door and opened it.

"But I am driving you out of my house. Go now."

And Isabel went. She had won, but the triumph was unacknowledged.

The cloak and hat were still on a chair and the packed valise still open beside the umbrella when Lyddy came back, and the door was open. Jessy was standing with her face against the wall and her arm over her head, like a child. The situation was as clear as a moment of good theater in a play, and the absence of Isabel was a dramatic accent.

Good honorable Lyddy went in and sat down. Breaking up a marriage was going too far.

She said unemotionally, "Have you thought what a dreadful position Mr. Edward will be in? Grieved. Humiliated. Neglected. Who would take care of him?"

Jessy turned around slowly.

"He's not happy any more."

"But you will be making him more wretched. New grief. New anxiety. No home."

Lyddy waited for a reply and, receiving none, went on.

"I think the worst is over. You have probably learned some things to avoid and some to do. You can be careful. You will want to be. A wife likes to adjust herself to her husband's people. Like Ruth in the Bible, you know."

Jessy did not know about Ruth, but Lyddy's good sense appealed to her. She was listening. The strong voice went on.

"You know, when a vessel has been banged around in a storm—stove in, mains'l down, maybe—they don't just let her sink. They patch her up and work her carefully till she makes the home harbor. Then they repair her good, and she sails for many a year. Marriage is like that—lots of times—more times than not, maybe. Your little vessel has thrashed around a good deal, but it is a stout one."

She paused and went on in unaccustomed expression.

"You're a good girl in spite of everything that has happened. And you two need each other. I don't know that I ever saw a young man more in love with a girl. And you are a handsome couple. Well matched, for all he is so big and you so small. You are as strong as he is—like a little bird that can fly as far as the big ones, maybe farther."

Jessy went out to the big window and Lyddy followed, and together they stood looking out into the November dusk. It had been an angry day on which the harbor gave notice of the gray menace outside. Now, the wind and rain drove in hard and waves slapped up high on the rocks and crashed over the reef. The water in the cove was black. The supineness of the falling tide was long gone.

She tried to tell Lyddy. All those were good reasons for staying. Only she never decided which way to take. She just waited; and after a while, found herself going along a road. There was something that started her going—the way music started her dancing this way or that. Maybe it was an inner voice. But what she said was not very clear in voice or in thought, and the only inner voice Lyddy knew was a conscience trained to the performance of duty and the cultivation of virtues known to be such. She had something to learn from Jessy and something to teach her, but it was too late for both.

The boat was coming round the point; she whistled twice for the landing. Jessy turned and as she did so, she put out her hand and grasped Lyddy's. The shadowy room was kindly—with warmth and order and the freshness of recent cleaning—murmuring in the stove and the tick of the pendulum. She stood intent until the clock struck six with its nervous shrillness.

She drew her hand away and walked blindly out of the room into the kitchen. Lyddy paused a moment; then she followed, picked up the hat and cloak and silently helped her put them on. The valise was still open on the floor, and as Lyddy stooped to close it, Jessy knelt beside her and took something out.

"I guess I'll leave him my book," she said. "I wish he'd read about Karen. It's on page twenty-five. ... Good-bye, Lyddy. Thank you."

Then Lyddy let her go. But she stood by the harbor window, watched the boat come in, heard the shouts as she tied up, and the slam of the gangplank; saw a few figures move aboard in the dusk; listened to the scraping of the gangplank as it was drawn up, the shouts of departure, and the pound of the engine. She stayed there until the stern light disappeared around the end of Queen's Island.

She could not decide easily whether to light the lamps for Edward before she left or not, but finally she did—in both rooms—and shut out the rainy dark with the window shades so that there were a few seconds of the bright warmth he had been looking forward to as he came down the blustery street.

"Hello," he called inside the street door of the empty kitchen. "Wait till I get myself wrung out and I'll be right in."

His hand paused with the wet coat above the hook—arrested by the blankness of silence. There was irrational alarm in it.

"Jessy!"

The coat fell from his hand. He made for the stairs and took the steep flight in clumsy leaps—calling up into the darkness. In the bedroom he fumbled for matches, got the chimney off the lamp, lighted the wick. The flaring showed the bed smooth and empty—brought a few seconds of relief. The smoking lamp in one hand and the chimney still in the other he strode into the study. It was as he had left it. ... She wouldn't play the mean trick of hiding. ... He put the lamp back on the bedside table and carefully set the chimney beside it. ... Downstairs he lifted the napkins peaked over the dishes on the table. The supper was there and ready. He took a cover off a pot on the back of the stove; its contents were simmering. The teakettle was full and busy—a strong column angling from its spout. The steam lifted the cover and caught his hand.

The east wind slammed the piazza door wide open and brought a second's relief. ... She was crazy enough to be out in the wind and the rain—even down on the beach, daring the tide to catch her. He ran out and down as far as she could have gone—to the rise where the birches grew. She liked to stand there, each arm around a tree to feel the storm spray till the last minute; to run up and in and shake her wet and salty hair at him like a gay dog. ... He closed the door, carefully, testing the deficient latch. "I ought to fix that," he had said several times. He said it now—aloud.

There was only one cup and one plate on the table! He took the napkins off again. And only one saucer of applesauce. He sat down heavily in the rocker. Everything else was as usual in the room—even nicer than usual. Except that there was a new basket on the table.

An oily sooty odor rushed him up the stairs again. The naked flame was smothering the neat room, black flakes in the air, settling on the counterpane. He fumbled the chimney on; then adjusted the wick with care, sitting down again to do so. The wicked little blaze quieted down, but his hand still moved the round screw slightly. ... Back and forth. ...

It was not a new basket! It was her sewing-basket emptied of the roll of white cloth and the fine lace and the spools and the thimble. ... He did not trouble to open the drawers in the chest nor the door to the wardrobe. When the nervous clock struck seven, he was still there, thumb and finger on the brass fixture.

Downstairs again, he stood looking stupidly at the framed motto. "God Bless Our Home." There was something wrong. His hand went out and straightened it slightly on its nail. Then he backed off—ridiculously like a connoisseur in a gallery—to look at it. ... The rosary was gone.

He took the same boat the next day. The mate had seen her when she came aboard, and when they landed he saw her cross the dock to the big coastwise steamer. But nobody on the big boat remembered her. They had sailed late and the morning landing had been busy.

In the city, there were only a few places to look in and a few persons to speak to—so centered they had been. He could do nothing but walk through the crowds and the lanes—looking at faces and into shadows. Somewhere, like a frightened and bleeding young deer in the forest, she was hidden from any hand—even a kind hand.

Back home in the dusty cubby-hole that was David's office he made a decision. He would not try longer to track her down. David agreed in his compassionate silence. Edward sat in the chair behind the littered desk—his head finally down. Words were choked in his cramped throat.

"She went because she had to.... She'll come back that way.... She can't help coming—no matter what has..."

"Do you know what happened?"

Edward did not lift his head.

"Nothing happened that I know of... to make her..."

"Did you have words?"

"No.... Sometimes little... anxieties between us. But no... break."

Finally the hand on which his head rested pushed it up.

"She had notions sometimes. But nothing between us. I had no idea.... She loves me, David."

Edward never saw page twenty-five. Lyddy had forgotten about the book when she left; and in any case she could not intrude upon him. But it was not necessary that he should see it, for he knew that Jessy was like Karen without knowing who Karen was.

He watched for her till late December. There were sometimes kindly knockings at his door at evening, but he opened to admit few but David and Polly. Isabel never came. Twice at the office he saw her. She smiled just the right smile—concerned but not insistent. He was grateful for that. As winter closed in, the boat came later and only on Wednesdays and Saturdays. He watched her come in, unload, depart—from the dimness at the far end of the dock warehouse—more and more regularly—his vigil increasingly eerie to the two men at work there—a ridiculous legend in the making.

At last, on an evening clear and bright from the winter moon already risen, they saw him leap the gap from dock to deck before they could draw the gangplank, disappear and reappear on the upper deck: and in moments before the mate could roar them into action, watched an unforgettable tableau against the bright white sky; and they saw him carrying her ashore. ...

"She was laughing," one of them remarked later.

"Crying," his friend corrected him.

There were a few days before the final parting...all present...no past...no future. There was no explanation and no need of it.

# CHAPTER EIGHT

He honored her at the cost of an estrangement that could not be hidden. She was buried in his family ground. His mother had threatened him; she would no longer live on the land if what he wanted was done. He used the weapon his grandmother had given him. He drove his parents out, the gossips said; they left the house and eventually the parish.

Father and son met for almost the last time at Lyddy's little village house for the baptism she had arranged. She had taken the baby home the first night; and a little later in the harbor house where Edward still lingered, dazed and helpless, had offered to look out for the baby till he could see ahead. The stony-faced young man stood before the stony-faced minister with the wailing baby in his arms. While the few sentences were said, tears for all of them ran down Lyddy's red face. Afterwards his father managed to say briefly that if Edward could pay "this good woman" for her services he could send him back to college. Equally briefly Edward accepted the plan with gratitude.

The harbor house he could not endure; he moved to the manse and lived as he could with the furnishings there—unaware of an awareness that had provided them, and oblivious to the tasks that little Jessy had added to Lyddy's life. Through the winter and the reluctant spring and the slowly burgeoning summer, he trudged back and forth to the quarry. Each week he took the money to Lyddy and looked uncomprehendingly at the baby.

He said goodbye to them both in September. Little Jessy, her head turned from Lyddy's shoulder, looked at him in an unwinking stare. Then the soberness broke into a smile and twisted lunge toward him. He could not take her into his arms yet, but he stood and kissed the top of her head.

"I think her hair is going to be curly," he said.

When the college work was finally accomplished, Professor Burcham helped him to a teaching position for the coming year. Edward went around to thank him and to say goodbye. That was the end of his college life, for he did not, could not stay for Commencement Week, not even to receive the old President's traditional blessing with the diploma. His father had refused to attend.

He hurried back to Bold Water. There was something he wanted to do—now. Finally, he came upon the spruce he wanted—a sturdy tree only five feet high. It had had a good start in life, for it stood in a small clearing with open sky above, straight and symmetrical. He went back to look at it more than once and sat on a pink boulder like an ottoman in a pretty room with a silvery deer-moss carpet. He continued to like it.

So David helped him dig it with a big ball of earth which they wrapped and tied tightly in a piece of old sail. And he helped move it and the pink boulder.

"That spruce won't know it's been moved," he commented.

Edward did the rest alone. It was good work—digging, carrying water, levering the boulder to the right position: muscular satisfaction in the doing. He found himself saying over and over in his mind lines from a Friday afternoon "piece"—forgotten when he left the school platform:

*Rolled round in earth's diurnal course*
*With rocks and stones and trees.*

There was first comfort in the old words—a fleeting cosmic companionship. Once again—and finally—she had strayed off without altogether putting distance between them. He could feel again the arrowed lines. ...

The next summer, without conscious decision, he opened the harbor house. Remembrance of peace, at least, began to come back. He could read and think in his attic study and in the room with the wide view. College discipline stood by him there. He tried to keep the house in order—not very successfully. Polly helped. Many people were kind now that he could endure kindness. Lyddy and the baby came—Isabel sometimes, quiet and gentle.

During his two years of teaching, she wrote friendly letters—not too many; they brought him home for all the vacations. He was young. Friendliness soothed if it did not heal, and they drifted into the old relationship—never very deep but often comfortable.

In the second summer vacation she manipulated an engagement on an evening of June moonlight on a placid sea, and a September wedding. Richer from a recent inheritance, she had made ambitious plans for both of them. He must resign his position and go on to graduate study—eventually at a foreign university. If he were going into business, she insisted he be willing for her to invest money in his enterprise and her point was kind and reasonable. While he continued his preparation she would build their house on his land. Then they would go to Germany together.

The handsome house won an austere compensation, a sort of respect, though tongues never ceased to be busy on the story. New details gave new material; the six bathrooms, the two pianos—the gold one in the parlor, the damask sent from Ireland, the artful thinning of the western trees to show vistas of sunset water and distant mainland hills, the handsome stable where the horses lived in spacious screened stalls with their names painted on the varnished wall over their heads.

Edward in his two years at the university shared a compensatory dignity and was steadied by a sense of direction in his studies, and finally in the big house by widening affections. His new little son was from the day of his birth the more precious because of his handicap, and Jessy's little girl was twice beloved for her gray eyes and lively dark hair. She was a quiet but happy little girl in the new establishment—devoted to both Lyddy and Isabel. The young spruce was thriving. His fears were quieted though not eradicated.

Isabel's—whatever they were, buried so deeply—should have been, but she could not rest until her triumph was recognized. She began a series of allusions and hints calculated to convey to him gradually what she was determined he must know, but his growing security and his absorption in present and future plans defended him—for a time, at least, from clear realization. She watched for a decisive chance.

It came with Professor Burcham's letter. Edward read it to her with a healthy and enthusiastic pride (for which he apologized). He had received a foreign study fellowship for which he had not even applied. The award had been given him over the claims of a needier man, because the Fellow was looked upon as a representative of American scholarship. Edward Smithpeters was the unanimous choice; there was to be no second choice.

"So I don't even have to be generous and resign in favor of the other chap!"

Isabel's joy made him soar the higher. She had much to say about her increasing faith in him and about the brightness of their future.

"The money is unimportant, of course," she went on. "It is the recognition that will do so much for you. And I am a little proud too that I could help you get that recognition even though your own ability earned it."

He still stood before her with the letter in his hand. She rose from her chair, took the few steps between them. Reaching up and on tiptoe, she kissed the dark cheek—glowing now. His arms closed around her for a moment that warmed them both.

There was much repetitiously happy chatting during the day; it continued in the evening as they sat on the terrace. Edward was not listening too acutely some of the time. Suddenly, her cultivated voice cut into his revery.

"Jessy would have loved you dearly, but she never could have given you other things you needed."

"I can't talk about Jessy, Isabel. Ever."

That tone was wrong—or perhaps right. Isabel dropped the sweet subtlety she could assume so well for arrogance—quiet arrogance.

"You know she couldn't have given you a suitable standing nor a proper home. Nor brought up her own child to be a credit to you. And I knew. That was why I helped her to decide."

"You did what?"

"Helped her decide. Talked to her about the difficulties. I knew it would be for the best. And it was, wasn't it?" She fully expected him to agree.

His voice was terrible like his father's.

"You drove her out!"

Isabel laughed her pretty laugh.

"Oh, no! Nothing so melodramatic. She began to realize. ... "

"You drove her out. And she knew it. And I wouldn't believe her."

He leaped up and pulled her to her feet, his big hands grasping her shoulders. She stood before him—intrepid. He took his hands from her shoulders and held them out before him.

"I could kill you with these. Right here. Quietly. A better man would do it."

"You are weak." She said it coolly and walked unhurried into the house.

That night set a pattern for the rest of his life—in one way. He crashed through a thicket, plunged down a rocky defile to the beach; crazily set out to walk the precipitous and tangled shore— jumping, clawing his way, gasping in a sudden pool; swinging his weight from uncertain handholds, mile after mile, hour after hour.... Isabel was gone from his consciousness. He was the criminal. If only he had listened to Jessy! The irreparable would not have been done. Old trouble would have been blotted out by new happiness. His wise deep action had come with her, and he had not been man enough to recognize and keep and adjust it. He had let himself be made a culprit. His stupidity had ruined Jessy's life—had killed her. She was strong. She need not have died but for the hardships and neglect of those last months. ... His parents could have held up their rigid heads in their sort of pride. And little Jessy would have had her father and mother together to grow up in love. ... Without knowing it he circled back to the house. ... Back to the house.

Physical escape was available. He got off to Germany with little delay. Little Jessy started to school, much pleased with her new slate and pencil box. Isabel maintained as usual a life of beauty and dignity for herself and the children. Perhaps she thought to retain her dominance and develop a time-bought reconciliation. But the separation wrought that night on the terrace ruled the rest of her short life and afterward. ... Edward did not come home when she died.

Financially she was generous. The house was hers, built with her money on his land, the title a joint one by virtue of which it went to him.

Her will provided lifetime resources adequate to support him and the house, and a smaller income for Jessy. Her brother and her son were the principal heirs. The Sparks family won an easy victory on the matter of her burial—the kind she hated.

When his work abroad was done, Edward came back to his property. With the something of his mother that was in him, he regarded his legacy as reparation. The study was pleasant and orderly the day he arrived and the day was clear. The blue cone of mountain seemed close. Work now progressing would refresh him, and he could teach his children, a plan he had found appealing in the German household where he lived. Jessy was an eager little student—but shy, he thought. ... The arrangement was not a success.

The great spreading house with its turrets and piazzas was Isabel's. The state in which its life moved was Isabel's ... carried on by Lyddy now manager and ex-officio executor. She was Isabel's and so was Sinbad. The formal service at table, for instance, was maintained for a silent man who tried not to be silent—and for two little children sitting quietly in high-backed chairs, meeting only once a day as a family, and an effort at the "conversation" that Lyddy was trying to teach little Jessy always had to be carried on. As soon as the children went to bed, their father returned—fled—to his third floor study. As the weeks went on and on, the oppression did not cease.

# CHAPTER NINE

"Little" Jessy had always been an outsider even in Isabel's regime, though not in so decided a way. The size of the house and its dignity of life had set her apart from the other village children, and no city children had come in the constant stream of guests. She was still an outsider. On Sunday, she always, little Eugene sometimes, went with their father to church where they sat quietly in the pew. They did not stay for Sunday-school—sociable Sunday-school—any more. Less and less did they go to other children's houses and other children to theirs—even for parties. It had been different when their father was away; Lyddy saw to things then.

To Louisa—Louisa Blake—the Smithpeters house and the Smithpeters family seemed just like the houses and the people in the novels she was reveling in, when she was eleven and Jessy was nine, and Eugene was five. Mr. Smithpeters was as awesomely real to her as Mr. Rochester. She wanted to play with Jessy, but openings were few since she did not come to school any more. When her papa had come home from Germany he wanted to teach her, her mother explained with anxious reservations.

Once when she rode his route with the fish man, he took her up the hill. Jessy and Eugene were tossing a ball to each other and a spaniel was watching. Louisa seized her opportunity and climbed down from the cart. She organized a four-sided game, having established friendly relations with the dog, Jippy—a game so lively that she let the fish man go without her. But very soon afterwards, Lyddy came out to say that Louisa had better go now.

She gave them each a nice fat cookie though. Louisa scurried down the hill somewhat abashed at being sent home.

The situation was no romance to the older Blakes and other friends of the Sparks and Smithpeters families but a calamity which was becoming a legend. David Blake, because he understood most and could help little, had been increasingly anxious about his old friend for a good ten years now.

"Good God!" he said to Polly, and she had never heard a real expletive from his conscientious mouth before. "The children talk as if he were an ogre, and spiteful gossip makes a graybeard hermit of him. He's only thirty and he's six foot three and weighs 190. He's brilliant and promising. Nice and friendly, usually. Remember that housewarming party?"

"I wish he'd take the children and go somewhere else." Polly's concern was ten years old, too. "Maybe he'd be happier. Why in the world doesn't he?"

"I don't know exactly. Some of his father's obstinacy in him, maybe."

"Maybe strength. More likely weakness," Polly amended his judgment. "Thank God for Lyddy!"

Lyddy had always been the bath-giver, the maker of doll-hats, and the comforter. So the personal changes made by Isabel's death had not been too sharp. Isabel, after the first, simply seemed to have moved from her big "morning-room" with all its pretty things—which the little girl wished she could see more often and longer—to the gold frame over the white marble mantel in the parlor—her father in his high study more remote. Each day she made a little ceremony of saying good-morning to that portrait in its dignity. She always entered the room from the far door, so that she saw the standing figure in the right perspective—imperious and dainty in the fussily elegant evening gown. She remembered admiringly that blond hair—elaborately puffed and curled and braided. Sometimes she led Eugene in.... The house itself was a congenial companion. She was not actively unhappy. She had almost everything she had ever had and what she no longer had she could think about.

And she could always look at the books. The house was full of them—in Isabel's room some pretty ones—up in her father's study where she went to be taught—in the library downstairs. She liked the pictures in *Oliver Twist* and in *Pilgrim's Progress*— Oliver with his bowl asking for more and Christian trudging along with his burden. She was proud when she could read in these books—and satisfied. She would re-read them.

One rainy afternoon, she found a box of children's books in the attic. On top were old arithmetics, geographies, first Latin books; underneath were little girl and boy books, brought together by some whim of household arrangements—the *Arabian Nights, The Greek Heroes, Black Beauty, Uncle Tom's Cabin,* and the Alger books. They were like her books except that some of these the adored Isabel had owned and others had belonged to a little Edward who seemed to have died long ago and was here kept alive. There was satisfaction in prim old stories in which children were treated with the most considerate love and understanding; in which fathers provided good times, the grownups were always wise and good and polite.

At the bottom of the box, the books were harder to get out. One she was reaching for was jammed. She found it necessary to balance herself in the edge with her feet off the floor, and in her effort lost balance and tumbled in, but she got out the obstacle that caused the trouble. It was a faded little book of rough paper and crude illustrations. She sat on the bottom of the box and read here and there. Then she clambered out.

It was *Andersen's Fairy Tales.* On its flyleaf was written in a penmanship not a bit like that in her Spencerian copybook the name "Jessy." At first she wondered about that, but she never asked Lyddy, and after she settled down to read, the book was so much hers that the other Jessy was almost forgotten—so much hers that she stepped into the book to join the disgraced, the imprisoned, the driven out, the bewitched, the disguised. She was a foundling separated by many difficult miles and impassable circumstances from her father the king; she was the little match girl hungry and cold, looking at gay warmth and plenty inaccessible beyond shining windows; she was the ugly duckling in the tragedy of oddity. She was awaiting the liberating prince.

And always there was escape or release or redemption: the disgraced were brought to honor; little Klaus triumphed over big Klaus; the eleven swans became princes again at sundown. It was true in the other books, too. Uncle Tom went to heaven and Black Beauty to a green pasture with a brook in it.

"Always," she instructed Eugene, "the princess is in captivity, or she does not know she is a princess. She must be delivered from the cruel stepmother or the witch. Now you are a prince whose cruel fate is lameness, but you shall be delivered. I will be your fairy godmother."

Eugene's faith was great—so compelling was her earnestness.

# CHAPTER TEN

Decoration Day that year was just the kind of day that Jessy liked—until late afternoon.

Quite early, Uncle Eugene Sparks—the quarry office closed for the day—came spanking up the drive in his smart trap, gay black horses shining in the sun, and Spot, the coach dog, trotting between them. He had come to take Eugene to see the soldiers as they marched up the street with the flags waving and the band playing, on the way to the monument.

Eugene was excitedly ready at the top of the wide flight of shallow steps, proud of his new hat with the blue ribbon on it, Lyddy and Jessy behind him a little way.

"Good-morning," Uncle Gene called to Lyddy, and to Eugene: "Ship ahoy, my hearty! Come aboard!"

Lyddy gave Jessy a little nudge forward. "Help him down," she whispered.

Jessy did, holding his left hand while his right held on the iron railing, the little foot in its heavy-soled shoe bumping awkwardly down. When they stood on the bottom step between the stone lions, she looked up and said politely, "Good morning, Uncle Eugene." Whereupon Eugene raised his new hat, as Sinbad had been teaching him to do, so unexpectedly and so elegantly that they all laughed. So Uncle Eugene's smile was still on his face as he glanced at her.

"Want to come along, Jessy?" he said gruffly.

Jessy glanced at Lyddy and Lyddy nodded. "Get your good hat," she said, and when Jessy came out with the good hat on, she stooped to give it a twitch and to say, "Something nice is going to happen this afternoon, too. Surprise!"

The morning was good enough without the promise of the afternoon. Uncle Gene bought popcorn and a flag for each of them. He found an intersecting street corner where the trap would be first in line to see everything perfectly. Right away the parade began to come—first, the carriages with the minister and other gentlemen in high hats and some soldiers who Uncle Gene said couldn't march because they were wounded in the war—only one leg, maybe.

"We're here to honor them for what they did for our country," he explained, "and the dead, and all who went to fight. ... Here they come—from all over this part of the state."

It was all so spirited that Uncle Gene had to gave a big boy a quarter to control the excited horses' heads; he braced Eugene, standing on the seat beside him, in his strong arm. Jessy, in the "trap" part behind, danced up and down a little, but the more the soldiers went by, the quieter she became. She liked it way down deep in her heart.

"When was it, Uncle Gene?" she inquired suddenly. He told her.

She liked memorizing "1865," resolving never to forget. She liked it as she liked the old stone jug in the store room, marked, "A. McFarland, 1818," glad for Mr. McFarland that the jug was still such a good jug, with his name so clear. Somehow it made her think, too, of Eugene's baby carriage up there—rattan with many curlicues and a round silk and lace parasol.

When the fife and drum corps, the last of the parade, had gone by, all the people fell in behind on foot. Uncle Gene, carrying Eugene, moved toward the monument, too. Jessy tagged along. They stood there a little while. There was more music and praying and some gentleman yelling very loud. One sentence he yelled the loudest Jessy heard:

"The world—will not forget—what they did here."

It made her look up at the gray monument—very high it seemed—a soldier on the top with a caped coat and a funny little round-topped cap and a musket.

"Will it last as long as the pyramids, Uncle Gene?" He did not hear; he was up too high. She hoped it would. And pretty soon they went back toward the trap. Uncle Gene bought a bunch of pink roses made into a flat piece and more flags on the way.

Then they went up the steep street that curved around the "big" cemetery.

"We're here ahead of the crowd," Uncle Gene pointed out.

Jessy was glad he let Eugene carry the roses, "For your mother's grave," he had said. She had some of the flags.

"Wherever you see those little iron markers, that's a soldier. You can stick in the flags, if you like."

She stuck them all in except the one that had been given her first and then she looked out over the harbor—blue and sparkling—all the boats and vessels at anchor for the holiday. She looked for schooners so as to tell Sinbad how many there were—systematically separating the tangle of masts to see which vessels had "two or more" and lingered so long that when Uncle Gene called her, he was starting Eugene toward the drive. She ran down to the Sparks lot, just the same. She wanted to see the pink granite stones and the slate ones for earlier Sparkses—with weeping-willows and verses on them and "Sacred to the Memory." She had wanted to stand for a few minutes by the one that said: "Isabel Sparks, wife of Edward Smithpeters." She had not been there very many times—not the day of the funeral, even.

"I guess they thought I was too little," she reflected.

The pink roses lay on Isabel's grave, and flags waved over two others.

"Sacred to the Memory," she said to herself, twice.

The surprise was a real surprise: Louisa, smooth bangs, black pigtails tied with red bows, blue plaid gingham—Louisa and a little basket of lunch packed by Lyddy.

"You girls go over to the woods and play. Take Jippy." She shoved them benevolently out. Jessy was carrying her flag again.

They had a delightful afternoon, but they did not really play together. When they hurried through the gloomy region where dead spruces reared gaunt out of many inches of springy needles, Jessy was playing Inferno as she ran, at the same time dropping pebbles like Hansel and Gretel. Louisa was racing Jippy and Jippy was following a wild smell over the forest floor. When Jessy talked about the gulls who were enchanted persons and the wise man behind the mountain who could release them, Louisa said, "But how could we play it?" practically enough.

They ate their lunch in Jessy's bosky dell. And Jessy's appetite was not a state of mind. The apples and the ginger cupcakes were good and there was a nice bone for Jippy. She folded up the two little fringed red napkins before they left.

Late in the afternoon they met Sinbad on the main path, and he sat down affably with them on a log. Louisa wanted to see his tattoos.

"My father says you've got 'em all over you," she remarked.

He ignored that suggestion, but he rolled up his sleeves to show the anchor, the star, and the lady in very short skirts almost out of sight at his shoulder.

She inquired about the name Sinbad. Jessy was a little scornful about that. When he lighted his short pipe he looked like a pirate, she thought, on the quarter-deck with a cutlass in his hand. Had he had any adventures, she inquired. He hadn't.

"Did you have a sweetheart in every port?" Louisa demanded.

"I haven't been in every port."

"But you would have had one in every port if you had been?"

"You might say so," Sinbad said with becoming modesty but changed at once to a more seemly subject. "Miss Jessy, your great-grandpa fought pirates and was in a war. Why don't you girls play pirates over in the cove with the cave in it?"

Louisa snapped at that suggestion. "What can we use for gold?"

Shells, she and Sinbad decided, could be sorted out in various denominations and nationalities, and some for pearls and diamonds.

Jessy had heard only one sentence.

"Was my great-grandfather in the 1861 war? It doesn't say so on his stone."

He was in another war, Sinbad said, and his adventures were such exciting ones that he had heard about them when he was a little boy from his grandpa.

"Come on," Jessy said. "We'll put this flag on his grave—all of us."

"We'll play that instead." Louisa's assent was vigorous. "Parade and everything."

"This won't *be* playing," Jessy said.

She insisted on their stopping at the house to wash their hands and smooth their hair. Louisa could not change her dress, so Jessy wouldn't either. But they did put on their hats. She got Lyddy and Eugene to join the procession (Lyddy demurring somewhat; she wanted to work on her afghan) and started it moving from the side port cochere up through the hay, Sinbad at the head playing "When Johnny Comes Marching Home Again" on his mouth organ; Jessy carrying the flag and Louisa next; Lyddy in the rear helping Eugene.

She yearned to ask her father to join when, glancing back, she saw him swinging off for his daily walk. But she could not summon the courage. "Johnny" lasted to the gate. Then Sinbad began mournfully "Tenting on the Campground" and played until the group was gathered at the schooner tombstone. He and

Eugene removed their hats; Jessy thrust the flag into the sod over the gallant captain; Sinbad led the assembly in one verse of "My Country, 'Tis of Thee," and the ceremonies were at an end.

The little girls lingered on in the warm sun. Jessy watched the flag horizontal in the stiff breeze and Louisa went from stone to stone trying to figure out who was what relation to whom and was somewhat disturbed because she could find no wife for the captain. She counted the number of stones with "Rev." on them and read aloud one Scripture text: "I have fought a good fight. I have finished the course. I have kept the faith."

She moved on to the edge of the plot.

"Whose grave is this without any stone?"

Jessy did not know. She went over to look. It was nearer the woods than the older stones, and there was a pretty young spruce at the head with a shapely boulder under it.

"Somebody killed by the Indians, I s'pose." Louisa went imaginative too. "Or an Indian maiden."

"Maybe it is the grave of the little match girl. You know she died and went to heaven. Or maybe it is Karen, the dancer in the red shoes. She died, too."

But Louisa did not know those stories. So they went down the hill, and Jessy ran up to her room, and brought down the book.

They sat down on the bottom step of the *port cochere*, and Jessy began to read.

"The Red Shoes," she announced.

*"There once was a little girl; she was a tiny delicate little thing, but she always had to go about barefoot in summer because she was very poor. In winter she had only a pair of heavy wooden shoes, and her ankles were terribly chafed.*

*"An old mother shoemaker lived in the middle of the village, and she made a pair of little shoes out of some strips of red cloth. They were very clumsy, but they were*

*made with the best intentions, for the little girl was to have them. Her name was Karen.*"

Jessy stopped to explain. These were not the real red shoes. The rich old lady who adopted her bought her some red morocco shoes like the ones the Princess had. They were made for an earl's daughter, but they had not fitted. The old lady could not see very well and had not the least idea they were red, or she would never have allowed Karen to wear them for her confirmation. She did, though.

"*And she thought of nothing else, when the priest laid his hand upon her head and spoke holy words. And the organ pealed solemnly, the children sang with their fresh sweet voices and the old precentor sang too; but Karen thought only of her red shoes.*

"*By afternoon, the old lady had been told on all sides that the shoes were red; and she said it was very naughty and most improper. For the future, whenever Karen went to the church, she was to wear black shoes, even if they were old.*

"*Next Sunday there was Holy Communion, and Karen was to receive it for the first time. She looked at the black shoes and then at the red—looked again at the red, and at last put them on.*"

Reader and listener were too absorbed to hear steps on the drive. All at once, Jessy's father was high above them. They both sprang up.

"I am sorry I startled you." He spoke in the voice Jessy loved and was not afraid of. "You were having a very good time. What are you reading?"

Louisa was surprised to see how pleasant he was—not a bit like Mr. Rochester who never smiled till the end of the book.

She was a bigger girl than he had realized, he remarked.

She said politely, "I guess mostly I've gone to bed when you have to come and see Papa, Mr. Smithpeters. I grow then, too."

"You'll be tall like your Papa, I expect." Absently he took the book and glanced at its dim gold lettering. "Oh, fairy tales," he said. Then he opened to the flyleaf. His dark face turned a strange and terrifying white.

"Where did you get that book?" His voice was terrifying, too.

"It has my name in it!"

"Not yours! Not yours!"

He took it away—up the steps and into the house.

Louisa said, "I guess I'd better be going. I have had a very pleasant time. I hope you will come to see me."

Jessy could say nothing nor respond to the quick hug Louisa gave her. She watched her down the hill before she went in. With one glance at Jessy's face, Lyddy swept her lapful of crocheting to the floor and held out her arms where she sat in her walnut sewing chair. It had been a rocking and cuddling refuge for nine years; it folded up too and made a very good floor boat—till she outgrew it.

There were no tears nor any anger this time, but the more dreadful to Lyddy and to Jessy was this tension of hurt and bewilderment. The dreadfulness increased when Sinbad brought word that Mr. Smithpeters would not come down to dinner.

Lyddy held her tighter and said nothing. Minutes moved slowly in the sunny quiet.

"Why didn't he want me to have it?"

Lyddy thought maybe it belonged to somebody he used to know and he wanted to keep it—"the way you like to keep the plaid waterproof your mother wore when she was a little girl. You know how that is."

Jessy did, indeed, and she thought about that some little time.

"Maybe he feels bad, too," she ventured.

"I guess he does," Lyddy replied. "It's better to be sorry for people than mad at them or afraid of them."

Jessy had never thought of feeling sorry for her father.

"Maybe he is enchanted by a cruel sorcerer. Maybe he is a captive in a dark cave."

"I guess he is." And Lyddy let another silence fall gently and rest in the room before she remarked that she would buy another fairy book.

"But it won't be the same!" The wailing came back into Jessy's voice.

Lyddy knew what to say and do.

"No, it won't be. Things aren't ever the same, but we have to go on and enjoy the new ones. Lots of things get taken away."

Then she rose and slipped Jessy to her feet.

"Let's get supper on the round table by my window for you and Eugene. Do it ourselves, shall we?"

"And you, too!"

"And the round cake in the middle of the round table! And cambric tea!"

"Will you lie down beside me when I go to bed?"

Lyddy did, and lay tense long after Jessy had dropped asleep with a few overdue tears on her cheek. She did not go to her own room till she had made up her mind how to make the pendulum start swinging the other way.

At eight o'clock the next morning, her blue eyes bluer and her red face redder, she did an unprecedented thing; she took the breakfast tray from Sinbad and carried it to the third floor. She knocked his knock, walked in, and set down the tray. Edward stood in the angle of seaward windows bigger even than usual in his maroon dressing-gown, but his face was not formidable to Lyddy, nor his voice. She answered his good-morning, and then she had her say.

"Mr. Edward, I want to talk to you about Jessica. I can't stand by and watch her growing unhappy and queer without saying something."

He did not reply and turned abruptly to the window. She talked to his back more fluently than she could have to his face with the old pain flickering over it—ready with her little speech.

"Mr. Edward, you can do as you like, of course, in your own life, but I am responsible for Jessy. Miss Isabel made me so.

"You know and I know that I was loyal to the Sparkses in the bitter days that are gone, but I tried to be fair to you, too. I tried to help you more than you know. And I am faithful to my duty here. Especially to the children. I know how Jessy ought to be brought up. Miss Isabel was a good mother to her. She started her and she started her right. She made her life as nearly what a little girl's should be as was possible under the circumstances. There was no grudge in Miss Isabel. And Jessy loved her and her ways.

"She ought to go back to school. And Sunday-school! She needs to be with other children and she ought to go to other children's houses, and she ought to have a party. Miss Isabel gave her a birthday party as soon as she was big enough—four years old, four little girls—five years old, five little girls.... Ice cream. Games. Cake. Things have been getting worse and worse these last months. She ought to have a party! Now! We can't wait till December for her birthday. More and more you hide her away—you make me refuse her permissions time after time. We've got to have a change. Something dreadful will happen if we don't."

Her task was suddenly done: his silence was astonishingly broken.

"I know. I know.... You're right.... I don't know why I do it. I hide myself like a frightened dog—craven that I am. And I shut her up with me—for a comfort I never get.... I shut her away from me, too. Something dreadful has already happened—is happening, and I cannot help it! This place both condemns and imprisons me!"

Lyddy's face, turned earnestly up to his, was twisting. She could not bear to stay, and she knew he did not want her to. She walked to the door. Then she turned, like an emotional actress, her hand on the knob.

"Well," she said as placidly as she could, "we will have the ten little girls next month." But her voice shook and so did his when he called before the door closed, "I think she likes my lessons sometimes."

# CHAPTER ELEVEN

After Edward's grandmother had made her will she wished that she had provided for something else. So she penciled a request after the signatures that, especially on dark nights, her lamp should continue to go into her east parlor window—a sharp point of friendliness for her neighbors coming ashore after dark. Martha thought it nonsense, however. So sailors no longer could say, "There's Mrs. Smithpeters."

Jessy as a little girl would have enjoyed putting the lamp in the window—not so much for the aid of a fisherman out on the dark water as for the continuance of her great-grandmother. That was one reason why what happened at the "birthday" party in July was so great a calamity.

The ten little girls came, but they did not come to Jessy's house. Lyddy in her anxiety had, for the first time, talked to Mrs. Blake. "Louisa has told her, anyway," she excused herself. Mrs. Blake's plan seemed a good beginning for the hoped-for new regime: Louisa gave the party and the jolly Blake atmosphere made it a foregone success.

Jessy wore Isabel's amber beads, and her dark hair made into long ringlets over Lyddy's practiced finger was much admired and envied. Her dress was the right blue for her gray eyes and happiness the tonic to make them sparkle. She was the leader in all the games and tore around with abandon. She received a nosegay with a frill around it from Mrs. Blake—a pink rose in the middle. She sat at the head of the table with a little air of dignity which impressed the guests favorably.

It was a beautiful party—"a very pleasant time," all the guests told Mrs. Blake, Louisa and Jessy.

Jessy was the last to leave and Sinbad was waiting for her in the surrey.

As she came down the walk, a strange lady in a phaeton called to her. "Is Ella coming pretty soon?"

Jessy said that Ella had gone, and the lady said, sociably, "I'm Ella's Auntie—visiting at her house. Which little girl are you?"

When she heard "Jessy Smithpeters," she said, "Why, of course, you look exactly like your mother."

Jessy said nothing. It was Eugene, she knew, who looked like his blonde mother. Once an old gentleman had said to her, "You have your father's upper lip," but she had heard little about resemblances. She said nothing, however.

"How old were you when your mother died?"

"I was seven years old."

"No, I don't mean Isabel. I mean your own mother."

Jessy did not speak nor move.

The lively lady called to Mrs. Blake in the doorway, "When were Edward and Isabel married?"

Mrs. Blake did not hear.

"I guess she died when you were born. You were named for her, of course. ... Where is she buried?"

And Jessy replied, "In the cemetery up by our house."

Lyddy had not come back from the Dorcas Society when Jessy went into the house, followed by the worried Sinbad. She had not acted like a little girl coming home from a party at all, he said later. It was part of the dreadfulness of her trouble that she felt glad that Lyddy was not there. She did not tell her then— or ever—what happened at the party. What she had to do did not concern Lyddy nor the big house nor anything she had ever known about—only a book, a grave with a spruce on it, and her father. She went directly upstairs—the two flights—her hat still on and the nosegay in her hand. She knocked and then opened her father's door.

Without preface, she said, "The other Jessy was my mother, wasn't she?"

She saw a face she had not seen before, and he saw once more gray eyes and dark hair under a wide hat, and anguish in a pointed face.

"Yes, my darling, she was," and he held out his arms.

She came swiftly around the big desk that stood between them. For a little while she stood beside his chair, his arm around her. Then somehow her hat was off and she was in his lap, the nosegay crushed between them, his arms around her, his head bent over her. She felt him kiss her curls. She and her mother belonged here. There was solace in this strange experience. Solace was much needed.

The calamity was as complete as the devastation of a hurricane that flattens forests, sweeps away bridges and scatters the contents of a beloved home over miles of ruin—leaving maybe only a few prisms to be picked up later. Jessy did not have even the prisms, and all her shelters were demolished. Her nourished memories were destroyed and those she should have had had never existed. The clear amber beads were meaningless, and the plaid waterproof—which was not at all like Isabel's pretty clothes—belonged to nobody.

On Decoration Day, Louisa had said, "You live just like a girl in a book." And Jessy was pleased. If Isabel had been unkind to her there would have been one miserable place to hide, but she had not been a "cruel stepmother." This was no story-book. It was a dreadful and confusing reality that she could not bear. The fairy book had lost its flying power.

The portrait was no longer a gracious presence. It was dimmed out by an enchantment that would never be lifted; and her mother—her mother—was under a spell of invisibility—a formless person lost in time—no stone on her grave like the captain's or Isabel's—no dress hanging in a closet—no bottle on a dressing table—no picture on somebody's wall. Her mother who had died only ten years before was obliterated. "A. McFarland" on the jug meant more to her.

"I don't know her," she whispered. "I can't find her the way I could find—Mama in the parlor."

So Edward stumblingly told how pretty she was and gay. And good. She was never afraid. How she loved music and pretty colors and good times and—dancing. How alive she was. Jessy must never forget her.

She listened hungrily and quietly till that last sentence. Then she got down from his lap.

"You made me forget her." She stood, and looked, and spoke accusingly. "Why did you? Why hasn't she any stone? Why weren't there any flowers for her on Decoration Day?"

He did not reply.

Her little-girl indignation grew brave. She fought for her mother.

"They shouldn't have pushed her 'way off. She had a right to be remembered. Why did they push her out of sight?"

"I can't tell you that."

The very wrath of the child was like hers. He could not continue or repeat this scene—Little Jessy so much like the other Jessy in his arms.

"I can't tell you that." He repeated it. His voice was strained and distant.

But Jessy's insistence like bleeding little fists pounded upon it. Where were her things? Where was her picture? She had a right to be remembered. Dread pried into what her father could not tell and was multiplied.

He sent for her soon—a Saturday morning at nine o'clock, the time she came for lessons on other days. She stood on the other side of the desk as he spoke, kindly but distantly—about her new dress, the brilliant blue sky, the fresh wind.

Jessy obediently looked out at sky and water.

"I have something for you," he said. He reached across the table and handed her a box. "These are things of your mother's. You can have them all—to keep. Except the ring. Please send that back to me."

She knew that the conversation was closed. She thanked him politely and closed the door with care, but he opened it and called her back. He was holding out the little gray book.

"Wouldn't you like to have the fairy tales, too?" he said.

Once in her room, she stood by her table with the box unopened—hope and apprehension welling up together. Pretty soon she was going to touch things her mother had touched. Would she find her? And keep her? These things were hers to keep. He had said so. Maybe she could keep her mother.

She opened the box, quickly laid the small wrapped packages on the table and felt of each one anxiously. She hoped there was a picture. She waited again and then unfolded the silk handkerchief which made one wrapping; there lay on it nine coin spoons with spidery initials interwoven on the handles. She could not make out the initials but there was no J. They were somebody else's spoons—some other one lost.

The ring was in a gray velvet box held between two firm little cushions—a gold ring with a garnet framed in pearls. She looked at it long. Then she took it out and put it on her biggest finger with a surge of sweetness—as though her mother had said, "Yes, you can put it on. Be careful not to let it fall off."

But that she could not keep. She must take it back—send it back. How she loved it—and the box, too.

There were a pair of fur-trimmed carriage boots which were not very much too big for young Jessy's little girl feet, and a fan, a thimble, a black book—a leather book like a Bible with gold edges—but it was not a Bible. She could see that it was about God and Jesus and Mary, but it was not like any church book or quarterly she had ever seen. There was nothing she could wear like the amber beads. There was no picture.

"I guess I don't know her very well yet," she thought, and then tears came and sobs—so desperate an outcry that Lyddy hurried in. In one glance she saw the objects on the table and the prostrate little figure on the bed. She comforted her as best she could and the tumult subsided, but there was no healing talk.

Nothing ever was said about the spoons and the ring and the other things, but Jessy hung over them with daily devotion lest her mother slip even out of memory again. She worried about the lack of a stone on her mother's grave, and before another Decoration Day got up courage to tell her father so. He could only say, "You are her only memorial. You are Jessy. Spell it with a Y."

Lyddy had feared she was defeated when Edward told her briefly what had happened; she knew she was when she realized that Jessy was not going to speak to her about it. She was shut out from the climactic experience of the child's life. Her kind of comforting was no longer adequate. She herself belonged to Isabel, and the change that had dethroned Isabel had pushed her away—not a long distance but an impassable one. She had helped Jessy along to that tenth summer, but she knew that their relations would not be the same in the sixteenth—even to some degree different in the twelfth.

Not outwardly different, of course, ever. Lyddy boiled with zeal to make life pleasantly normal for the children, and Edward tried to cooperate as when, at Lyddy's suggestion, they bought a pony and a cart. Jessy named the pony Merrylegs, for he was a jolly little beast. She and Eugene took turns in driving him around the place. She obligingly drove on errands which Sinbad concocted for her. Occasionally but not as often as Lyddy wished, she took Louisa to ride and let Louisa drive. But she seldom came home late as Lyddy hoped she would, and once, when she let Louisa and Ella have Merrylegs and the cart from Friday till Monday, she told Lyddy she guessed she wouldn't go on the Saturday picnic they had planned.

"She looks exactly like her mother," Lyddy said to Mrs. Blake, "but she is taking her father's way in trouble. She gets quieter and less sociable all the time just like him. And I'm afraid she is unhappier down underneath than she knows. ... And she'll be a woman before long." Lyddy wept as she said it.

There was no party the next summer, for on a June evening that year little Eugene died—his "blue-baby" struggle with his other handicaps brought to an end.

Early on the second morning, Jessy woke with an urgent plan in mind. She had something to do and something to take to Eugene. A little time and sleep had calmed the terror of the death night; she was not afraid now. Nor distraught.

By the big staircase window on the landing she paused a moment to look out just as usual through the one clear pane in its pattern of color. A seal was heavily looping in and out of the water, reappearing each time at a surprising distance away. How Eugene would have exulted in its score. "Cat in the window counts ten. Cat and kittens twenty-five. Seal—one hundred." And how he would have liked the dozens of green pendants on the pear-tree coming up toward the window. There were more pears than his counting could count.

Downstairs she let herself out of a side-door. The air was fresh and clear, though yesterday's fog bank had moved nearer. Everything was quiet—only birds' morning songs and the sound of oars—a rhythmic plumping on water. Merrylegs was pleased to see her over the bars of his pasture behind the stable. He didn't know about Eugene; that was why she wanted to see him just now, and all the places. The old shell of the locust was still on the gate. Sinbad had seen it first and called them to see: the locust just emerging from it, tugging to break one at a time the power-ful filaments that held him. His wings came out like fans and slowly opened in iridescence. The children watched till supper and when they ran back afterwards, the locust was still straining forward. Next morning, he had gone on his wings.

Back in the house, she paused in the music room door for a moment. Eugene's violin had been in its case for some weeks now, but his exercise book still stood on the piano rack before the stool where he sat to practice. He had stood beside it the day he had played "The Blue Bells of Scotland" for her surprise.

Across the hall, in the parlor, the lady of the portrait was no longer a queen in a yellow dress, she was a little boy's mother. Eugene would be proud when he learned who that most beautiful angel was. That was why she had wanted to go to the library with something of his mother's for him. Sinbad was there but when she came he slipped out, only stopping for a moment to lay his thick hand on her head.

Eugene lay where the morning sun flushed his face a little. It made him look a little younger than six—like the picture of him in his Fauntleroy suit. He hadn't liked that suit until they played a story in which he was a king's son who wore velvet and had millions of diamonds. He had on his good Sunday suit now. She tucked the pitch-pipe into his pocket. She could remember how beautiful Isabel was when she sang in the choir—leading them all with her high clear voice.

She sat beside him quietly and watched the far-off fog bank and thought about Heaven and Eugene. And the music there. And Eugene's mother and her mother and the captain and all the ministers and the soldiers.

> "A noble army, men and boys
> The matron and the maid"

they had sung at Sunday School, and she sang it now, very softly,

"Around the Saviour's throne rejoice
In robes of white arrayed.
They climbed the steep ascent to Heaven
In peril, toil, and pain. ... "

She stopped to think about that. Did Isabel have peril, toil, and pain? The other Jessy did, she was nearly sure.

Then she heard the bell—the bell across the bold water. It was Sunday at six in the morning. She listened acutely as long as it rang. ...

Again the old graveyard was the subject of controversy. At nine o'clock, Eugene Sparks walked into the house and into Edward's study unannounced.

"It's not too late to change yet."

Edward, behind his desk, raised his head from the prop of palm beneath his forehead. He looked dully at Eugene.

"I say it's not too late to change yet. I don't want my nephew buried in that god-forsaken place."

Edward only said briefly that the arrangements were all made.

"But I won't have it! He's my nephew—my twin-sister's son—my namesake. I won't have it!"

Edward got up and stood behind the desk.

Eugene broke out again.

"I want him buried by his mother! He's her son! A mother has her rights!"

Edward's voice swept in.

"He is my son—my father's grandson—my grandfather's great-grandson. He will lie with those whose name he bears. His mother had more than her rights—always!"

"I won't have him up there by that damned woman! She smutted up. ... "

Edward walked around the desk and thrust his face close to Eugene's, his head lowered. His years with the Sparks family had focused into fury. The voices rose—Eugene's shouting. Edward's fought hard and long. Sparks pride had defeated him before. This time, he stood his devastated ground and won.

He had gone back to his chair when Eugene left his threat in the air and slammed the door behind him.

"I have it in my power to make you and that bastard girl very uncomfortable. And I'll do it if it takes me ... "

Jessy in the room below did not overhear the words—only the voices—the strife and disgrace in them intensified because unclear.

Fog came in with cold and surrounded the private service at the grave. Afterwards a little pointed stone was set up.

To her father the place had become intolerable and he could give no comfort to Jessy because he had found none. He took a college position and Jessy went back to school.

There was a surprising satisfaction and solace in his teaching. He was eager—at ease in the classroom. Eager students crowded about him. In time he enjoyed the fellowship at the Faculty Club and played tennis and sailed and sometimes dined out. Perhaps on that campus he might have found his fruition. But he could not forget the wise man behind the mountain, and perhaps he was stubborn in his own plan of justification. In vacations he was impelled to circle back to the house, and having arrived there he was always caught in the poisonous web of the past and his flow of thought impeded in that high study, though it had many windows for a high solitude. ... Finished chapters of his book, however, piled up—slowly.

# CHAPTER TWELVE

Lyddy's anxiety never slackened—especially after the "birthday" party. Her zeal never flagged either, though her notion of her duty changed. Her loyalty was never blind.

"Miss Isabel started her and she started her right," she had said hotly to Edward, but she had partially repudiated that slogan. What occurred after the wedding she called a crime—with no compromise.

"But she started her right in manners," she insisted to herself. "And I must see that she knows how to do. She'll live in this big house and go places. She must know how to do."

That was why she advocated boarding-school—the one that Isabel had attended. But Edward had flatly closed that subject; his usual consideration cut off in command:

"I won't have it."

So Jessy went to the academy as a day scholar; Sinbad drove her back and forth. It was a bad plan: She had no social life there and lost touch with the Bold Water children as they all grew up. But she went to an occasional taffy-pull on a Friday night or a rare winter party; Lyddy saw to that and to the "entertaining" she considered necessary—mostly in the summer. Her clothes were bought and made where Isabel's had been with the good advice that Isabel had always been able to pay for—with equally charming and appropriate results.

"But it isn't enough," Lyddy worriedly told Mrs. Blake at intervals. "I wish she had something her mother had. ... It is just as I've told you before. That trouble when she was ten made a mark on her. And she'd take it as her father did if I'd let her. She seems to have a place to live by herself anyway."

"It will be better maybe when she goes to college," Mrs. Blake often replied. "Maybe she needs to get away from home."

When that time came, however, Lyddy was not sure.

During her two college years, Jessy wrote home about the girls; the classes and the teachers; games she had been to; class parties and chafing-dish spreads at midnight; excursions into the city to see pictures and plays and hear music. Lyddy read and re-read those letters and in her eager though stiff replies would inquire, "How did Helen get on in the algebra examination after you helped her?" or "Is Sara's sprained ankle better? I guess she won't be playing basket-ball in this next tournament, will she? Who will take her place?" She suggested that Jessy bring one of her roommates home for a holiday visit at Christmas, and before Easter she repeated the suggestion. Jessy replied that maybe she would ask Emily in the summer when they could be outdoors more. Lyddy read and re-read; her anxiety was abated sometimes, but it always came back. There was something about those letters she could not put her finger on.

They were good letters, however. Jessy enjoyed writing them: she liked the angle they gave her on the pretty rolling grounds, the elms, and the willows around the lake; and the organ and stained glass in the chapel; the whirl of girls on bicycles—a few daring ones in bloomers; the five-pointed net of motion the basket-ball made from girl to girl; the lofty library, all of whose alcoves were open to every student.

She thought she knew better than most of the girls what books were for. She walked through the cool dim rooms with assurance—often to the table by a diamond-paned window where she read for fun. Sometimes study reading led to "fun-reading," into realms of gold discovered from a clue in a sedate textbook. Sometimes she read old-fashioned novels and poems—sometimes new books—*When Knighthood Was In Flower, To Have and To Hold, Three Men in a Boat, The Dolly Dialogues,* and *The Light That Failed.* Somehow, now, she wanted to tell her father about what she read and what she thought about it. He would be interested too to hear of her new zeal in college algebra, she thought, and about the professor of Latin who made Roman life so real that Jessy liked to think of herself as a nymph or a vestal virgin. Her father was interested and pleased with the letters—partly because she wrote so well and was entering so zestfully into what he called the "world of the mind." But more than he realized, he was warmed by the illusion of a new companionship she could create.

But that illusion disappeared when the household was assembled again—Edward home from his teaching for a few months of study. They talked politely but there was no flow. She was glad he was away when she came home from the visit in August.

"I don't know what it was," Lyddy confided to Mrs. Blake when Jessy had gone back to college. "She went to visit her friend Genevieve. There were several other girls and some boys there. They called it a house-party. I was so pleased. And she planned to bring Emily home with her. But she came home after the third day! All wrought up! Said she didn't feel well. She always is well! And nothing was said then or at any time about what happened or about Emily. ... I'm afraid she is getting stranger and stranger."

"But she had lots of pictures of the girls in her room, Louisa told me. And she wrote a great many letters during the summer."

"I know. But she might have done all she's done at college, and still not be any better off than when she was fifteen. It's inside."

"She goes around with the Bold Water young folks more than she used to, and she is a perfect lady. I have been hoping she would improve Louisa's manners. And she's good in her studies, isn't she? Gets high marks?"

"Yes. ... But somehow it seems as if a college ought to do more than give them knowledge and make their minds work and mend their manners. There's a deeper place where they need education. I am afraid Jessy is all twisted somehow in that deep place. ... I don't know."

"But still," Mrs. Blake reminded her, "she certainly had a good time rowing that boat with the other girls. And this fall she is going to be in a play."

"Yes, she's looking forward to that play. She wants her papa to come. She wrote and asked him last May, and he planned his sailing date so he could."

Then again, encouragement swung to anxiety.

"I'm afraid she thinks she is an outsider wherever she is. And if she thinks so, she is."

Miss Amidon, who directed the play in Jessy's sophomore year, was a wise woman. She did not produce plays to give the girls fun, though that was part of it, nor to prepare them for the stage, though if any were so minded, she helped them to shorten their apprenticeship. Her idea of education was like Lyddy's; there was more to it than knowledge and logical thinking and clear speech and good manners. There are places, she thought, about which psychologists are finding out—places wise men have always known but not named—hidden places with no outlet—troubled.

She thought of her plays in that connection—hoped that they would open up new channels by means of the long and many rehearsal hours and in a final evening of imaginative living.

"That's all acting is," she said frequently.

Once she flared up when one of her scholarly colleagues referred to her work as a "mere skill" and unadvisedly used the term "play-acting."

"Don't you know that there is something therapeutic in vicarious experience?" she demanded—and said no more. There was no use, earlier experience had taught her. But she thought it out later with fervor. ... Strain and monotony are forgotten and relieved as the thumping romance creates new tensions and new rescues. Music brings the loveliness of yearning sorrow and the gold of love into a drably contented life—for a time. A teacher back in the hills sees London with Dickens and Paris with Balzac and provincialism irks her less. There is something of the effect of having consummated—more fully perhaps than in actuality. Vicarious courage may become real courage—vicarious dignity, real dignity—by the creative power of egotism.... She was strengthened in this formulating of her creed.

So, as always, she studied the girls as keenly as the parts they were to play and the stage design in which they were to move, and she saw what not all the teachers saw about Jessy, even when she pointed it out.

"She is lonely. Not one of the obviously ugly ducklings, of course. She's pretty, well-mannered, well-dressed. Good student. And she does what the others do. But she's blocked somehow.... Falling in love would help her, but there's more to it than that.... Somehow she makes me think of that crazed old Miss Damon in her cluttered house."

"But that is ridiculous!" her friend broke in. "That lovely young girl. I think there's something bewitching about her!"

"Maybe Miss Damon was bewitching once. She wasn't a crazed old woman to begin with, you know. Maybe she was only a little solitary at first."

Once Miss Amidon made a suggestion to the dean about Jessy and the others like her—always a few—maybe more than anybody knew. The college, she thought, ought to have someone who would care for the inner life of the girls, as the physician and the gymnasium teachers straightened backs and cleared up skins and eliminated needless colds and fatigue; someone to build up defense against graver ills.

The day of the play was Jessy's greatest college day; and in a moment of cessation on that day came the clearest joy she had ever known. It began in the "math" class. She sat in her end seat by the window—not too attentive. No lesson, she thought, would help her to keep the mood she wanted to create and hold until the play was over.... The quiet clock was something to listen to while Professor Ash commented on a recent test. He stood on his little platform, nonchalant but incisive, the sheaf of papers in his hand. The girls laughed—some of them ruefully—at his sallies. She need not listen; her paper was good, she knew that already. She must not get too interested in anything real, must not think too hard. She needed a form of escape from actuality for that imaginative living behind the lights. She knew how to achieve it—had long known. The pale November sunshine with its shimmering haze and the line of red ivy leaves waving in the stone frame of the window would help; and so would the tranquil song of the blue-bird she could see on a gatepost—on a gate-post as though he knew he was taking leave. He did, no doubt, in the way a bird knows in Indian summer. She would not think of her lines in the play. She could say over Keats' *Ode to Autumn* or think the airs of the "Unfinished Symphony"—first movement and second. And as she thought of how she would achieve, she had done so; she had reached the place where she was alive.

The door was on the opposite side of the long room near the middle. It was recessed by cases on either side—cases on whose shelves stood mathematical models wrought by toiling students: cones, parallepipeds, spheres. A light but sharp tap on the door drew her eyes in that direction and they rested on a sphere on which the sunlight lay: its pure beauty held and intensified her mood. The door opened, and in the seconds her father stood there, the glory came. He was as brilliant an image as if she had never seen him before; more distinction in his magnificent build, in his fine head and in the keen eyes under the heavy brows than she had ever perceived; bigger than she had realized—smarter in his English clothes—easier in manner.

Professor Ash stepped off his little eminence with hand outstretched.

"Professor Smithpeters, this is great!"

"No, no! Don't let me interrupt! I'll just sit down over there in the back."

But his modesty was not indulged. He took a chair on the platform while Professor Ash was handing back the unfortunate papers; and as he sat there his eyes ran over the big roomful of girls till they found Jessy. His smile was so brilliant that she knew a miracle had blessed him, too.

In a few moments, he was standing before the class at Professor Ash's insistence.

"This is what is bothering them." And Professor Ash explained. "You tell them."

What he said she tried afterward to remember—to treasure, but she never could. She did not hear. As he spoke, she did not see him on the college platform in his tweeds, but in the maroon dressing-gown behind the desk of the third floor study. Special times. The day he used the globe that stood on his desk and a big apple on the bookcase and a horseshoe magnet that picked up nails to explain about tides; and told her about the great incoming rush of the water at the Bay of Fundy.

The time he explained about the print of a fern on a piece of rock he used as a paper-weight; how old that fern was and how big the dinosaur that may have tramped it down. ... The morning when in the arithmetic lesson he tucked in a magical trick of algebra. ... The terrible day of the party when she found out, and the rush around the desk into his arms. ... And the beautiful day he played the flute and she read aloud to him,

"All in a golden afternoon
Full leisurely we glide
For both our oars, with little skill
By little arms are plied."

and he was in that boat—with her.

He was with her today—in this room with a blackboard behind him and a length of crayon in his hand—relaxed and full of friendly zeal. The girls broke into a patter of clapping when he finished his explanation.

"This," commented Professor Ash, "is the first time I have heard applause in a mathematics classroom. This is a great day."

"Yes!" Jessy was almost afraid she had called out her exultation aloud.

Three years afterward, with a new fluency, she told Stephen about those moments in the classroom.

"That is precisely what I mean. That was it," he told her in his easy gravity.

She told him about the play, too, and about Miss Amidon:

"She made me the princess! And an arrogant princess at that! Much admired for her beauty and brilliance and good deeds. Many suitors. But only one good enough for her."

"That's right," said Stephen, "and a lucky guy!"

Jessy was not halted by persiflage.

"In the end, the arrogance was burned away. I was left faultless and the center of my beautiful world."

"That's right, too."

"The girls in my corridor sent me a great bunch of yellow roses. They thought I was good. And I was."

"I'll bet you were."

"One of the girls said I seemed enchanted. But that wasn't right. I was delivered, Miss Amidon said. That was the way I felt."

"That's it," he said. "She was a smart woman. You were delivered. I suspect your father was, too."

He was, and his deliverance came in a shock of joy and pain at the first entrance of the dramatic star for the moment which awaited her. Jessy walked into the throne room with royal assurance—the eyes of the queen, the courtiers, the minstrels, and the visiting princes upon her. She was stately in a green velvet gown with court train and standing gold lace collar. On her high-piled hair rose a diadem jeweled in many glittering colors. Before her royal parents, she made obeisance in a slow deep curtsey, her great fan held against her breast, its golden feathers gleaming; her proud and slender neck bent in proud humility. She spoke her first lines with confident graciousness, waving the fan in a slow and fascinating rhythm.

He did not see the fan; he saw the turning of her hand from the wrist—a slender hand with an oddly long index finger. He did not see the green gown but the flowing of the slender body which made the velvet lovely. He did not see the diadem; he could not for love of the way her hair swept up in a springing vitality nor the gold collar for the pathos of the proud line of her neck. It was as if he had never seen her before—almost as if she had never existed—nineteen hard years obliterated.

But the years were not obliterated; they were wasted. He had been away from home too much—and not enough. He thought it out bitterly as the play went on and he watched only for Jessy.... They could have lived in the harbor house—if he had realized.

Jessy's success grew. Her important exits were vigorously applauded, and her entrance brought life to the commonplace play the girls had written. The electricity of double awareness— she of her audience, they of her—built up the power.

"Where does she get it?" he heard a girl's voice behind him whispering.

He knew where she got it. He had seen it before—giving magic to a tawdry stage. He knew how it worked between one and one. He would never lose it again.

"I came home to bring you something to ... keep," the other Jessy had whispered.

He had not sensed the full value of the bequest. But, thank God, he had not lost it.

The curtain came down amid much enthusiasm; rose and fell for curtain calls in good professional fashion—the star in her ascendancy at the last.

She was appealing, alone on the big stage, but self-possessed in the sureness of success. The gold roses from the girls went over the footlights from an usher's arms to hers, and then the chrysanthemums he had had at least the good manners to bring. They were big and there were many of them—yellow bronze; her arms were loaded to the shoulders. She smiled and bowed; then, suddenly stepping forward, she tossed the roses over on the chrysanthemums with that loved airiness of hands and arms and, thus freed, looking straight at her father, threw him a kiss.

He returned it behind the scenes with a kiss of which he was a little ashamed—so mixed were his emotions and his sense of time. He swept her from her feet—green gown trailing—holding the doubly loved body against him.

Long after twelve o'clock had struck, the golden coach had still not become the pumpkin. The prancing horses were still prancing, and Jessy was still the princess—in nightgown and bathrobe. The lines she had given best were echoing in her mind, and the rhythms of her entrances and stage business still beat in her nerves and muscles. But far beyond and above the excitement of imagined living glowed the transcendence of new reality.

She was careful not to go to sleep before she had to.

"Usually I hate to wake up when something beautiful is happening," she thought, finally drowsy.

They had an hour next day in the stiff college parlor to get things clear and to say good-bye. Shy talk it was—stumbling and sparse—but momentous: he would be back in the late spring … next summer at home … next time, could she go? … letters like her college ones … something pretty from Italy … really like the play? … she loved college … just like her mother … the stage.

"Bend over," she said when the time was gone. She put her arms around his neck, and once more he swung her up in the new comfortableness.

"My daughter." He said it with grave sweetness.

She never forgot that moment nor the one when her eyes moved from the sphere to the classroom doorway where he stood.

# CHAPTER THIRTEEN

He sailed at noon, and she lived in the transcendence until the February day when David came to tell her. It had shone in her college living and in her long letters.

David came. He agreed that he must, for Lyddy said, "I can't. I belong here. She won't know me there."

But on the way he changed the plan. He went to the college dean with his sober dignity to ask for someone whose presence might be support. So it was Miss Amidon who told her—gently but without suspense. Her father had gone sailing with friends off the coast of Italy near Spezia. The boat was found capsized ten miles off shore. There was nothing more to tell.

Jessy made no outcry—did not weep. Her gray eyes darkened.

"And all she said," Miss Amidon's voice broke as she told it, "was Romeo's line when he got the dreadful news about Juliet, 'Is it even so?' We had it in class just yesterday. She didn't even have his bracing defiance. She just thanked me and went to her room."

Later, David talked with her. He had a message from her Uncle Eugene. He would see to her affairs; Mr. Atwood would see that the money for her expenses was sent. Later, they would talk things over and Lyddy had a memorandum from her father about things he wanted her to have. She had sent something now. ... It was the garnet ring in its gray velvet box between the two little cushions—the pearls around the garnet. David thought she should stay right on in college. There was nothing to call her home just then. It might be easier there with the girls and her studies, he went on. Her father would want her to. Jessy said she would. And her good friend, Miss Amidon, would help her all she could, he knew.

She would, indeed. Jessy treasured the warm-hearted concern and the calm wisdom offered her, but she had her own technique of meeting loss.

Once, she suddenly asked Miss Amidon, "Where was Shelley drowned? Where did they build the fire on the beach?"

"Near Spezia, I think it was." She was sorry she had said it. But she realized in a moment that she had brought some sort of comfort. What sort it was came to her later. She might have know sooner, she thought.

Lyddy made a mistake.

She did not know it, but she saw the results. She thought Jessy would be interested in the "obituary" which had appeared in the county paper and enclosed it in one of her letters—now even more faithful than before.

"Edward Smithpeters was born in Bold Water in 1863, the son of Thomas and Martha Smithpeters, and died in Italy by drowning on February 28, 1905. He was educated in the schools... " It ran on to college and the honors received there. Then, "He was twice married, first on June 23, 1884 to Jessy Arnell, who died on December 21, 1884. His second wife was Isabel Seymor Sparks, daughter of Jabez Sparks, whom he married in 1886 and who also preceded him in death on April 2, 1891. He leaves a daughter by his first marriage, Jessy, now in college. The son of his second marriage, Eugene Sparks, died. ... "

She stopped reading. Her mind jerked back to that first marriage. There was something about it. She had never known her mother's surname before. Jessy Arnell. It was pretty and gay, but she did not stop to enjoy it. There was something else.

It was her birthday! December 21, 1884, the day her mother died, her mother who was married on June 23, 1884!

She did not finish the remaining paragraph—"Although still a young man, he had already... great promise... serious loss. ... " She could not read about honors. Her mother's memory was dishonored, and everyone must have known all these years. And her father! She could not gainsay the youthful necessity of blame—desecration though it was. And she herself. She was what she had heard somebody call a "child of shame"—a hard-visaged old woman it was.

That was why Lyddy had always been so solemn as she told her about things. First about mothers and their babies, cats and kittens, colts. Later—quite a while—about a father and his part. It was all very beautiful and very sacred, Lyddy told her, and Jessy thought so, too. So a girl must always be very careful—not be too free with the boys. A girl could get into trouble without meaning to. The seventh commandment warns us against one of the worst of the sins. As Lyddy talked on, Jessy went through all the first six commandments to get hold of the seventh. ... Her father and her mother had broken it and everybody knew. ...

The boy from Yale. They all paired off at the house-party, and he was her beau for tennis and dancing. She liked him. ... Very handsome be seemed at first with his sleek hair parted in the middle and the highest stand-up collar she had ever seen—so high its points seemed to pinch a fold of his neck when he turned it, over his fashionable blue satin Ascot tie. The party was lively. She had never had such fun. Being one of the four girls to be invited and the chosen girl of the handsomest boy was emerging into the life she read about in *Susan Jane at College*. It was exciting. They danced well together—two-steps and waltzes. She loved the waltzes and after one they would stroll out on the veranda and watch the stars wheeling their way. Sometimes he forgot they were not still waltzing and kept his arm around her. Sometimes he said what he should not say and touched her where he should not touch her. And she liked it. ... That was the awful thing, she now knew. ... It led—to moments she could not bear to remember. Once a nasty child had told her things about boys and girls. She had forgotten till the boy from Yale suggested what he suggested and did what he did. The old memory made her fling away from him with disgust.

"Go away. I never want to see you again." For the first time in her life, she stuttered—on the g's and on the w's.

He laughed.

"Well, g-g-g-goo'bye then. Meet me in St. Looey-ooey. Meet me at the Fair!"

She fled into the house and up to her room. The other girls were already in, and the boys were out in the orchard, practicing their serenade songs. She heard his loud voice requesting a "special number." He sang himself.

"I gathered me a lemon in the garden of love
Where they say only peaches grow."

That moment of stammering hung on through the rest of the summer and her sophomore year—recurring in a crowd of young people; when she was with a young man alone, especially; not with the girls often; not with her father. Not at home. She came to think of it as a warning—Puritan daughter that she was. ... Now she knew that it was. The taint was in her blood. She tore the obituary into bits. ...

She went home in June to stay.

All that Lyddy feared seemed to be coming to pass. Sinbad saw what she meant at first.

"Seems as if she's kinda blasted like that old spruce the lightning went down inside of. Didn't tear it where you can see. A few little chips around—one root torn out. Exploded inside, sort of."

But there was something that Lyddy could not understand.

"I wouldn't have thought she'd grieve so for him. They had never been very chummy," she reminded him. "He was away from home too much. And upstairs too much when he was home. They tried too hard to be pleasant and polite to be real good companions."

"She's born and bred in the shadow of death," Sinbad said solemnly, "death and memories of death—all alike and all different. They helped to tune her up the way she is. She feels awful bad about him."

"I'm afraid it's more than the deaths." Lyddy's voice was close to tears. "Something alive is tangled up in it. And I don't know what it is. She's been home six months now and I don't see much recovery.... She wears that ring of her mother's all the time," she added.

In time, Jessy grew restlessly active—an encouraging sign, Lyddy thought. It might be nice, she suggested, if Jessy had her room done over—replace the bird's-eye maple furniture and the frilled dressing table she had loved so long. But Jessy planned otherwise. She wanted to leave the little-girl room the way it was and move into Isabel's rooms. They gave her a sense of refuge though she still felt timid there. Maybe she wanted to feel timid, she considered. So she worked absorbingly to freshen the rooms and include her own things without changing the tone. The parlor with Isabel's portrait in its fussy frame still hanging over the white marble mantel had a commanding stillness that she liked. Later, she played the piano diligently. It was something like acting. In the music room, little Eugene's violin in its case had been put away, but Lyddy got it out for her. There was a new dog—a yellow and white pointer who had replaced Jippy. His name was Bingo. New horses lived in the handsome stable. Isabel's phaeton was gone, but a new and modern one was waiting for Jessy when she came home. Uncle Eugene had thought she would need a proper conveyance. She drove out in it—as she used to drive Merrylegs—sometimes with Louisa and her mother, sometimes alone. She walked, regularly, too. The grounds were well cared for now—even the meadow mowed to velvetiness, as it used to be in Isabel's day, Jessy remembered with sudden sharp pleasure.

She had forgotten that detail. The trails into the woods were clean; she followed the familiar routes with Bingo circling ahead.

For some time she worked on her father's papers in his study. There was a neat pile of finished chapters—seventeen of them—titled and numbered; and there were many less intelligible but no less important looking sheets. They were systematized notes, she could see.

"I wish I could finish his book for him," she said to Lyddy. "He had done so much. It seems dreadful to leave it so. But I can't. I can't even understand most of it."

Lyddy did not reply for a moment. Her fine needle and thread whipped the napkin hem in five more strong and tiny stitches.

"We all will leave something unfinished, I suppose."

Jessy thought about Schubert, but she said nothing. The room was quiet. She watched the cannel coal in the Franklin stove. Lyddy went on.

"I have a basket full of patches my grandmother made for a wedding-ring quilt. She'd sewed some of them into blocks. But she couldn't finish it. She expected to, I know, for she'd quilted her needle in neatly the last time she worked on it."

"Why didn't you finish it, Lyddy?"

"Well, I have always had my own work to do. . . . I guess that's the way it is. . . . And a pretty good way, too."

Jessy thought about those patches and her father and Schubert. Then she bent over and took another napkin from the round basket at Lyddy's feet.

"I'll fold it down, and then I'll get my thimble, Lyddy."

Lyddy made an uneven stitch; she could not see quite clearly.

The next spring Mrs. Blake interested Jessy in gardening, the first step in a mental hygiene she practiced, pretty shrewdly, though the term came too late for her. Nothing gives a philosophic perspective like transplanting, she often observed. So she was triumphant when Jessy took to it with zest. She bought imported English seeds and raised plants over whose flats she hung with passion and infinite patience. She never threw away a plant no matter how spindling. It had its chance. She was pleased with the gift of lemon lilies from the clump which had come from Mrs. Blake's grandmother's garden—so much so that Lyddy collaborated by bringing phlox and lupines—big clumps now—that Isabel had set out in her father's garden. The tops of the plants looked dead except for tiny pale stems beginning their climb, but the roots were thick and strong. Jessy looked at them intently. Then she turned and put her arms around Lyddy and kissed her.

"It's the loveliest thing we can do for her—and for me, too," she said. "My flowers will be monuments."

Lyddy gave a purple mat of thyme for her memorial, though she was not certain she should.

The garden was laid out in two long panels on a slightly rising slope. It led one up to the clump of big birches where the hammock swung—and to next spring.

Louisa coaxed her to teach a Sunday-School class the next winter. The children never did arrive at the thrilling intimacy of hanging on her arm as was usual with most of the teachers, but she had the class party which was in the ritual—a very successful party. She played the organ sometimes too. It was harder than ever, however, to get her to come to any social gatherings where there were more than half a dozen people. There were flourishing card clubs, but only occasionally would she attend. Now and then she would play chess with old Captain Blowers. She liked his pieces—the kings six inches high and Chinese—with regal pigtails and slant eyes. Her knights made fierce attacks and her queen rushed up into the thick of battle. She never spoke while she played until she could say "Check!" That was not often. Captain Blowers was good.

Mrs. Blake and other kindly concerned matrons thought she was making progress. So did Louisa. Lyddy was not optimistic, but she talked less of her anxiety, partly because it was so hard to explain.

"She *does* all the right things." She had thought it out. "We taught her how to do and the college folks helped that way, but nobody taught her how to *be*. All her troubles would not be troubles if she knew that. I am afraid she is all banked up like a fire, and neither she nor anybody else can scatter those ashes. That kind of fire isn't much good either. It just keeps. ... She stands on Sunday mornings listening to the church bell across the harbor. I don't know why." The occasional stammering troubled her also.

Jessy settled, however, in a twilight satisfaction of her own making—in the gardening and in the music; in the books, especially the books and the place she could find for herself in them. She liked to think about the land and all the Smithpeters women who had lived and died upon it.

Uncle Eugene had stopped in one day soon after her return home. She saw him in the stable talking to Sinbad when she went by looking for the dog. He stopped her as she came back.

"By the way, Jessy, I suppose you want to go on as you have been doing—for a time anyway. Lyddy and Sinbad carrying as usual. Your income from your stepmother comes in promptly, I think. She was generous."

Jessy said it did. She was unnecessarily vague about the money and the property, though she had signed some papers and matters had been duly explained.

"Let me know when you are ready to make any changes in your plans," he called over his shoulder as he turned back to Sinbad.

One point was not vague in her mind: she would never be ready to change her arrangements.

# CHAPTER FOURTEEN

Everybody in Bold Water—even Jessy—knew when Stephen came, for he drove up the street in the first automobile ever seen there—high and red and shining with brass-work. Even the horses were demonstrative.

He drew up at the sign, Seaside Home, creaking before Mrs. Spencer's big boarding-house, set his outside brake carefully with both hands, and dismounted. So great and so unconcealed was the interest that he went up the steps with an embarrassed suggestion of a bow toward the high piazza. Interest was not diminished by a surprising pause halfway up the steps, where he turned and looked out over the lively and sparkling harbor.

Mrs. Spencer's new guest was the high point of the summer. Even before his arrival he had made friends. Halfway across the moist causeway, his ponderous vehicle had suddenly stopped, the back wheels caught in a trough of sand running crosswise of the road. More power produced only a terrific churning—no advance. The situation, examined from the rear, was still some-what disconcerting: the suction on the tires as vicious as quicksand. Still it could not swallow down the whole machine, he reflected cheerfully, and, no doubt, somebody would come along before high tide. ... Certainly no one could pass by on the other side. Any traveler must become the helpful Samaritan.

He climbed back in the car and got out his lunch—the wild strawberries picked on a sunny slope where the first wide view of the bay and islands had spread out before him. The berries were good; he had learned in the process to pick only those that acted as if they wanted to be picked—came off in his fingers with no resistance.

Lunch done, he pulled his book out, though he never could read outdoors. But he kept it in his hand, a finger moving a little between the pages. His head was tipped back to search the new deep blue of the sky and to listen to bird-cries and beating wings.

From a wooded point across the mud and the shallow pools came the call of his old friend, the wild dove. "Tolling," he had heard some one call the sound, but he was not sure the word was just right; there was no dragging melancholy. He never called it a mourning dove. There were two tones separated by a little interval—with a feeling in each hard to identify. One higher—unresolved—looking forward but quickly gone. Then three insistent lower seeking notes. It was so haunting that it sometimes made him sorry he had ever shot that "wandering voice," but it was wonderful sport, so fast was the flight—seventy-five miles an hour, an old naturalist had told him. A dove is built for speed.

He was so absorbed that he did not know when the little boys climbed up the side of the causeway behind him. They were standing in a row of four, pails in their hands and clam rakes over their shoulders—abashed but eager.

They were not chatty little boys, Stephen soon discovered, but they accepted promptly the invitation to climb in when he got out and sat in a solemn and crowded row on the wide seat, the fattest one sitting partially up hill against the door. When, at Stephen's suggestion, the one nearest pressed the bulb to make the horn sound, they laboriously and speechlessly shifted positions until each had made the rewarding squawk. Each then took a turn under the horizontal wheel.

"How do you start her?"

Stephen explained that you pull out a little thing and you push that one and you turn this, and then somebody down on the ground turns a crank, "and then with any luck she goes."

"Let's do it!"

"We're stuck, you know. Got to be pulled out."

"We could do all those things up here in the car and you could turn the crank. We could hear her go." Twelve-year-old curiosity was breaking down local reticence.

But Stephen still did not think they could.

"How would you like to see the works?"

As this inspection went on the Blake buggy approached. Only discreetly near, David halted his uneasy horse and looked with silent enthusiasm till Stephen, catching sight of him, waved a friendly hand.

"Come over here," David called. "I can't leave my horse."

Stephen snatched off his cap when he saw Louisa on the seat beside her father and, to her delight, stood holding it in his hand while he talked, his bronze-auburn head bright in the sunshine.

"I have a committee over there," he said gaily, "looking into the subject of automobiles. Very efficiently interested, it seems to me. The only thing is that I can't make it go for them, and I am afraid I'll have to have help before you can go by or anybody can follow me." And he explained the predicament of the rear wheels.

David knew that spot. "You can fill it every spring, and every summer it will be as bad as ever," he said. "But if you fellows start coming over here in those things we'll have to find a way to fill it permanently."

They fell into conversation, full of facts and prophecies, David eager to add observation to his reading. An easygoing conversation it was, running companionably until another buggy came up behind the car with another astonished horse halted at a safe distance to be held by a capable wife while three men continued the conference at David's buggy—a ways and means committee, he said jovially. He was in high feather.

"What do you do?" he inquired. "We generally can move things that have to be moved. But this is a new kind of a job."

A team of horses and a good rope—strong horses—Stephen thought would do it, though he had not yet had much experience either, he said.

"Oh, if it is a matter of pulling, we'll get a team of oxen." The remark was made in virtual duet by the local men.

Louisa was lady-like during these considerations—a danger sign which her father should have noticed. She had an idea.

So she was somewhat crestfallen when he suggested that she drive to the village (he would turn the horse around for her) and send back Captain Henry Blowers and his oxen. He added that she could go on home then; the errands could wait until tomorrow. She saw the point; he wanted to ride home in the car himself. Three really could ride in it, she estimated, though not so desirably. And besides there was the horse.

She thought of saying prettily, "Oh, Papa, I don't believe I can drive her over the causeway," not in the hope of fooling him but merely to let him know that she did not care for the plan; but she was saved from the necessity. There was a yoke nearer than Henry's, John, the newcomer, said—just off to the right at the other end of the neck. He could turn his horse and his wife would drive back.

It was a long time before they could see the oxen starting their glacial progress. David found a way to tether his now placid horse while Stephen, after clearing the boys out of the car, handed Louisa into it with a flourishing deference.

"Queen Elizabeth never had a coach like that! And if I may say so she wasn't nearly so pretty!"

"She wasn't pretty at all! Neither am I!" Louisa was always both saucy and downright. She played up to her present role, however, regally erect on the seat until her father came over for the inspection Stephen had promised.

Then she could not resist descending to see what Stephen showed the men and hear his enthusiastic though none too expert exposition of the workings. The little boys wove in and out of the group. David answered as many questions as did Stephen, his own and John's—and Louisa's.

"She's a good sewing-machine mechanic," her father explained.

"And I took the clock apart!" she added with an expectancy which Stephen took up.

"Get it back together?"

"Yes, sir! It goes better than ever!"

"But it strikes only once a day—eleven at three in the morning," David snapped the practiced joke, and everybody was very lively and friendly—even the boys, until a raucous horn sent a blast over the flats. The fat boy seemed dashed.

"Gosh, my mother wanted them clams for dinner," he ejaculated with gloomy alarm.

Responsibility infected the other three, and they departed.

"You'll be seeing me around," Stephen assured them.

The dinner horn reminded Louisa. So the four sat on the piled stone coping at the edge and shared the lunch her mother had packed. Afterward, when David drew out his pipe, Stephen got his from the car and they sat in philosophical silence. Louisa climbed into the car again, this time under the wheel.

"I expect we will have to get one of those so that you can ride," her father called unguardedly.

"So I can drive, you mean!" She took the pose—her hands gripping the wheel.

"I'll take her home when I get started," Stephen said around his pipe, "if you are willing."

"That would be mighty clever of you!" David took Stephen at full face value on sight. Then a rare selfish impulse seized him. "I don't know what her Mama would say, though. I guess she'd better go in the buggy."

He did not say "with me," Stephen observed.

In due time, the oxen arrived, were maneuvered around the car and, after due adjustment of tackle, moved it and Louisa the requisite few feet. After the pause of triumph, there was further inspection for the benefit of the owner of the oxen. Louisa watched her chance to speak.

"I guess you'd better get Whitey farther up the road and headed for home. Don't you think so?" Her manner was modest and girlishly anxious. "I'd go but I don't know what she would do."

She and her father understood each other perfectly, but he could not very well assign his daughter to a task that sounded ticklish, even though they both knew she could handle it competently—especially when she said sweetly, "I'll catch up with you when you are ready."

She hardened her heart as he trudged off, and Stephen called after him, "You can drive this car whenever you say the word, Mr. Blake. I'll be around to see you!" Then he smiled at Louisa.

After some directions, John bent over, his hand on the crank. He was both proud and startled at his instant success, for the engine, on his first attempt, got into terrific action. Even the oxen were restive, and John set off to the aid of his wife and her excited horse at a run.

Whitey, ready none too soon, broke into a gallop. She was not running amuck; she was not that type of horse. She was a staid matron who heard something behind her that she did not like and saw the road to her barn stretching out straight before her. She slowed down when she felt calmer, not at David's guidance, for she had the bit in her teeth; and, after a few rods, stopped, somewhat winded in a middle-aged way.

At that, from the car following slowly came another blare of sound. She lingered no longer but put out for home with the steady persistence of the race-track and with very creditable speed, too.

"Why, that rubber thing blows the horn, doesn't it?" Louisa spoke with excellent surprise. "What an awful noise it makes! I don't blame Whitey."

And then they burst into laughter, Stephen as wholeheartedly as Louisa. So, to Polly's astonishment, the red and brass novelty made its first stop at the Blakes, and a strange young man handed out her daughter.

Stephen turned up everywhere as the weeks went on—at the wall where the old salts sat in the sunshine looking over the harbor shipping and forecasting the weather; at the ball game between the seventh and eighth grades; at church and town meetings; at the parties and picnics that bloomed all summer. He liked the boats ashore or on the water and the men in them. His red car roared up the cliff to the lumber camp, and the two operators ceased operating to examine "her" with silent enthusiasm.

He set the girls to dreaming on golden afternoons. His gay deference was enchanting; and so was his trick of playing the piano so that each one felt that the music was intended for her alone. He systematically gave each girl a ride in the automobile—sometimes with her beau, sometimes two or three girls at a time—through the birches to the mill to which young people had always traveled—by ox-cart, buggy, or bicycle.

Sometimes as they set off, he would sing:

"As I was going to the mill one day
I met Julia Glover going that way."

but its rollicking refrain

"Sit down there, Julia Ann Glover.
Lord a massy, oh, how I did love her"

usually died down before long. The road narrowed as it turned into the thick of the woods, and the light was clear and pale—like light through old stained glass between slender columns.

# CHAPTER FIFTEEN

Jessy first saw Stephen as one sometimes meets a new person in a book. The page is turned and there is Eunice or Nathaniel. He came around the point toward the sandy cove below her seat under the big spruce; she watched him as he walked along the seaward rocks. There was elasticity in his straight, tall, slender figure. He seemed to feel it, for, as he paused on the high rock, he rose on his toes and stretched his arms upward; then dropping his arms he sank on his heels; then rose and sank again. As he did so, he was whistling a melody she knew—the whistling of a wood-wind that emerges from a background of instruments like the sea.

He was a lithe figure by a fountain, she thought, except that he had on a turtle-neck sweater with a college letter on it.

Suddenly she called down, "Why, you are the flute that plays the air in the scherzo, aren't you?"

He turned and found her at first glance.

"I am that! How do you like my performance?"

His face was as vibrant as his figure, down there with the sun upon it and the bronze hair.

"I ought to have opera glasses so I could see the artist better," she was astonished to hear herself saying.

"The soloist will come up to the box where the audience sits, if the audience is agreeable." His voice had a tang of accent.

Given the word, he took the roundabout upward path to her perch, though she pointed out the hand-holds up the tree and up the face of the little cliff.

He had a handful of mushrooms when he appeared again. He sat down beside her.

"Do you know (he spoke as though in the middle of a long conversation) once I saw one of these as big as a pie! A ripe lemon color."

As he spoke he took out a clean handkerchief from a back pocket and tied up the mushrooms.

"A present for a lady." He turned toward her and she toward him.

His face was quiet and clean-cut—with wide-set eyes under a smooth forehead—eyes like brown water in a clear woods brook with sunlight in it.

"*I'm nobody. Who are you?*" she said. "*Are you nobody too?*"

And Stephen, still looking into her gray eyes, replied, "*Then there's a pair of us—don't tell! They'd banish us, you know.*"

She laughed and was off with the rest of it.

The seat was as comfortable as a settee for Jessy, its cushion six inches of spruce needles, her back and feet supported comfortably. But Stephen did not sit long. He stood on his end of the footrest, looking out to the rocks where the seals were sunning themselves at low tide; at the birds perching above them; at a schooner on the horizon line.

She watched the slight turnings of his head and saw what he saw. The schooner was a four-master, she noted, going east, and the patriarch of all the seals was lying on the flattest ledge in the late sunshine. And as Stephen watched, his long slender feet in the tennis shoes rose and sank.

He was Quicksilver! He could walk off that ledge if he wished. She might get glimpses of the wings at his heels and cap if he did. He would skim over the sands and the rocks to an old Baucis and Philemon somewhere, and for their kindness, returning kindness, would start the white fountain in the old milk pitcher, and more than that would avert the calamity which was about to overwhelm them, and they would live on—the old linden tree and the old oak, whispering "Baucis," whispering "Philemon." He would slay the terrible Medusa with his sword in one hand and flashing mirror in the other. ... He was Quicksilver! But who was she?

Still there was no speaking and no need of it. He turned and looked down at her and then up the dark wooded hillside. She did not turn, but she knew what he saw; the great rock, its tons split and separated, first by mighty movings and then by an ambitious sapling that grew into power; trunks fallen on the needles and the deer-moss; the planes of light from the sunny meadow around the house cutting into the darkness.

Turning back, he began to play—not a magic flute—but a magic harmonica which he took from the rolled fold at the bottom of his sweater. He played the place, she thought; rhythms of trunks, of branches and twigs and cones. He played darkness with threads of light. He blew hard for the rock of ages and the breaking waves on the stern and rock-bound coast. And running throughout was noise as of a hidden brook. There was no real brook, though, Jessy thought.

When he had finished, he tucked the harmonica back into his sweater with his right hand and as he did so, he dropped the left to Jessy. With hers in it, he drew her up to stand beside him, and they looked across the harbor where castles were forming against the sky—vast and temporary. A bird took off from that shore and moved swiftly toward them. As they watched it, their heads tipped slowly till they were thrown back as far as their stretched throats would permit. They watched that swimming blue even after the bird had disappeared, Stephen longer than Jessy. Then, still without speaking, they went down the roundabout path, across the cove where the tide was beginning to come in and along the rocky shore toward the point.

In the narrow path above the pool that was always deep, Stephen laughed. The big seal had come to cool off and was lying on his back luxuriously—his venerable whiskers bristling above water. Jessy laughed, too, in a laughter that raced over her whole body like a sip of an exhilarating drink. And from around the point came the gayety of the clam-bake.

"Say," said Stephen. "Maybe we'd better get around there. It's time for supper. I ran away till they got all the work done."

"And I am on my way over there. My house is on the other side of the woods. My name is Jessy."

"Mine is Stephen. And how do you do?"

(Several weeks later, she said suddenly, "What is your last name?"

"Geddes," he replied without surprise or comment.)

It was not until they came into the lively group that Jessy realized she had not stammered once when she spoke to Stephen.

But she did again in that bantering circle—though she was near Louisa and her Doctor Greenleaf, Abby and her beau. The derisive shout that had hailed Jessy and Stephen as they came around the point developed into systematic "joshing"—uproarious and broad. It was lively and friendly, but a kind of liveliness she had never been able to enter into at college, or before, or after. And she knew it was likely to degenerate into mawkish sentimentality with a good deal of "spooning."

"Oh, look at that moon," they would say later, and couples would stray off into nooks in the rocks or shelters in coves, though she and Louisa at least were always "careful."

Abby's beau called Stephen with facetious insistence.

"Hey! Somebody wants you! Looks lonesome!"

But Stephen was busy helping serve.

"I'm busy. Chaperoning these clams," he called.

Jessy tried to say something about her plate of food, but she stammered badly. It was stammering that had nothing to do with her throat. She knew that very well, and she knew when it began exactly. She was clear-headed. Nobody paid her any attention, anyway, she thought with illogical sensitiveness.

The clack grew louder around her as the evening grew quieter, she noticed, and she thought Stephen did too, because when he played his harmonica by noisy request he followed "Pop Goes the Weasel" by "Swanee River" and that by "Stars of the Summer Night." The sentimental phase of the evening was at hand—the moon already half above the notched line of the woods.

Then Stephen played "Good Night, Ladies," put his harmonica away, and announced, "The motoring party must now withdraw. Doctor Greenleaf has professional duties," and crossed the circle to Jessy. "And if she will enjoy it, we will take another passenger."

He put out his hand and she took it, but he did not lift her. She was standing beside him before any of the others had scrambled up. He kept hold of her hand on the path through the woods to the road. The hilarious crowd behind was singing, "I was seeing Jessy ho-o-ome. I was seeing. … " but she had already walked away from them farther than she had ever been before. Only part of her listened.

Stephen handed her into the front seat, and Louisa piled herself into the back. Tom Greenleaf did the cranking with the expertness of recent practice.

"Maybe some day you can start it—just press a button the way you make a bell ring and drive right off," Stephen said to Jessy.

But she could think of nothing to reply. Anyway, Louisa was loudly boasting as Tom jumped aboard that she could crank her right now.

Jessy said little in the progress up the main road. She was disturbed, she thought, by the incongruity of this noisy and noisome vehicle at Bold Water. It played an entirely different tune from that of summer evening; from creaking of gear and harness. She hoped that not many automobiles would come. Of course, steamboats were new and startling once, too.

But when Stephen started up "Julia Glover," she unexpectedly found herself singing a duet with him.

"Where did you ever learn that?" Louisa demanded.

"Lyddy used to sing it to me when I was little. I guess I've not heard it since."

Then she started Stephen on the second stanza:

"I kissed Miss Julia by the road.
The fool she screeched and screamed so loud,
The ox ran away and the cart tipped over
And threw out I and Julia Ann Glover."

and her voice rose in the beat of the hearty chorus:

"Sit down there, Julia Ann Glover!"

In the quiet spot, Stephen stopped the noisy car—without comment. By and by the birds and the squirrels forgot their terror; little movements and notes made a pattern on the twilight silence like leaf shadows on light.... But Jessy did not see that pattern. She was wondering if she should have sung like that—what the others thought. And Stephen was holding her hand again between them on the seat.... She recalled with familiar sickening remembrance that he and she had walked away from that hooting crowd hand in hand.

Next day, the red car roared up to the Smithpeters house—the first one to travel Isabel's fine drive. Lyddy, answering the door, and his smile, ushered him elegantly into the parlor.

"I thought maybe Miss Jessy would like to go for a ride. And you," he said with a bow. "I am a careful driver. I have to be. I don't understand the thing too well."

"I'm sure she'd enjoy it," she said, and then refused her own invitation with delighted promptness, Stephen observed.

Jessy entered the room with grace—dressed for the afternoon in a thin white ruffled dress with a long and flaring skirt. Its length and the high collar which arose from a lacy yoke gave her dignity, and the high-erected pompadour height. She greeted Stephen pleasantly and coolly and seated herself in a high-backed chair.

"She's a little lady," he thought. "She's been to boarding school or she has a strict mother. Or else she likes to play lady."

She chatted easily about the mushrooms and how good they were; the weather and how the view usually quite fine was blurred by the advancing shower; about the pointer who, he said, had greeted him on the steps.

"Seemed to like me, I flatter myself."

As conversation drifted on, he watched her as one listens for motifs.

The regal chair and posture were not all there was to see. Each of the fragile ruffles from the hem of her frock to the waist was edged with narrow lace, and over her shoulder was a Janice Meredith curl that would not hold its formal shape but softened into tendrils and fluffiness.

"She has on a straight front corset, though," he considered analytically. "Lots of petticoats. Bones in that collar up behind her ears."

The gray eyes were fortunate in the sheltering long lashes, for they were not altogether candid—nor serene. She was not at all the girl in the plaid gingham dress above the cove, her head turned back, staring into the sky.

"And I'm not the same fellow, either. Those minutes were on a mount. I'm glad she doesn't call from here to there... and doesn't bring back her discomfiture with those chumps at the clam-bake, either. ... That woman in the portrait had something to do with her, but I don't believe she is her mother, and I don't want to know."

After some turn in the conversation, he found himself playing the gold piano—strange music that Jessy liked but did not understand. She did not understand either why she had been so unusually easy in talk. But she did know, she thought, why she would not go for the drive. It was because of the boy from Yale.

# CHAPTER SIXTEEN

Jessy did not go for the ride with Stephen that day nor for some time afterwards. He was not precisely sure why; nor sure what a seemingly trifling episode on the Fourth of July meant. They had set out through the wooded path for High Point to see the display of fireworks on the mainland ... quite exceptional, for the Governor was to be there—an unofficial and friendly appearance in the middle of his fishing trip.

She suddenly said they had better go back.

"Why, all right, let's do," said Stephen easily. "I like the Lord's fireworks better anyway."

The terrace was cool and quiet. There was no moon and the sky was clear and black. They let the moments drift on in silence for a time—then into intermittent talk. The Lord shot off a rocket or two, and off in the north there was a suggestion of his wonderful Borealis set piece.

But Jessy stood up abruptly. The mosquitoes were at their worst, she said. They were—their terrible worst, but Stephen would have stayed on even so—beside her on the bench.

As he rose, he realized that as he looked upwards he had stretched his arm along the back of the bench behind her, his hand around her shoulder, unconsciously.

"But she'd never believe it was," he thought as he walked meekly behind her up the steps, across the piazza and through the French windows. He had "put his arm around her" as his sister Victoria used to put it accusingly.

He paid a great many calls in that parlor through the summer weeks. He drank considerable tea, sitting on a gold-colored sofa. Sometimes, cup in hand, he had to walk about the big room—wings on his heels. It was pretty tea with a slice of lemon in it. The cup and saucer were very thin, the cup deep and narrow and slippery: he was afraid of it. Once Louisa broke hers and scalded herself besides.

Jessy sat behind an elaborate tea-tray, looking exceedingly pretty and apparently much at ease. Her hands were "fluttering over the tea-things" like ladies' hands in English novels. And Sinbad brought in and passed things like a butler in a play. ...

Conversation was decorous—frequently what Stephen thought of as "naming authors."

"Have you read Mr. Tarkington's new book?" Mrs. Blake to the minister's wife.

"No, I haven't. I've been so absorbed with Mrs. Deland. I love *The Old Chester Tales*."

Stephen once thought of inquiring whether any one had read *Mrs. Warren's Profession* but desisted. Probably nobody had; so there would be no fun in it. And if they had, their code would be outraged, bless 'em. He amiably "named" Kipling to the relief of the minister who, feeling solid ground, opened up on *The Bear That Walks Like a Man* and *The White Man's Burden* and their political implications. As he did so, Stephen put away a good-sized slice of cake. ... He was amused at himself for being there, but there as a rightness in his presence. He knew it in the way he knew important things.

He played the gold piano for Jessy and her guests on various occasions, and played duets on a better piano in the music room with her—surprised how soon and how much he liked Jessy *a deux* and how intelligently she played. He walked in the grounds, holding her ruffled parasol; he helped cut and arrange roses for the church.

"In fact," he reflected, "I have done everything but beat fudge in the kitchen and lick the spoon. She may treat me like poison ivy, but she lets me come."

He was amused at himself but not at Jessy Her clouded charm was fascinating, but it made him sober. Once Tom Greenleaf said, "I guess I ought to tell you about Jessy," but Stephen cut him off nonchalantly. He did not want to hear gossip; he did not even want the outer facts to begin with. He wanted to use a sort of intuitive stethoscope that he had. He did not need its perceptiveness to make one observation, but it was too apparent to be basic. He waited genially—not always consciously; his stethoscope worked without supervision.

Back in Bold Water after a few days' absence, he made a belated discovery—with regret. He was at the Smithpeters door within an hour. For the first time, he was taken to Jessy's second floor sitting-room—pleasant on the rainy morning with a birch fire snapping.

Jessy lay on a long white wicker chair wrapped in a crimson robe—her face white and her eyes dark-ringed. Instantly, his hand went into his pocket, but it came out empty. He would wait a bit.

She held out her hand, and greeted him pleasantly without apology or explanation, and asked him to draw a chair up to the blaze.

"This was my—step-mother's room," she said unexpectedly.

"She was the beautiful blonde lady downstairs?" he asked and went on to say, "I think I can tell which things were hers. That embossed silver inkstand for one."

"Yes, it was." She was game, he thought. "I used to watch her writing with her gold pen. It had a very slender pearl handle. Do you remember those old pens?"

"I do indeed. My Aunt Luella had one. And I would say that the Frenchy vase was hers and maybe the red glass was her mother's."

"Good!" said Jessy. "Go on."

"The etching in the white frame, and the books on this side of the case."

"Right. The first one on the top shelf is *The Lady of Shalott*. I loved it—just the pictures then. Once I got fingermarks on its white binding."

"Did she scold?"

"No, she never scolded, but I knew when she was annoyed. I adored her but I stood in awe, too."

"Still like *The Lady of Shalott?*" he went on easily.

"I love it," she said. "It is—comforting."

"Comforting? That's a new angle. I was always sorry for the poor Lady. Nice poem, though, like a piece of music. Doesn't make much difference what it means."

"I think it is ... " her voice and manner broke. "Stephen! I've lost my mother's ring!" Her face was twisted like a child's when it is getting ready to cry.

Stephen could not bear it, and besides he had waited long enough. He went over and knelt down at the head of the long chair.

"Hold out your hand and shut your eyes, and I'll give you something to make you wise." His left hand was in his pocket again.

She looked at him intently for a moment and then obeyed the childhood bidding. He dropped the ring into her outstretched palm, and watched the pathetic joy wash over her face and the devotion in her hands as she slipped it on again. She lay still in the chair for a moment—eyes closed—her expressive body very touching to Stephen.

Then she swept upward, twisting sidewise, and kissed him, clinging afterward, her cheek against his and a hand on his hair. He knelt unmoving in the awkward embrace and as passive as he could make himself. He did not return the kiss. It was a great moment, he knew that, though sweeping perceptions confused him.

She wanted to know, of course. He had found the ring that morning pushed down behind a slipping cushion in the car.

"Why didn't you give it to me at once?—Just to tease me?"

"No, not to tease you. I just—awaited the moment. And it paid me," he added, dangerously but hopefully.

She played up in a good laugh. There was no silly embarrassment nor squeamish reaction in it. They were past the poison-ivy stage—for a while, at least, he thought.

She swung out of the long chair, trailing her crimson gown, sat down nearer him by the fire. It was astonishing how joy had healed her face and strengthened her movements. But the devastation which had been wiped out was still alarming.

"How old were you when your mother died?" Stephen said gently.

"I was just a little baby—not many hours old."

They sat in the quiet which Stephen liked as always, whatever it was he needed. Then she began to talk—the rush of her words eloquent even without their sense: the ring she had had to give back and how Mr. Blake brought it to her in the velvet box two years ago. Her mother's prayer-book, the carriage-boots, the spoons that were not hers, which belonged to another lost person whose initials even were unknown.

"I used to hold some one thing in my hand and try to think back to her. Stirring her tea with her spoon. Only I didn't know what the room was like where she sat. But her hand had held the spoon. I'd try on the carriage-boots and try to see her walking across a snowy walk to the opera house. Only I didn't know who was with her nor whether she sat in a box or where. My father told me after I was in the college play that she was a dancer. That year in college I went to her church and took her prayer-book. But I didn't understand it much. Maybe I can find her that way now."

"Might be the best way," Stephen commented. "The background is unchanged, and the experience is an inner experience. You could share it, maybe."

She looked at him intently.

"How old were you when you started on your search for her?"

"Going on ten."

He considered a moment and then said,

"You must have been like a little lost princess in a fairy tale trudging through terrifying woods."

"I was! I was! And it comforted me to know I was! I liked to find people like me in the books. I made up little plays out of the stories for Eugene and me—Louisa sometimes. Lyddy helped us."

"Eugene the little chap whose violin is downstairs?"

"Yes. He was lame."

Stephen felt his eyes suddenly stinging: two little lonely crippled kids in the woods.

"Eugene knew by heart the part where the ugly duckling became a swan. He made up a little tune for it."

"Big Klaus and Little Klaus. Great relief to have the little fellow win, I remember," Stephen carried on.

"My favorite was *The Little Match Girl*."

"Yes," said Stephen. The good quiet came down again except for the interwoven sounds the flame made.

It reminded her of the book she had found in the attic box.

"She had written her name in it. Just Jessy. In pencil. I'll show you."

She brought the book from a desk drawer. He turned the rough pages absently. Then he read aloud:

*"In heaven, though, when she had flown there with the sunshine, nobody asked about the red shoes."*

"I never cried at that part," Jessy said, but there were tears in her eyes as she said it.

Stephen only said, "You liked that attic, I bet."

"Yes! I did! I like it yet. I like to think about people up there. There's a portfolio of pencil sketches somebody made. And a carriage parasol. Things sacred to the memory. Somebody who put them away carefully thought so each time. There's a doll carriage that belonged to the little girl mama was. My father's collection of arrowheads. … That's why I like this room so much. Sacred to the memory. Like my great-grandfather's tombstone with the schooner on it out there. She used to let me play wand with the pearl pen. Do you want to see it?"

He held the pen, turning it gently between thumb and fingers. Perhaps he ought to snap its silly little handle into bits and toss the fairy tales into the fire. He crossed the room and wrapped the book in the tissue paper from which she had taken it and tied the blue ribbon in a bow; then he put the pen in its narrow box. He stood for a long minute by the windows that flanked the desk, looking up the hill at the cemetery and the dripping trees.

"Are they all buried up there?"

"All except my stepmother and my father," and she told him how he was drowned where Shelley was drowned.

It would be better if those stones were removed and broken up, he was thinking as he listened, and the ground leveled off.

"How old are you now, Jessy?"

"Twenty-two." She was not surprised by the unconventional question.

"So you really had *him,* didn't you? About twenty years."

She did not reply so volubly, but she told him: her father's absences, his seclusion, the darkness around him, the time he took the book away.

"I don't know what made that darkness. I think now it was blacker than it should have been."

"He'd lost both his wives and his little boy."

"Yes, but there was another quality to it, as I think of it now. Something I don't know."

"God, hold that part back!" Stephen was thinking as he replied, "Maybe he was seeking in the wood, too. Most of us have to."

"Lyddy thought so," she said absently and went on.

"I lived twenty years while he lived, but most of the time he was not so real to me as the 'mother' I never knew and the 'mama' I had lost. And now that he is gone he is more real than when we sat at the table together. The things you never have and the things you lose you keep."

She said it with conviction.

"But there were a few times. I can't talk about them now. Maybe never. Once when he was surrounded by ... golden light. I don't need anything to keep him as he was then. ... And if he had to die, I am glad he died as he did!" Her talk had worked out of childishness. She did not seem unstable nor rebellious. She had come farther than she knew in the sudden release the morning had brought, he suspected, and she had thought it out more clearly than ever before. But Stephen was appalled.

"The things you never had and the things you lose you keep," she had said.

Out of one of those tea-parties of genteel conversation, a gushing voice (unembodied now) rippled back to him with devious relevance.

"Let's each of us tell what is our favorite poem!"

There was a somewhat blank silence under which, he suspected, was a scrambling to mention something not too discreditable to knowledge and taste. Louisa burst in with "Hiawatha" to get it off her mind. "Crossing the Bar," the minister said.

"And yours, Mr. Geddes," the relentless gusher went on. He never had a favorite anything, he said. Too many favorites.

Jessy cut in clearly before she could be called on. She wanted to say, he noticed, the only one who did.

"Mine's the 'Ode on the Grecian Urn,' " she said, seriously.

The gusher gushed on and somehow the triviality wore itself into oblivion.

*The things you never had and the things you lose you keep.*

"She is trying to live on a Grecian urn." The sentence came into his mind a formulated judgment, rushing into words.

She loves the silken heifer, forever silken, her garlands fresh; and the lover in the moment of ecstasy before the kiss.... She misses the sequences: the beauty of the crimson sacrifice and the burning of the kiss. She remembers more than she lives.... She is stuck in stanza one.

And "The Lady of Shalott." The lady who never looked at the river or the road or the passersby except in a mirror. Not even for a long time at the gallant and handsome knight. When she did look, she died.... Jessy finds it comforting.

*I like to find people like me in the books.*

It was a comfort that her father's last cry bubbled out where Shelley's did. And she would like *bubbling* because Byron said it.... Her virginal squeamishness was only one detail.

Jessy was weeping gently. She seemed oblivious of him as she looked into the fire. He did not understand for a moment; it was so long since she had spoken. Then he remembered: "...a time when he was surrounded in golden light." The tears were healthy ones, he hoped, but he could not watch her through the keyhole of the door she had closed.

She did not know when he left.

# CHAPTER SEVENTEEN

Stephen, like Jessy's mother, did not often make a formed decision. He had learned not to. If he stood before three open doors, he waited unhurriedly. By and by, one door would close and then the second. Or if no door closed, he would in time find himself pushed gently through one of them. But in mid-August his system did not seem to be working well. There were two doors; both stood open and both drew him. The power that had so often moved him was turned off.

The boarders were beginning to go with the zest for home and work that a good vacation gives, and the Bold Water folks— so he learned from one of his cronies—were looking forward to the long quiet of autumn and Indian summer and the hush of winter and the concentrated business of each. His dilatoriness would not fit in, and he did not want to be dilatory any longer. He had followed directions carefully for the whole summer—not apparently, however, he prided himself; and he had not been merely marking time. The sea, the clear air, the color and, above all, the rhythms had been working deeply for him in the great enterprise. But if he were going, it was time to go. He must make his money last: he must do with it what his mother had saved the premiums for so zealously. He was the heir of her ambition. That door was open wide and was urgent.

Jessy was beyond the other door and he could not turn and walk away. He wanted to kiss her for the kiss she gave him when he returned the ring—and many more times, he knew that clearly enough now, and he thought that in time she might want him to.

He thought, with a kind of Messianic urge which, too, was part of his inheritance from his mother, that he might be able to help her.

"I sound like an ass," he thought, "as if I were the gallant prince or the handsome cowboy come to the rescue. But just the same she did some real living that rainy morning. And there was no silly reaction of embarrassment, either."

Maybe she needed him, but more and more he sensed that he needed her. He knew it when he entered a room where she was—even with others; when he looked down at her standing before him or when she walked beside him, "the smaller of the two"; when he recalled deliberately the twisted and awkward embrace by the long chair, her hand on the back of his head, the little-girl kiss. … After all, the sharp closing of an important door had sent him to Bold Water. Perhaps the Push was moving him to her.

It was moving him in any case to the church on a Sunday afternoon for a rehearsal. There was to be a sacred concert; Jessy, somewhat surprised, was the chairman through the collusion of Mrs. Blake and Lyddy. They had also added a strain of match-making to their efforts.

"It's the only way she can be saved," Mrs. Blake had said earnestly. Louisa, eagerly in love, thought so, too.

The plan for the afternoon worked out well, as separate preceding efforts of the chorus, the quartet, the duets and the solos culminated in the final rehearsal. Stephen rejoiced in the good time that the chorus was having and in the really lyrical quality of the quartet. Jessy sang in a contralto whose color told him something new. He saw a new Louisa as she stood in front of the chorus for her solo. "She's a church-social diva," he thought. The tawdry Holy City had an honest hosanna.

The vocal rehearsal over, he abetted Mrs. Blake's plan without knowing it.

"I guess I'll stay and practice for a while. I'm not sure I have all those stops under control."

Louisa struck in not too subtly but effectively.

"You'd better stay, too, Jessy. You know those stops better than anybody."

Jessy was not kinder but socially quicker-witted.

"Not nearly so well as Miss Sampson!"

Miss Sampson, however, knew what everybody knew, and she loved a lover from the standpoint of sixty-three years of spinsterhood. And Jessy had upheld her organist's reputation. So she was very sorry, but she had to hurry home to feed the chickens. Louisa was taking the whole group to her house for popcorn and herded them out, urging Jessy and Stephen to follow.

Jessy contributed something from her efforts with the stops, and experimentation taught him more. Then he settled down to play.

"Do you think they'll like Bach?"

"Play it to me."

She listened from a pew in the middle of the church. He thought he had never played better, though the organ was wheezing a little and the pedals rattled "Jesu, Joy of Man's Desiring."

When he had finished, he sat still facing the organ, his hands on his knees. He had nothing to say; he had said it. Jessy was silent, too, for a time. Then she said,

"Play it again."

The second time, the yearning aspiration lifted him so high that he forgot the organ and his own uncertainty and even Jessy. But when he had finished, he turned the revolving top of the organ stool and sat facing the pews.

"Jessy," he said without hesitation. "I am going to stay all winter—maybe a year in Bold Water."

He rose then and stood facing her. She too rose and walked down the aisle toward him—like a bride.

"Will you be glad?" he said when she joined him by the organ.

"Why, yes. We all will be." Her polite formality was glorified by her eyes. They were darker and shining.

"Will you let me kiss you—in the church?"

She stood quiet a moment and then moved a little toward him and raised her face.

It was a gentle kiss, but when it was done, he was trembling. His hands were still unsteady when he closed the organ. When he turned back, Jessy was gone—out into the "lecture-room," and she did not speak or move when he joined her. He knew how she felt—at least, he thought she felt as he did: he could not walk right out even into the Sunday afternoon quiet of "the street." They stood in the front of the awkward room without awkwardness. He was staring at a big book of Bible pictures on an easel. Like wallpaper samples, he thought—a picture for today in view, preceding ones thrown back over the top. A Golden Text was at the bottom.

"Do you know," said Jessy suddenly, "all those old gentlemen—or most of them—are my ancestors?"

Around the room were framed portraits—several enlarged photographs and some hard and shiny paintings—"hand-paintings," local pride called them—portraits of solemn, sometimes grim, worthies in clerical dress of various types—the older ones with bands or stocks.

"Most of them are Smithpeterses. That big one by the door is my grandfather."

He looked at the picture she pointed out.

"Gosh," he said definitively.

They both laughed. She knew how to resolve a situation, he thought.

"But if you climb up on a chair to look at him, you'll see more than his chin and jaw." Stephen did so. "Look at his eyes," she went on.

"You're right. Savonarola's eyes. Some St. Francis, too. But I don't believe I would have wanted to live with him. His eyes knew more than he did. I guess he lived in the wrong part of him."

He circled the walls—reading the neat name-plate on each frame.

"How is it that this church seems to be a family affair?"

"It *is* remarkable. There was an article about it in a church paper once. It lasted until my father broke the sequence and a stranger became the minister. He was a philosopher—my father. Have I told you? ... The very first minister was a Smithpeters. He was the one who was ordained out at Ordination Rock. You've seen that, haven't you?"

He had not.

"That's a good story."

"When the first pastor came there was no church, really no pastor, for he was young and not ordained. His zeal could not be delayed, however. He began to preach from the big rock after he had hewed out steps so that he could mount with seemly dignity. Before his first summer was over, brethren from the nearest parishes came and ordained him—on the rock. A tablet commemorated that solemn day. He was a Smithpeters."

"Should you like to drive out there in the phaeton with me? Now?"

He was glad to. He did not mention Louisa's popcorn.

It was sunny on the pulpit. Jessy sat in the chair hewn out by her ancestor and Stephen on a seat of moss, green and plushy. The young pastor had chosen wisely, for his pulpit faced a slightly sloping area of rock like a segment of an amphitheater. All around, the trees had advanced but the first church of Bold Water was unchanged.

"Stephen," Jessy said. "I know you, but I don't know anything about you. I'd like to get acquainted."

"Pleased to meet you," Stephen replied. "My life is an open book. What would you like to know?"

"Where is your home?"

He sat down on the moss, knees drawn up, hands clasped around them.

"Michigan. Upper peninsula. You remember? Lower peninsula like a mitten? Upper one peaked out north-east? Up where the copper is mined.... You'd like Michigan. It's like this region—cold, clear air and the blue water and spruces. We haven't any ocean, but we have Lake Superior. It's big and deep and cold—always beautiful summer and winter but terrifying sometimes."

"Is your little accent the way people talk in Michigan?"

"No, people don't talk any particular way in Michigan. I talk a little like my mother, I guess. She was a Welsh girl."

"And your father?"

"He is English. They came together to America after their wedding. Two children—Victoria and Stephen. He is in the copper mining company and loves it. He's never made much money though.... He likes to have little copper things around the house—paper-knives and bowls and trays...a little copper-sheathed clock on his desk. He is a hunter—and has a dog like Bingo only with liver-colored spots."

His hand was burrowing in a pocket, and then was stretched out towards her, palm up. On it lay a ponderous English penny. "Hold it a while. It brings luck."

"What kind of luck?"

"Luck in living. He has a knack for it. So did Mother."

"And your mother?"

"She died two years ago."

"Is she buried in Michigan?"

"Yes, in a country graveyard. Like yours."

"Is it pretty there?"

"There's a view of the lake. Sky-blue water as far as you can see."

"You must like to go there."

"No." He was speaking now more carefully. "I sodded her grave myself. She loved grass. And I had a big boulder set there with a copper plate on it. Her name and birthplace and date. Another little piece of copper for my father. ... Like your grandfather's schooner, isn't it? ... No, I didn't go there much. I don't believe I will go any more."

"Why not?"

"Because everything there seems so irrelevant. The real things—" He suddenly broke off. He could not charge in like that. She did not pursue the question anyway. She had another.

"And what is your sister like?"

"Like her name."

Jessy did not pause on Victoria.

"But you, Stephen, who are you? 'What is it that you do?' "

He laughed carefully. Always quotations!

"You make me feel like The Leech-Gatherer."

She laughed, too.

"What is your occupation, Mr. Geddes?"

"I am a musician. Semi-professional. Would-be professional. I can play the piano, the pipe-organ and odds and ends—bassoon, oboe, glockenspiel—."

"Harmonica." Jessy finished his sentence, she thought, but he added, "Bass drum."

"Go on," she said quietly. "There's more to tell. Tell it all."

He did. He had to begin with his mother and the eisteddfods—in Wales and in the Michigan choral society.

"She was a great conductor. She really was. I know it now better than ever. How she could make those miners sing 'Men of Harlech'! They weren't Welsh, either. They sang abstractly."

"She had started me out early, in infancy. She said she knew which songs I liked and didn't like when I was six weeks old. Howled dismally at 'Hush, my babe, lie still and slumber.' I hate that tune yet—makes me feel like a dog when the bell tolls."

And she had sat him up to the piano, tied in his high-chair, and wouldn't let him pound—took him down if he did; showed him how to play one note with one finger till he got so he liked it. "I grew to be quite a legend all around the neighborhood—little Stevie Mozart."

To his everlasting gratitude, she had given him his first piano lessons and she played and sang all the musical beauty and grandeur she knew in countless family recitals. She loved the promise of the phonograph. "Not much yet, but some day they will be wonderful for children to have at home—if they don't stop the music lessons to listen," she used to say.

She built up a good-sized class of pupils. She read music magazines and went to music-teachers' conventions, made a local name for herself; and saved up enough money to send Stephen to the conservatory.

"That's about all. They gave me scholarships after a while, but she had earned them."

Jessy said nothing for a time. She was watching something beautiful in Stephen's face as he turned it up to her from his humble seat.

"Could she ever hear you play in college recitals? Come to see you graduate?"

"Yes, thank God, she could and did! I played the 'Appassionata' at my graduation recital! She loved it. Afterwards—" but Jessy did not pause.

"And now?" she prompted him.

"I'm composing now," he said simply. "I studied with good men in composition. They encouraged me. I've had a little recognition of my few publications. I am getting ready for my first ambitious attempt."

"Opus No. 1," said Jessy. "What is it?"

"A sonata. ... I have accomplished a good deal today."

"Today?"

But he did not reply. The wind blowing through the warm spruces brought fragrance to Ordination Rock. A delayed thrush was singing back in the woods.

"Stephen."

"Yes, darling?" He said it absently.

"You are going to stay in Bold Water all winter, maybe longer. You are getting ready to compose your sonata."

He was glad she asked no prying questions on the obvious dilemma and made no reply which might lead to one.

Immediately she did ask one.

"Do you compose at the piano?"

"Some of the time. I want one handy."

"Then you must give up either the sonata or Bold Water unless ... Stephen, will you use mine? It is a good one, you said. The music room is secluded. You will not disturb or be disturbed. Will you, Stephen?"

The Push had outdone itself this time. He had gone through both doors into a pleasant room of double satisfaction. It had given him unthought of ways and means. It told him that Jessy wanted him to stay.

The plan was so eternally right that his polite demurrings were feeble. He accepted with jubilant restraint.

# CHAPTER EIGHTEEN

Lyddy arranged the details with Stephen—charmed by his thoughtfulness of a housekeeper's problems. Of course, he need not vacate on cleaning day. That room could be done early—before he wanted to come. And he need not bother with a key. She would see that the French windows were unlocked so that he could slip in from the side. And there was a foot-path through the woods from the village—not so steep as the road if he cared to walk sometimes. Sinbad or the stableman would be glad, however, to help him start his car any time. He could play the piano in there as loud as he wanted to. Miss Isabel had meant it to be soundproof.

"That's fine," said Stephen, "but I won't really play much. If you ever hear me, you'll probably think I'm tuning it!"

Lyddy would be glad to send in his lunch on a tray if he ever wanted to stay on. That attention he declined. He couldn't think of putting her to that trouble. It wouldn't *be* any trouble, she insisted cordially.

"She's my ally whether she knows it or not," he thought. She thought the same about him.

Neither she nor anybody else in the house knew on which morning he started coming or at what hours he arrived and left. She was not even sure whether he came every day or not. That lack of observation was wonderful for Stephen.

"When I work, I'm like an old mother cat that is going to have kittens," he had once confided to his mother. "I don't want anybody to know anything about me till I have something to show. I go under the barn."

No girl ever gave her beau so good and perfect a gift. The room was quiet and not intrusive in spite of its handsomeness; there was stimulating warmth in it because it was Jessy's and she had lent it to him. He had forgotten to tell Lyddy that he would need a desk, but a pretty cherry writing-table with emptied drawers appeared, standing at right angles to the piano and between it and the windows. It had never been there before. So Jessy was thinking about him, for he was quite sure that Lyddy knew nothing about the business of composing. Or Jessy either, but she could think it out. He stowed away his materials and went to work regularly, pleased but not surprised to see how fertile the summer had made him. If he couldn't compose under such conditions, he never could anywhere.

"And I am in love besides," he found himself thinking, surprised only at the codification of his feeling.

It was pleasant to think of her—somewhere in the house with him. He had little notion how she ordinarily occupied herself except for gardening and reading and playing the piano. Now, he could only surmise reading, her gardening being largely done till covering time. She couldn't read all the time. There was a hovering satisfaction, nevertheless, under her roof, better because of vagueness.

He thought, at first, she felt as he did, because when they met in afternoon or evening as before, she made no reference to his work or his place for work—not even when he dined alone with her one evening, she in her high-backed chair. She was graciously at ease, pleasant, and interesting in conversation but as coolly remote as she had been the first day he called upon her. Once she took a long drive with him alone—in the same genial but distant friendliness. He followed her lead—let her set the key.

He speculated about her, though, as days went by and she still kept her distance. After all, they had recently had together two rare experiences, one close after the other—by her fire and in the church—each heightened and deepened by a kiss. Two very special kisses, he considered them—epochal kisses. It was incredible that her complicated girlishness had not been profoundly moved. It would not have been so hard to understand if she had seemed embarrassed or stiffly restrained in the reaction; her earlier squeamishness would have been made logical. She simply acted as if nothing had occurred.

Sometimes he wondered whether her habit of luxuriating in memory was so set that she was thus cherishing even recent experiences—the hour on Ordination Rock a bas-relief on an urn; was re-living the moments in his arms by the church organ. Maybe she translated them into a story and so enjoyed them. "I liked to find people like me in books," also meant that she liked to find herself like them. Sometimes, he was skeptical about that book-obsession idea of his. Maybe it was not so acute as he had thought that day in her sitting-room. After all, there is many a normal girl who has a habit of lugging in literary allusions—just a mild form of intellectual vanity. But just the same this habit had bothered him several times in a way he always paid attention to—though the Dickinson introduction had seemed so charming—*I'm nobody. Who are you? Are you nobody, too?*

"I'm no psychologist," he thought, "but there were many who didn't know the terms. Common sense ought to help."

One day at his desk, his mind trailing off from his task, another conclusion settled in his mind: she was living her life in separate compartments. The idea grew more tenable as it came and went. It explained the ease with which she could ignore what had happened. It interpreted her obsession for the Grecian Urn. It made her escape into memory and books reasonable—and disturbing.

And the compartments in which she tended to spend the most time were not the compartments of real living. She enjoyed acting, she had said.

"I'm no psychologist," he thought again, "but I'll go to bat on that point." Somewhere he had read the word *dividedness*.

He had a refuge which he called his outdoor studio. It was a low ledge on the cliff where he could sit in a rocky nook, sheltered and yet enlivened by the vibrancy before him: leaping fish and soaring birds and the gorgeousness of the cobalt streaks in the water; the sudden appearance of a sloop around the point off-shore, poised and sure in her beauty and power; or a vessel as she swung at anchor. Occasionally, when he could not strike his pace, he went down there to await the impulse he needed or the idea he was groping for. The swinging walk, the clear air, the fecund sunshine set him going again. September was gorgeous that year and warm. Sometimes he ate there the lunch that Mrs. Spencer gave him on request.

He was just finishing his sandwich when he heard footsteps on the easy little path, and in a moment Jessy came around the tall rock that gave seclusion, as surprised as he was.

"I never noticed before," she said after mutual welcomes, "that there are places for two to sit here, and there is a tiny table between us."

She sat down on her rock and he on his. She was dressed in a plaid blouse and a thick heavy skirt—a "golf skirt" he seemed to remember it should be called—smart woolen stockings and stout oxfords. He had not noticed before how much summer had tanned her face to a good ruddy color. She looked vigorous. And unhurried.

Stephen laid his two peaches on the table—a clean paper napkin beneath them.

"Dessert," he said.

The peaches were good and ripe—and large. Eating absorbed them. There was no conversation in the general juiciness. But when the peach stones were tossed down into the pool and fingers wiped on the one napkin, she said,

"Stephen, how did your sonata get started in the first place?"

He fell into step at once.

"I got one little melody—it came to me."

"Where were you when it came?"

"I was at home. Shaving. In the bathroom."

She giggled.

"Let's call it 'Sonata Tonsorialis.' "

"Or 'Sonata Saponacia.' "

The giggling developed into laughter. He liked to laugh with Jessy. It died down and broke out again with his "Sonata Razorina" and diminished into a refreshing sort of silence.

"I suppose," she went on, "that the little tune will appear a good many times and in a good many forms."

"That's right. You've learned to pick 'em, I see."

"What happened next?"

"I played around with it in my head and on paper and at the piano to see what I could make of it. Like moulding all the things you could out of a sphere of soft clay."

"And then?"

"I collected some more as they came to me—wrote them down."

"And what are you doing in our music room in the mornings?"

"I am trying to see what I can do with all my various ideas. I throw them into different forms.... change 'em and yet keep 'em.... Change the rhythm, the key ... break 'em up ... make the folks think there is something new and yet let them have the fun of hearing the same thing. You know. You have listened a good deal."

"Yes.... And then you make a complicated web. Everything woven together—like a tapestry. Is that right?"

"That's it. And the hardest thing—for me at least right now—is getting a sense of direction. Where is it all going to? ... Sometimes I come down here to get it."

"What I think really important to know is this: where do you get a musical idea in the first place?"

At that moment, Stephen had his great idea—not a musical idea, but it came like one and would have to be developed in the same way. If he could explain—if she could see. It was not more formed than that, but it both excited and relieved him.

"Well," he said brightly, "all of a sudden there it is and you grab it."

"I never grab them. Nor even hear them. Why not?"

"My old teacher used to answer the beginners who asked that question by asking another, 'Why don't dogs meow and cats bark?' He said it all depends on how you naturally express yourself. If you don't naturally meow you'll never be an important cat."

She did not reply at once. Then she said slowly (and he liked the tone in which she spoke), "I don't think I ever expressed myself so well—and so freely—as I did in the college play I told you about."

"That's the way I feel when I play or compose."

"I've played in pupils' recitals and I was always too scared to know what I was doing."

"Stage fright at the play?"

"Not a bit."

He stood up on the ledge. Jessy watched his heels for wings again.

"But where does that first little melody come from? That is what I want to know."

That was what Stephen wanted to tell. He sat down.

"I had a wonderful teacher in composition. He used to let us sit around with him and talk and smoke our pipes. He gave me my first one—said it would make a philosopher out of me. ... Good old German he was. Sometimes when we were talking he'd get up without a word, play something on the piano, and then resume the conversation. Only for him it had been no interruption at all. I heard that once in a fiery committee meeting—teachers—he got up in the midst of an argument and played *Am Meer* without a word before or after. Then he made a motion that was carried. Wolfgang his name was. He loved to sing—in a bellow. But what a hand he had on the piano. And how he did glory in composition!"

The memory brought out Stephen's pipe. Jessy waited quietly while he strove to fire it up.

"I want you to know how I felt about him before I tell you that on one point I was brash enough to disagree with him. Still do. About what you have just asked me. He always said that a musical idea was a gift from heaven. It came or it didn't come and there was nothing you could do about it." The pipe was not yet going.

"The lightning strikes you or it doesn't."

The bubbling puffs were finally effective.

"Uh huh. But I thought and still think I know ways to make one come. … It's all indirect. I'll say that. You don't go at it as if you were writing a book on the French priests in northern Michigan in the 17th century—a history book. In that job you'd collect all the stuff in the books and explore the country for old graveyards and ruins and legends. Just go get it—direct means. … As for a musical idea, there it is and you grab it."

"You said you knew ways to make them come."

He paused before he spoke again.

"Did you like *The Arabian Nights* when you were a little girl?"

"Yes. I do now."

"Well, I have a slave of the lamp. He makes up my musical ideas and gives them to me. Not so instantaneously as Aladdin's did. … He's good, though. You have one, too. Everybody has. Does big jobs and little ones. Gives you the name you have tried to think of and given up. Wakes you up for the early train. Works out a solution you need."

"He works at night sometimes," Jessy struck in. "There was a trigonometry problem I couldn't do. The next morning I could."

"He's the one. He tells you what you ought to do, too, and you know he's right. All dressed in gray then and called Conscience. Some people don't know him otherwise—except as Love, maybe."

He slowed down into silence. The easy motif was started, clearly enough he hoped. Development would come.

She perceived it, he could see, for then she asked a good question.

"Is he working for you in the music room?"

"Not so much. I have another slave there. No lamprubbing for him. He has a spade and a crank that he turns. He is the good old reasoner and arranger, figure-outer. I have to have him, too.... Everybody knows *him*. The teachers advertise him all the tme. Sometimes, though, something pops up from the slave of the lamp—a new little rhythm maybe. The turning crank connects with him somehow."

"Both working at once.... Stephen, how do you rub the lamp?"

"Lots of ways.... Do you know, Jessy, you could help me with that if you would."

He knocked out his pipe and pocketed it.

"You know I will if I can. Maybe I can learn how, too."

"Maybe you can," said Stephen quietly.

His hands were busy, collecting spruce twigs and a few cones. Then he crumpled a sheet of music paper, and with his tiny fuel, laid a fire on the flat rock, handing Jessy a match.

"Will you light it? The luncheon table has become a hearth, or is it an altar?"

The little blaze sprang up between them.

"Perhaps it is all three," she said, "though I don't know exactly what I mean by that remark.... Maybe it came like a musical idea."

"Maybe so. Musicians don't always know what they have caught."

He fed the slender blaze just enough to keep it active—one twig or cone at a time.

"A fire is a means of communication, isn't it?" He put the big cone on. "Wordless—for all the crackling and snapping it does. Unformulated, too."

They watched silently till the fire had become a fuzz of warm ashes.

"Let's come here again," he said finally. "Soon."

She did not come for several days, however—at least when he was there; and he would not ask her or arrange a meeting. He was laying the little fire when she suddenly arrived. He gave her a match to light it at the right moment.

"Aren't you ever going to tell me how to rub the lamp?"

"I want to tell you about the idiot first"—and he did—the idiot who took all the hands of his clock to the repair shop and laid them on the counter. They wouldn't go, he said, and he wanted them fixed. "I must have the whole clock—the works," the repair man said. "Go home and get it." But the idiot refused. "You want to make a lot of changes and charge me a lot. There's nothing wrong with the clock but the hands. They won't go. Fix the hands."

"The works," Jessy said slowly, "the works."

"Yes," said Stephen.

He was often that kind of idiot, he went on after a pause—not all the time, he hoped. Lots of people are as bad.

"Parents," Jessy said. "Teachers."

"My mother wasn't."

"I don't believe that mine was either."

"Neither do I."

"Am I?"

He considered for a few seconds. "Yes," he said, "sometimes."

There are various methods to get the works going, he pressed on. He knew now pretty well how to start the wheels and springs and cogs that produced his musical ideas—God-given at that, though not in the sense that old Wolfgang meant. He could have known much sooner if experience were not the best teacher. His mother knew how, too, and she knew that she knew. She rubbed the lamp.

"Same thing," Jessy commented and Stephen nodded.

His mother whistled—beautifully, he went on to say, so much so that someone once asked her to give a whistling concert. She refused—said it was silly. Her notes sounded more like a veery than any orchestral instrument but a particularly versatile veery with a flair for composition. Her little tunes were enchanting and there seemed no end to them or the combination of them she could make, as she sat crocheting. The miners' wives were always having babies and she was forever helping get ready for them. Little coats and socks.

He used to ask her how she got her tunes and she always replied that she couldn't do it unless she were crocheting. She knew all the time what it took him so long to find out. He remembered that crocheting one day when he caught his love-liest melody. He had been rowing a boat by himself on a dull day.

"That is one way, I think: try to keep your active attention lightly occupied. ... Keep doing something unimportant ... something monotonous. That's the rubbing. After a while there comes up what you asked the slave for ... maybe a long time after. No matter what you asked him for."

He had worked it again and again, Stephen continued, though not often, if ever, with immediate results. Sometimes none. And not always could he trace the source of the success when he achieved it. But too often for discounting, musical material—live, vigorous, reproductive—had appeared opportunely when he had somewhat recently been doing his kind of crocheting. That was why he liked his outdoor studio.

"You can do it with music," he went on. "That is one thing music is for."

Or sewing. Or walking. Or sitting on the shore. Or dancing. Or playing solitaire. Or manicuring. Or listening to the clock. Or waiting and watching in a station.

They tossed it back and forth.

"Indoors or out," Stephen concluded, but Jessy added, "Hemstitching."

His teachers were always trying to make his mind think hard, he said, concentrate. Hers were, too, except one. But somehow there seem to be certain times when you shouldn't, when your top mind ought to get in the background.

Stephen thought she might light the fire at that moment. She did not move, however.

"The tide is rising," he said.

There was motion but imperceptible motion. One small pyramidal rock was submerged except for the sharp peak. A sloppy red jelly-fish. Thick furry weeds on the base of the big rock still high above the water. The light burden of slowness. Indistinct notions of the moon and the expanse of oceans around the globe.... After colorless wanderings of attention, measurable progress: the sharp peak was under water—visible, however, in the pale clarity ... jelly-fish gone. She leaned her head against the rock behind her and closed her eyes. The tide is coming in—is coming in. She stated it to herself. Suddenly she sat upright, leaned forward, struck her match and lighted the little fire. It snapped instantly into blaze with such vigor that she put on more of the bits of fuel. When she glanced up, Stephen was watching her, his brook-water eyes luminous. He smiled but he said nothing. His harmonica was in his hand; in a moment he began to play. He played the tide of love and exultation in living, and running in and out was a melody she had heard before.

"Why, I know," she said when he had finished. "That is the noise as of a hidden brook. You played it the day we met."

"It is one of the chief themes of my sonata. You name it perfectly. We will always call it that."

# CHAPTER NINETEEN

There had been thirteen days of storm. The wind swept around the compass—drove cold fogs in and drove them out. Black clouds piled up in the west and brought thunder, sharp lightning and hard rain. Evenings, if quiet at all, settled to thickening fog and dreary drippings and chill.

On the fourteenth day, a Saturday, Stephen did an unprecedented thing; he opened the door from the music room into the hall. Jessy, by gracious fate, was coming down the wide stairway, just turning at the landing. She paused.

"I am the Gentleman of Shalott! I am sitting in there at that piano, and outside the whole world is gorgeous and brisk. Come down and see." He flung open the front door. He was right. It was a triumphant morning—a coronation morning—a heavenly morning—gold like clear glass, garnished with jasper.

"Jessy," he said solemnly, "you have an apron on. If you insist on staying home to wear it, I am disappointed in you. Let's board the *Water Gypsy* and go wherever she goes. She gets back about sundown. Leave your apron on if you want to but come on!"

She looked at the chatelaine watch on her breast.

"We have three-quarters of an hour to get there," she said, and was running back into the house and up the stairs calling for Lyddy. ...

The *Gypsy* came out of the lee of the outer island, and the whole sparkling vista opened up before them—water, islands, sky, and the long range of hills blue-misty on the mainland. They sat right up in the bow, Jessy's feet on the anchor.

"I'm pressing right out into the breeze." There was seclusion in the wideness and Jessy was conversational. "I feel like my great-grandmother. She started out on her first real voyage after she was seventy. My father remembered the day she went. I like her. So did he. He was six."

The vessels they passed were gayly active after the thirteen stormy days—a workaday schooner loaded with lumber as well as the pleasure craft out for what was probably the last Saturday of the season—late-stayers and week-end returners aboard. There was always a polite exchange of greetings in passing. Always, somebody on the sloop waved a friendly hand, and everybody on the steamboat thought he was being waved at and responded. "Nice to be out again," the hands said. Stephen waved to everybody.

"Your great-grandmother—" Stephen said, "is she buried up at your place?"

She told him the rest of that story and explained about the captain, her husband, and stern Thomas, her son.

"Old Savonarola? He doesn't look the way she sounds."

He waved his hand to a lobster-man homeward bound. The lobster-man waved the lobster he had in his hand.

"That old Savonarola, Jessy. There's some of him in you. And a strain of your great-grandmother, maybe."

"I hope so. And a piece of my mother."

A gull skimmed the water on some errand of his, or in sheer delight. They both watched him awhile.

Stephen went on. "It isn't so much what traits you inherited. It's the gift of life. The impulse that starts everything moving in you. Everything! Life! Jessy! Life!"

She did not answer. Ahead was a bell-buoy rocking irregularly in the wind and the waves. She tried to listen to the broken cadence of its tones and the beat of the engines and the cutting swish beneath the bow all at once—a kind of counterpoint of rhythm, she thought. The wash of their boat set the buoy rocking more deeply with a variation that helped her "composition." She kept on listening to its clang long after they had passed it. As it grew slower, she found herself fitting Stephen's words to its sway—Life. ... Life. ...

The *Gypsy* was slowing down for her first stop—steaming through the passage between two islands—so close that the handsome old summer houses spaciously set in lawns and among trees above their little docks and boat-houses seemed cordial.

"It's a grander place than Bold Water," said Jessy, "but I don't like it as well. Nearly all of these folks go home for winter— nobody but caretakers left. We stay and we have stayed since I don't know when. Why, there was a famous company of Bold Water men in the Revolutionary War, and some of their descendants you know! There isn't a summer house in the place. But these places are nice to see."

"There's a splurging one," said Stephen. It was large and elaborate, rather impressively painted dark green. "Know any of these people?"

Jessy stood up—her little figure prominent in the bow.

"Marie! Marie!" she shrieked. A girl in a sailor-suit was standing in a dinghy at anchor watching the steamboat pass. "Marie!" Jessy called again, but the wind was off-shore. Stephen jumped up and trumpeted with great vigor through his hands, "Marie!" Marie got the call then. And the yelling was two-way yelling as long as possible.

"Who's she?" Stephen inquired. "I ought to know. We were on chummy terms there for awhile."

"A girl I knew at college. Marie Sands. She's awful clever with that dinghy. They're tricky little things—fast. She's probably going out—maybe regatta today. We won't see it though. The boat lands around the point."

Stephen pursued the subject of Marie.

"Was she one of your best friends?"

"Why no." She spoke as if surprised. "I don't know her very well and didn't really like her much.... I used to feel rather snubbed with her. ... But she was nice today, wasn't she?"

It occurred to Stephen that snubbing could not be done very effectively by yelling across a stretch of water and that Marie had done the only thing she could do—short of turning her back—answered inanely Jessy's inane remarks. But he was much pleased.

Jessy went on about the dinghys. Somebody back from Italy had started the fashion of colored sails, and the whole little fleet took to the idea with zest.

"It is pretty to see them darting around on regatta day— lively—sails dark-blue, light-blue, red, coral, leaf-green, orange, yellow. They all come home at the end in a procession. The skipper of the fleet is at the head in his turquoise boat with a white sail."

"Know some of 'em?" Stephen was persistent and then he was sorry he had been.

"Yes. Not very well, though." She spoke with an overtone which he caught.

But it was gone in a moment, for as the boat came close to dock, she was delighted again—to see a pea-green rowboat with pea-green oars flashing her out to a pea-green yacht.

After lunch, there was an hour's wait at a dock for the unloading. They went ashore, walked up and down the short and crooked little street, climbed a hill for the view. There was not much to do. All the prettiest places were hidden and tall iron gates shut them in.

So they went back to the dock-house and watched the unloading. It was low tide, and everything had to be hauled up a steep gang-plank. There was a pulley and a rope with strong hooks at each end—hooked into the barrows. Constantly one man was running down with an empty barrow pulling the rope that helped haul up the man with the loaded one: bags of grain, crates of live chickens, bundles of shingles, a crated ice box, kegs and barrels, trunks. It was incessant and hard work—only a half-minute pause occasionally, and only an hour between jobs. They had no breath to spare for songs or jokes like leisurely river stevedores, but they were zestful in motion and attitude. In their rhythms, Jessy thought.

There was quite a little audience on either side of the oblique pit the two gang-planks made—shopkeepers, servants waiting for goods or luggage; citizens idly inspecting the world's work going on in that tiny spot; easy and leisurely and elegant summer people watching for week-end visitors to come up the passengers' gang-plank.

"My dear God! Isn't she beautiful?" Stephen said. He was looking at a tall, well-built young woman, high-bred and gracious in manner; unaffected; unselfconscious. Her skin was clear, her teeth fine, her hair shining and crisp. She was dressed in a full-skirted dress of dull blue, and she was holding a little girl's hand on one side and a little boy's on the other. It was perfectly apparent that next summer three children would come to meet a gay and handsome young father.

Jessy looked where he was looking. She said nothing. She was embarrassed, he saw.

"Why, Jessy darling, the Romans would have made her a goddess. And Christians ought to have made a saint of such a woman—not of a pale nun. She is Easter!"

Aboard again, they sat in the rush of sunlight and dazzling water—somnolent.

"Like those big black birds on that rock," Jessy said.

"Yes, but how their wings will beat when the time comes."

Somewhere, six young people with picnic baskets got aboard—very noisy and very happy. They wanted to dance on the deck to the music of the piano in the little cabin. But there was nobody to play. They wanted to dance at once. It was made known to all. Jessy looked inquiringly at Stephen. He looked very sleepy and said nothing.

The six were crowded behind them in the bow chattering over their heads but oblivious of them.

Suddenly, she stood up and turned around.

"I can play 'Waltz Me Around Again, Willie,' if you want me to. Will that do?"

It would indeed. The whole group escorted her to the piano, lowered the stool to bring her feet to the pedals and opened all the cabin windows. She and Willie went to work with a raggy rhythm. Her sense of an audience made her beat that tinny instrument as she had never struck keys before—so loud that she could not hear the feet outside, but the feet were rejoicing. She was good, they called. She played it over and over again, trying, as it grew too wearisome, to remember another tune she had occasionally played for the girls. She got one and, after a pause, broke out with "When That Midnight Choo-Choo Leaves for Alabam." It was greeted with a whoop. She played it over, too, very sure she was nearly if not altogether at the end of her repertoire of popular dance music.

They wanted another waltz. She played "The Blue Danube" with saccharine romance. As she played it the third time, Stephen came in and leaned on the piano. When she paused, he bent down and said, "You are a young woman of infinite capacities. Don't you ever forget it." He looked both gay and earnest.

Her audience was enthusiastic and loudly grateful.

"Too bad, though," said one hearty young fisherman, "that you can't dance with your girl."

Stephen took his harmonica out of his pocket.

"I'll tell you what," he said. "You dance with—my girl. And I'll play and your girl maybe will sit it out with me!"

Out on deck again, he said, "I'll just perch on this thing with the rope wound around it."

He had no gap in his repertoire. He played all the dance hits of that summer and for several summers before. The four-man crew took turns coming up to listen and to rescue the young woman who had to sit out for Jessy's sake. Dances were "traded" until she had danced with each young man.

He drifted from tune to tune. Jessy was glad she was with the best dancer when Stephen played a new tune—so enchanting it was—with gypsy in it and fun and tender romance. Part of the time it was waltz and part two-step. Applause kept him playing it until the boat put in for the six to go ashore. They wished Jessy and Stephen could go too, but they were sailing back after supper with a fellow who'd been fishing there. The parting was merry and warm.

The sun went down in furious glory—so that the east was all pink and black as they swerved in toward Bold Water—pink in sky and on water—black mass of trees marching down to the shore.

"It was a good day, wasn't it?" Stephen said.

"Mm-*hmm*!"

"Good day to rub the lamp!"

"On that noisy boat?"

"Why, yes! There was living there. Free. Zestful. Lots of kinds of life on that noisy boat. On the dock. And the water."

Sinbad was there to drive them home in the surrey, very professionally reserved. As they went, Stephen continued the conversation begun on the deck.

"I got immediate results for once. Didn't you hear my new tune? Even got the title."

"I liked it! I danced it four times with that young man. He was a butcher. What will you call it?"

He did not answer. He was whistling again the melody the butcher liked so well. ...

Before she went to bed, Jessy ran up her window shades to the top and opened the window wide.

Mars was coming up as brilliant as the Star of Bethlehem on a Christmas card, with as clear a form—so large that it made a path of light in the quiet of the harbor water.

Sunday was always a good day for Stephen. He rather thought the commandment and the church, blue laws and all, had him in mind—solemnity, cessation, and hush ends and means for him. So he kept it holy in his own way. Being with Jessy was part of it.

They were sitting on a bench built close under the lee of the high rock in the mowed circle, facing the woods and down the harbor and out to sea. Only there was no view that day—constant view, that is. The fog had blotted out yesterday's brilliance. It was a white fog. Sometimes it fluffed up densely, sometimes drifted past so thin that it seemed little more than air in motion. Spruces were soft darkness and pointed laciness. Stephen liked the timelessness; the misty seclusion drove out both the clock and the calendar.

There was little conversation at first. It was not necessary, he thought, but he listened alertly when Jessy said what she did.

"I am rubbing the lamp without intending to. Here in the fog. And I love it."

"You're quick to learn."

She had been doing some late gardening, she said. Transplanting and setting out bulbs. She thought it was like his mother's crocheting though no whistling tunes came to her lips.

"There's something special about transplanting," she went on. "I've often thought about that. It's absorbing. I forget what time it is."

At the end of her sentence, a fawn stepped through the fog-curtain. An autumn fawn slender and strong. It gazed at them, alert and unafraid; silent and motionless they watched. Then in long, slow-motion leaps, it crossed the diameter of their circled isolation and disappeared. No comment was made except a turning of their heads for a shared smile. Presently, Jessy drifted back to her transplanting.

"Sometimes I think it is the touch of the earth—crumbly and damp under my hands. I imagine I feel fertility ... and—something else I can't name. ... I remember once lying on a sunny hillside on new spring grass—with my scarf over my eyes to shut out the light. And I could feel the world revolving and all the worlds swinging through space."

Stephen waited before he said as casually as he could, "What else happens inside you while the transplanting goes on?"

And she waited before she replied.

"Why, I don't know precisely. I am happy in a special sort of way. It's a small happiness—concentrated, I guess. ... Like a seed!"

He thought wishfully that she was going to say more.

She did. "There's urgency in it. Not urgency to do more garden work exactly. Though I always think I'll put in a few more before I stop. It's an urgency—"

"An urgency of life maybe? Really like a seed?"

Jessy laughed.

"I guess so."

There was comprehension and unanimity in the silence that closed in again, and the Push told him the time had come.

"Jessy," he said, "we are talking about something big. We both are getting inklings. It isn't merely a trick for a composer's daily job. It is no slave. Nor a relaxed musing. Nor a handy problem-solver. Though it's all of these. It is grand and fundamental.

"I think it is this: there is a Deep Place in us where the power is—the works of the clock. Not enough people know about it, or, if they do, how to utilize it. A Deep Place—capital D—capital P."

He must not address her like a public meeting. Selah, his mother once told him, means *stop and think,* and it is an important word on a Sunday morning. The Selah lingered—productively, he hoped. She was listening.

"Like electricity," he picked up again. "We've found ways to use it—lights, street-cars, telephones—but that is only a beginning, the imaginative scientist says. He has inklings, too."

He was trying to be quietly conversational.

"The ancients knew about it. Sometimes they said heart and sometimes bowels, but I bet they meant what we mean! The saints knew, and the seer, and lots of poor strugglers. Some of the poets. All the artists work from there whether they know it or not. ... Selah!"

Jessy's eyes turned toward him with a quirk of inquiry and then back to indeterminate gazing into the blurred trees, as he waited for grace to go on rightly.

"And yet millions of people have struggled and travailed—as if a woman in a house wired for electric lights turned a switch but toiled to render tallow to mould candles to sit in a dim room, straining her eyes to read and to sew. As if a man in a boat tugged at heavy clumsy oars with blistered hands while all the time furled sails were ready to be let out to a brisk and favorable wind."

Perhaps he should stop, but he wanted to put his conclusion in explicit terms which perhaps she did not need.

"It is a quiet place—in those depths, but it generates an even, constant flow of productivity. We need to find more ways to release it. ... And use it. And we've got to find more little homely human ways of turning it on—more crocheting and transplanting and dancing on a steamboat. Find times when our ordinary powers are in abeyance—to give these welling powers a chance."

He felt as he often did when he had played his heart out on the piano—drained but exalted. The fluffy hush cooled and quieted him as the moments moved.

"You mean," she said clearly, "that if you sit quietly on a Sunday morning and wait, a fawn will come out of the fog, don't you?"

He broke into gayety.

"And elephants and honey-bees and horses for the pony-express!"

She was quick.

"It isn't just a matter of moony, vague yearnings and pretty fawn ideas for poetry or music. An elephant will come to move the teak. That's it, isn't it?"

She went on after a pause. "Fog is a good way. It is soundless—isolating. It is so—present; nothing but here and now."

"But so is effort! And exercise! And whenever it happens all of you is focused. There is no dividedness—if you know what I mean. Whatever you are doing you are all for it."

It was then that she told him about those moments in the math class—her father transfigured in the doorway.

"That is exactly what I mean," he told her in his gayety. "You induced the suspension of the ordinary which a creative artist must have. You were living supernally."

She liked the formal respect he gave to her experience.

"That is the way you live when you live on that deep level." He had to say it again. "With every cell and fiber of your body and with all the forces of the part that isn't body. As you did that day—as we did on the boat yesterday. That tune," he went on, "I shall call 'Young Man with His Girl on a Steamboat.' "

She laughed without embarrassment.

"Will it be in the sonata?"

"Maybe, modified."

"In the third movement?"

"Yes, but it will be involved with other things."

It was more than he had hoped for, but it was logical. After all, she knew a sort of inner life. They had remembered the Sabbath Day. ...

She heard it first.

"The bell across the bold water," she said.

"What is bold water?"

She told him.

"Variations on a favorite theme," he said.

# CHAPTER TWENTY

Tom Greenleaf—science-absorbed, literal Tom in his severely new office—gave Stephen the variation that started the fourth movement. It was as if Tom's kind blunt sentences had obliterated all words. The concept swept in on deep chords of mystery and finality—awe with no strains of terror; into a chorale of glory: the chariot of fire, Christian crossing the river with all the trumpets sounding on the other side. And the sweet chariot, swinging low. ... Stephen listened—his head raised a little. Finally he spoke.

"Maybe it will be 'Opus Posthumous.' But I hope it won't be unfinished."

He had to voice it but not to Tom.

Tom's ears did not heed.

"Didn't you know—at all?"

Yes, he knew. He was sent to Bold Water for a rest. He had had an illness that left his heart pretty rocky. He thought he'd followed his directions fairly well. Tom nodded.

"And I've been happy—happier than—"

His voice did not break. He was listening again—parting music, unbearably sweet. ...

"I was careful. Early to bed and late to rise. Didn't climb—save on stairs. He said I could drive the car if I didn't crank it. ... So you other guys did the cranking."

"I thought it took two men always."

Stephen grinned. That was what he had hoped they would think. The harmonica and other things helped him to cover up, too.

"Doctor said maybe my—engine might get better if I slowed down."

"He was right," Tom replied. "It might have … but it didn't. And it won't now. I'm afraid it's done for, Stephen, as I said before. I guessed when you told me what happened last night, and now I'm fairly sure."

He was looking over Jordan and what did he see? And what did he see on this side?

"How … long, do you guess, Tom?"

"Hard to tell. Most any time. Might be quite a while. Might not. … Longer, of course, if you go to bed and stay there."

There were two things he wanted to get done, Stephen explained, reasonably. He would need to stay up most of the time. He'd rest all he could, though.

"And I don't want anybody to know, Tom. Nobody in the house knew what happened last night. I'd gone to bed. And the spell passed—fairly soon. Nobody needs to know, do they?"

"It's your business," said Tom with transparent gruffness. "Use your good sense. I'll keep you supplied with what you need."

Tom's clock was ticking loudly but Stephen lingered.

"Very busy, Tom? Anybody in the outside office?"

Tom opened the door: there was no one.

"Have to go on your rounds right away? Any baby imminent? Any old lady on the rampage?"

Apparently nothing was pressing. …

"Tom, once you offered to tell me about Jessy, and I didn't want to hear then. I guess I need to know now. … I'll light my pipe."

It was a pretty somber story, Tom said. He got it chiefly from the old doctor who'd started him out and who'd known all the Sparkses and Smithpeterses. He'd been in both households for years. He had delivered Jessy. … He was a wise old codger. He'd seen things going on that worried him—things he couldn't help.

Tom went on to a factual diagnosis of the persons concerned. Stephen listened sharply and with compassion. He asked a few questions. There were some facts that he was glad to know—facts that confirmed and clarified his deductions, and deepened his concern. He was grateful, he said.

The outer office door was opened and shut. Some one sat down heavily and asthmatically. But Stephen was still intent.

"I must decide what to do about Jessy, Tom. It's a good time. She's out of town shopping this week."

"Are you engaged?"

"No."

"In love?"

"Yes. I am and I know it. Jessy is, I hope and believe, though maybe she doesn't realize. She will be. I am quite certain. And now—"

He did not need to finish. It was clear. Something was growing that must bloom and fruit or be rooted out. There was no easy *status quo* to fall back upon.

Tom put it haltingly.

"Suppose you go on—making love—awaken her. Maybe marry. Why then, Stephen, she might be—"

"Say it, Tom."

He could not. Would not. A widow. Stephen went on without the word.

"Wouldn't it be another—throw her back to a worse state than ever? Might be too much, Stephen."

Stephen did not break the silence for a time. He was hearing rich wild voices singing about trouble—and a way of comfort. Nobody knows.

"And if I just drift off? Leave and not come back. Just stop writing gradually. What would happen then?"

Tom considered. His eyes looked anxiously at the ranks of new books and neat bottles on his shelves and then back to Stephen.

"Maybe the same thing. And if you tell her everything to help her through what's ahead, it won't help much. Just an indefinite period of dread. In the end she might be even more helpless. She's got to do it without you."

Stephen nodded.

"I guess it's a lonely job for you, Stephen. You'll just have to make up your mind what's to be done."

Tom could not know what quick help his futile remark was—the correction that Stephen needed. No, he would not make up his mind, but he hoped that before Jessy came home he would know the right plan or a first step. Or feel a direction forming.

He thought he'd go up to Jessy's house, and Tom's buggy took him to the door after puffing old Captain O'Brien was taken care of. The captain rode along as far as the lobster pound; Stephen sat forward in the seat to give his old bulk room, and Tom lowered him to the planks at the dock head.

He stood looking up at the two young men, his red face merry in its white whiskers. Then he turned and lumbered toward the pound, singing hoarsely his usual song:

We sailed two years to there and back
And we didn't sight a whale
And we didn't get a bar'l of ile
But we had a damned fine sail!

Stephen was whistling its salty tune as the buggy moved on. "Good doctrine, Tom," he said.

Lyddy was most cordial. She was sweeping off the broad flight of steps when Tom drew up at the carriage block and Stephen stepped elegantly out.

"My man brought me up," he said haughtily. "Home, Thomas. I will remain."

Lyddy giggled and caught her cue, holding the door for him with humble formality.

Once inside, her warm friendliness steamed up again. She was especially glad to see him, she said. Jessy was away, and Sinbad was away. So she'd let the cook and the maid have their vacations. It was lonesome. ... She was just about to have a cup of cocoa. Would he join her?

He would indeed. It occurred to him that he was more than hungry. And Lyddy thought that wet and cold were coming.

It was cozy and comforting in Lyddy's sitting-room, and the cocoa was spicy and hot. She produced some cookies, large and soft. Stephen was delighted.

"My mother made 'em, too! Mattresses, I always called 'em."

Lyddy watched him. He looks a little peaked, she thought—and said nothing. When the little meal was done, she asked if he would not like to rest on her couch. He would indeed do that, too. And almost the instant he stretched out he was deeply asleep. She laid her crocheted afghan over him and watched his quiet face for a few minutes as she stood beside the couch. He looked more than peaked. He was white with a bluish line at the edge of his lips. ...

He slept until late afternoon, and when he woke golden weather was gone. Rain drove in from two directions at once and wind howled winterishly around the big house. When Lyddy came in, he was standing at the window watching two counter-blasts of diagonal rain crossing each other in a lacy diamond-shaped pattern.

"It's going to be a bad night," she said with well-simulated anxiety. "All signs point to it and we haven't had any equinoctial storms yet. Could I ask a favor of you?"

She would feel much better if he would stay the night. He could use things of Sinbad's, and the down-stairs bedroom was always ready. Besides, he might miss the next day's work if the weather roared up worse.

He might, at that, and the kindness under the false timidity was too pleasant to leave. He was hungry and drowsy again—and appalling loneliness was not far off.

Stephen's night in Sinbad's stocky night-shirt was refreshing. He woke up thinking clearly about Captain O'Brien and his song. ... Perhaps few sailors, when the voyage is done, ever have seen many whales and barrelled enough oil.

" 'And I have had a damned fine sail. ... One bar'l is partly filled.' " His reflections moved on lightly and quickly.

He liked the rim between sleeping and waking, where lucid judgment comes without effort—poised judgment to be glanced at with welcome but without decision.

One judgment, however, emerged clearly final in those early minutes. What had been growing in Jessy and in him could not be rooted out. The bloom and the fruit must come. He wondered that his mind had ever put the question. ... He jeered at himself for his better-to-have-loved-and-lost attitude in view of his position in the situation, then jeered at the unworthy jeering—self-conscious and trivial jeering. Tom had seen the urgency, too. "You must make up your mind," he said, "what's to be done."

At least a damned fine sail for her, too. And when the sail was over she could sail it again and again—and would. He could outfit her with a poem—if he had to—to hold on to with more vitality than in her Grecian Urn cherishing. The Last Ride Together. She would like it—probably did already. He could provide all kinds of rides—literal and figurative ones so that time after time she could solace herself in recollection—of the opera, of football games. They ought to hear the biggest and best organ in New York and see spring come in the florists' windows, and skate and dance with crystal chandeliers overhead and mirrors all around; and see plays. Plays. He thought with quick concentration about plays—especially plays, he concluded. ... Ride, ride together ride.

Things to keep, too. He had his mother's ring waiting for her. She would cherish the double sentiment in its circle. The copper penny he carried. Special things to recall special times. He would find them and give them one at a time to put away like bonds in a strong box—bonds with memory coupons to be clipped and cashed. ... But memories are not much to live on, his swift judgment turned to say, and souvenirs are sentimental and should be transient. Hers would not be. Afterwards, he would be only another person she could keep because she had lost him—another picture in that airless gallery. ... Her way.

A poised rejection swung him to the other horn of the dilemma. She is coming out of that gallery. The rooms beyond it are busy ... real in joy and in sorrow. Their doors open out into sunlight and wind and the fertility of rain. ... His way. ...

When Lyddy brought his breakfast, Stephen's judgment was still unresolved in quick and undisturbed morning clarity. She laughed at his voluminous appearance as he sat up to receive the tray, but she saw the rested look that eased the pallor.

He was protesting vigorously, first, that it was an excellent night-shirt—warm and roomy; second, that it was outrageous for him to lie slothfully in bed when decent men were hard at work and be waited on by a noble-hearted lady!

"I will, however, consume this excellent breakfast with enthusiasm—just this once!" he concluded.

Lyddy sat in the slipper rocker. After the second cup of coffee had been poured, she said, "I don't think you look very well."

Stephen looked up sharply, she noticed, and then said casually that he wasn't altogether fit—a little upset as a matter of fact. She did no prying.

"Well, whatever it is, a few days' rest will be good for you. And you might as well have it here. Nobody to gossip about you. If you took a rest at Mrs. Spencer's the whole street would know it and wonder why and express their wonder. There's nobody in the house but me, and the men outside are used to seeing you around, anyway."

She had it all planned. She would write a note to Mrs. Spencer. (Maybe she should have last night. Stephen reassured her on that point. Mrs. Spencer never knew when or whether he came in and he slept late.) She would write the note and send it by The Boy.

"He goes to the village every Saturday afternoon. I am afraid he plays pool," she said severely. "I'll explain that I have asked you to stay a few days since I am all alone (and that is true)—and very careful to say that Jessy is not here, of course. And ask her to send your toilet articles and clean clothes. She takes care of your clothes, doesn't she, and will know?" And then she remembered her role. "She knows just how timid I am."

"I bet she does," Stephen thought and wondered what Lyddy would do if he gave her a good hug. Hug him back, he hoped. He'd do it some day before—long.

Those three quiet days and nights in the storm were a gift of great price—the days short and active, in a way, the nights long and contemplative, sleeping or waking. He walked through Jessy's spacious downstairs rooms, sometimes with the attitude of one seeing a great house opened to any who would pay a shilling—to see inlaid furniture, hand-tooled books behind doors of metal netting, mellowed portraits, and flowers in great vases; sometimes with a pleasant remembrance of Jessy on that graceful couch or with that silver coffee-urn before her on a damask cloth. Occasionally he played the gold piano in a spontaneous but desultory way, but he did no composing.

Twice he stood motionless at the bottom of the handsome stairwell, his head tipped back watching the carved balustrades curving to the third story. He would like to see the study where Jessy's father sought what it was he sought and the attic Jessy loved—clue rooms. There must be a far view up there.

He picked up *David Copperfield* on the way back to bed to read with practiced glancing delight, idly. There were long intervals when the open book lay face down on the counterpane. Bingo lay beside or under the bed, seeking and giving company.

Half-asleep, part of the time, Stephen's mind was full of pictures: a green intervale lovely in productiveness where bare-armed men labored until the farm bell called them home and children and dogs ran down a lane to meet them; an ice-capped area of total white loneliness, of impossibility, of precipitous rocks and narrow bottomless abysses. He saw a crowd where terror lurked and merged and drove a man mad; a ball-room with tinkling crystals overhead, where waltzing couples were smiling into each others' faces with kissing glances; a vast edifice where rolling music led in awe a stately processional of aspirants and suppliants; and burying-grounds—miles and centuries of burying-grounds, barrows, pyramids, catacombs, monuments and head-stones; lands where burying-grounds had been—graves levelled, stones fallen and removed, and business thriving on the consecrated ground.

But waking or sleeping, he was always travelling just above the terrain; his feet moved airily and invisibly just above the heads of those who toiled, loved and played, feared and fled, were buried and rose again—with interest but without personal concern.

"Appassionata days," he summed up.

They had had a balance like that of delicately precise scales whose pans weigh out materials of value. He was grateful to Lyddy.

On the fourth morning, the storm had blown itself out into blueness and crispness and vigor. Stephen, wrapped in a maroon bathrobe, sat by an open seaward window, the sparkling cold washing through. Lyddy had brought him the robe with anxious reprimand and something more in her face and voice.

"It was Jessy's father's." She said it gently. "He was a tall man, taller than you, even, and bigger. You can wrap up in it, though. ... And I think she would like to see you in it," she added with a shyness he had not seen before.

"I hope she would," Stephen responded.

She looked straight into his eyes, and he looked as steadfastly into hers. Their snappiness softened without loss of keenness. ... She might guess, but she trusted him. Perhaps she counted on him, and he could depend upon her.

He knew it when he found the letter in the pocket of the bathrobe, for she must have sensed it was something special—not to be delivered in routine fashion. It was special to see Jessy's handwriting and the kind of letter paper she used, and extra-special that she had wanted to write him during a few days' absence— that the absence had been to her a separation. And whatever the letter had to say, it brought him gladly back to strong purpose.

"I am coming home the day after my letter reaches you, Stephen, but I want to write it. I can say so much better on paper what I want to say.

"I have had a wonderful trip. I saw Jefferson in Rip Van Winkle and heard Paderewski. I've bought some pretty fall and winter clothes, and I went shopping with Genevieve. She's buying her trousseau, and we bought linens and dishes—really her mother did. And one day, by ourselves, we took a preliminary look at white satin. She's going to wear her grandmother's veil. She's asked me to be a bridesmaid.

"But that isn't what I wanted to write you about.

"It's about what has happened inside me, Stephen. I think I have learned what you have been trying to teach me. Oh, I *understood* all the time what you were getting at. When you told me that what we were talking about was something big, I thought so too. But it belonged to a lesson in psychology, then. I think I realized that all my trifling experiments in the fog and on the sea and in the garden were only a beginner's exercises. Once I did it listening to the clock, all the time knowing that it would be foolish to stop with clock-ticks.

"Now, I know. Experience is the best teacher, and somebody at college said it is the only teacher. It happened at the orchestra concert first. I only wish it had been with Paderewski. I enjoyed him, of course, in the way I've always enjoyed music. I read the program notes carefully. I tried to get the little printed measures of music with my mind's ear. And then I followed as intelligently as I could. Glanced back at the program occasionally. My mind was busy and happy.

"That was all to the good, wasn't it, Stephen? Knowledge and intelligence are all right and necessary, aren't they? Only at this concert, they were in the background. Before it began, I was looking at the curtain, idly, I guess. Anyway I wasn't studying the program. The curtain was a lovely rose-color, and I found my eyes dwelling on that color.

"I was still thinking about it when the music began. I was listening casually for single tones, for individual rhythms and melodies. For what separate elements I could hear in a big orchestral chord. Like a child. The way my conscientious teacher taught me to do.

"I don't know how long that went on. All of a sudden I was hearing what that music had to *say—to me*—in the deep part of me. I did not even know what they were playing. I was stirred and exhilarated—soaring. It seemed a long time. So much happened. And it takes so few lines to tell what I can put into words.

"There were some young men from the Conservatory in front of us, and when the music was done, they stood up and yelled, 'Bravo.' And I think I yelled, too.

"I want to hear Paderewski and Caruso and all of them and listen in this new way.

"I don't mean that I was rapt in ecstasy. It was more solid than that. And my mind wandered. I saw a pretty hat on a girl farther down and remembered a check I must write in the morning. (Guess why!) Things like that. But such thoughts were like ripples made by little breezes on a strongly flowing current.

"That's the way I heard it, Stephen, in the part of me that music speaks to—outside the range of words. That is the way you've always listened, I suppose. Why am I so far behind? And that's where your music comes from, too. And my acting.

"They were playing the Overture to Romeo and Juliet, I realized when it was over.

"And that wasn't all," the letter went on. "I went to church with my college friend, Emily. St. Stephen's Church, it was. (I hope nobody ever stones you to death!) I have been there before—when we were in college—and it always seemed a fancy sort of church after our bare little church in Bold Water and our plain service with its long instructive sermon.

"There was so much to look at. A little tablet on the wall beside me to the glory of God and in memory of one who 'followed the path of loveliness and beauty and found truth by the way and peace at the last.' I memorized those words while we waited. And the sun pouring through the colors of the resurrection window above. The beautiful serious face of the tall blond boy who carried the cross on a staff. A Celtic cross it was. Candles blooming on the altar as tall as the callas. Everywhere something to look at and think about—Alpha and Omega carved in the wood, embroidered on a white stole.

"And so much to hear. The far-off choir prayer and the increasing volume of song as the procession drew nearer. Majestic old words: Lift up your hearts. And music in the creed that ascended into heaven.

"Emily had asked me to go up with her to receive the communion and I did. An old, silver-haired man put a wafer in my hand, and held a great silver cup to my lips, saying gentle words. The only ones I remember clearly were 'with thanksgiving.' Because, Stephen, kneeling there in the seconds my lips were at the cup, I knew what religion is. That it is an experience in the heart. It means a meeting sure and intimate, doesn't it? With God. I guess I have experienced it before. I prayed a lot when I was a little girl and was comforted sometimes, and later, too. I guess I met Him sometimes but didn't know it. Now I do. And I know now that

I won't bother to pray *for* things but to meet Some One. I know what the word heart means, now.

"I guess my Mother knew. Once you said something about finding her in church. I've never understood her church very much, but I think I see now about the fanciness. The candle-flames and the pictures in the glass—why does that Crusader's lamb have its leg bent, Stephen?—the lofty arches and the vaulted roof—oh, all the things to look at and listen to—and to smell, sometimes—are tangible things for the part of us that loves tangibilities to busy itself with—tangibilities that stir the great intangible. And then—the miracle comes.

"You were right, I guess, when you said that I have in me something of those old Smithpeters, Stephen. Maybe they knew all the time what I am just learning. The one with St. Francis in his eyes, anyway.

"Oh, and the text, Stephen. The silver-haired old man in his fine white surplice and white stole with the gold fringe preached. And his text was, 'The singers also and the trumpeters shall make answer: all my fresh springs are in thee.'

"What a long letter. Maybe I will be sorry I sent it. But it has done me good to think it out, and I believe you will be interested."

There was a cell in Stephen's lungs that he valued. Some of his climactically drawn deep breaths reached it and some did not. It was his test of consummation. With Jessy's letter—her epistle of unrealized triumph—still in hand, he rose, reached that cell, held it, and let out the air in a long sigh trembling with strength. The dilemma—her way, his way-no longer irked him. He would swing vigorously and buoyantly from one horn to the other. ... She had brought a live coal from the altar of St. Stephen and laid it on his lips. He knew what he should do.

# CHAPTER TWENTY-ONE

He must complete the sonata. He must go on, almost sys-tematically, with his love-making—a good deal of it, too, before he asked her to marry him. These two activities would be involved with each other, and with both of them certain other threads must be woven. He would accomplish something even before she returned.

She knew tunes for the second and third movements. The fourth neither of them was ready for yet. It was another—color. But it was time for the first, and he felt like the first, and the first needed attention. He worked with clear zest. It solved left-over difficulties: slashed a dull passage, produced gracefully and eas-ily two effects he had toiled for fruitlessly, lighted up the sense of direction and suggested more to be done on another day. Then he made a "sample"—by selecting and re-arranging a bit—and copied it on a single music sheet.

Late in the afternoon he crossed the hall to the parlor. When he heard the wheels and hoofs on the turn just below the house, he opened the windows, raised the top of the gold piano, and began to play. He played with every muscle and cell and nerve in his body to pour the music down the hill, past the horses and Sinbad, to Jessy; and he played her into the room. The kiss he gave her was a part of his plan. He meant it to be matter-of-course and off-hand. It turned out otherwise, but that was all right, he thought complacently.

"I was answering your letter. I hope you follow me."

Her face was still turned up to his—more sober and more tremulous than he wanted it to be just then.

"Take off your hat while I wind up my letter and sign my name." He went on from where he left off.

Jessy was slightly astonished, but she was attentive to what she heard.

"You're answering what I said about ideas beyond the range of words, I guess," she said when he was done.

"So I am, but I didn't mean that."

She still looked seriously at him.

"Then you shouldn't expect words from me, should you?"

"No. But will you begin at the first and listen again?"

She would, if he would stay. So he played it again—after dinner, the whole movement, with special emphasis on what she had already heard. She listened from the tall chair.

At the end, he turned quickly and gave her no time for comment.

"What time of day am I playing?"

"Morning!"

"What kind of weather?"

"Crisp. Blue. Clear air. Like today on the boat."

"What landscape?"

"The Alps. ... Lake Superior?"

"Yes, Lake Superior!"

"What kind of people?"

"The French fathers on Lake Superior. People with ice-axes on the Matterhorn."

Stephen left the piano-stool and knelt down before her in the big chair.

"Jessy, darling, I hope all my audiences will be as good as you are. I don't care if I never have any other audience. I feel like crossing myself! .... And I must look like a fool kneeling at my lady's feet. And how in the devil am I going to get up?" Jessy laughed.

He did rise, however, and stood looking down at her quietly a moment or two. He had another question to ask.

"What part of your church service was I playing?"

The persiflage was done.

"Why Stephen—Stephen! You were playing the text—most of the time. All my fresh springs. You *are* answering my letter. Play it again."

He did, and it seemed to him that all the streams from the fresh springs poured down the mountain-side, united joyously and rushed on, joined the river and in the end, the sea, and the clouds again.

So it seemed to Jessy, undefined.

"Only," she said, "there's something else in it, something that struggles against the springs of—infinite capacities? Is that right, Stephen? Why do I try for words?"

"Why, indeed? You comprehend. Your Alpine climber slipped back, I guess. Lost his nerve and ambition for a while—right here."

He exaggerated the mood of the unfortunate climber and then swept with sincerity into the other theme.

"He's started up again," said Jessy. "Got his zeal back anyway."

"Right," said Stephen. "The class in ear-training is dismissed."

"There's something more in it," Jessy went back. "Almost hidden. Came out once—maybe twice. It is bewitching, Stephen—gay and very sweet—"

"This little thing?" He took it out as one separates and cuts a rose from foliage. It was gay and sweet and more than bewitching.

"It—says what I seem to want to hear, Stephen, but I can't quite—"

Stephen's eyes were shining in the depths of their brown clarity.

"You'll have many chances to find out! It's my favorite musical idea. It's in every movement, somewhere—runs through like a golden thread if I do say so as shouldn't."

"Aren't you going to develop it?"

"Oh, yes! With program notes besides!"

His eyes were as puzzling and as charming as the music—and something more was in them. She moved on rather hastily to practical questions which he answered matter-of-factly.

No, he did not plan to name the movements except with *Andante Con Moto* and *Scherzo* and that kind of thing. And the whole sonata would be called merely Sonata for Piano in B Major. For the public, that is. There was to be, he pursued the thought *ex tempore*, a special Jessy edition—with names—nice names on everything. ... Yes, she would hear it all—often, he hoped. She'd have to be like the wedding-guest who could not choose but hear.

Jessy liked the wedding-guest, of course, and Stephen thought he was an inspiration of technique.

"Can I ever play it?"

"I want you to. ... But it is no amateur's piece. You'll have to work. ... You can begin right now." He placed the single sheet on the rack and with a bow conducted her to the piano like a prima donna, her hand laid on the back of his outstretched one.

"It is a little piece made for you out of the sonata—a sort of prelude. I'd like to hear you play it right now."

She read the music through before she raised her hands to the keys.

"It's the hidden brook!"

There was silence when she had played it.

Then she said, "I know what to call it. Prelude for St. Stephen's. ... May I keep this copy?"

"You may indeed. Keep it always to remind you of last Sunday."

"And of today," she added earnestly.

Once more, Stephen drew a deep and satisfying breath.

His apostolic zeal burned on in details of his plan—spelled now with a capital P. All his thoughts were in capitals. He wanted to expatiate on many topics: Release, for instance, Disregard of Time, Receptivity, Rhythm. Ideas and apt expression were eager in his mind, but he choked off his garrulity before it came to speech.

"I'd be helping myself but not Jessy."

So, as September and October moved, he seized only offhand opportunities for carefully off-hand remarks—not too many of them at that ... as once when they were looking down into a pool.

"That is lovely color," she said. "Or is it color at all? Maybe merely green clearness."

"Aquamarine, I suppose. Just that." Stephen's voice was flatly literal.

"And those pinkish stones on the bottom. Edged with frosty white of barnacles.... White. Maybe not frosty, though."

He had encouraged it, in a way, but she had to see the difference.

"Jessy, if you don't mind my saying so, that kind of esthetics makes me tired. You know things are beautiful, darling. You isolate color and forms and outline and point them out to yourself in a finicky analysis. You fit words. You *think* too much about beauty."

He waited.

"And yet I miss it somehow, Stephen. I don't often get hold of it nor it of me!"

She spoke with a vehemence which Stephen welcomed, but he still said nothing; and the quiet moments faded it out.

"Too many program notes on sea-water," she said finally. "Just enjoy greenness." It was a perfect summation.

"And on love-making." He was not sure afterwards whether he had said that or not, but it made no difference. He would touch that point again and again ... and did.

"We are doing each other good, don't you know that?" he said when she protested at love-making that came too fast for her propriety. He shocked her when he added, "Renunciation is sometimes a worse sin than indulgence." But he disciplined himself.

Once he suggested with easy dogmatism that she take off her mother's ring and put it away for a time. She was unwilling—saw no reason.

"Oh, just because we sometimes get too tangled up in memory. Not so bad though as that old girl that stopped the clocks at twenty minutes to nine and wore her wedding dress ever after."

He noticed a focusing of attention in her eyes.

But she said only, "Great Expectations."

He thought they sat around too much. So he taught her and Sinbad to drive his car. He organized a choir of boys; she was the assistant and organist. He set her to work with regular lessons and solid daily practice on the piano—from her own impetus, she thought. She wanted to be able to play the piano, and he wanted her to, she repeated.

"Between us, we'll keep those pianos hot," he confided to Lyddy. She was delighted, and so was Tom. "Stephen has sense," he thought.

He rejoiced in her musical zeal.

"If I were paying for these long lessons, I couldn't afford you. You'd have to wear your watch. That mantel clock is purely ornamental," she commented.

"I haven't got a watch. I threw it away. Big old turnip that belonged to my Uncle Albert.... Say, my father wanted to name me for him. Mother wouldn't have it. Victoria and Albert! Gosh!.... His watch was heavy. It kept good time though. Too good."

Jessy couldn't imagine calling him Albert, she said. Then she turned the subject just as he was warming up to his discourse on Time.

"My Uncle Eugene is home."

Stephen was careful. He remembered something Tom had told him.

"And who is he?"

She told him. He had been away all summer—part of the time on a walking tour in the Bavarian Alps with his son. He had on tweed clothes—golf trousers—and there was a little feather in his hat when she saw him—met him by chance on the street. That feather seemed to annoy her.

"Stout party? Red-faced? Double chin on the back of his neck?"

She laughed but without much mirth.

"I think I saw him, too," he went on.

Jessy burst out, "I never like to be with him—even for five minutes on the street."

"It's probably a matter of rhythm," Stephen expounded. "You can't be yourself when he's around, can't call your soul your own. That means a lot more than independence, you know."

She did not know just then.

"You have to get away from some people, alive or dead," he said, "the way I have to with my sister. I like her but she is brisk and always active and unaware of what the important part of her is—and of me. I took a vacation one time because she kicked my chair and halted a nice rhythm."

"Did you get it down after you got away?"

"Oh, it wasn't a musical rhythm. . . . Rhythm is important, you know—rhythm inside of you."

"Certainly for a musician," she agreed.

"For everybody!" he declaimed and left it at that.

The lessons were a masterpiece of unconscious strategy, more from luck than good management. But it was the kind of luck that is not luck: the perfect plan which, after diverse labored effort, springs into easy accomplishment of itself—always a surprise, no matter how often and how clearly it happens.

Stephen's mind went naively eloquent on the obvious, suddenly personalized into the miraculous: everybody ought to be a musician, for musicians are liberated—himself at the age of eight playing Oh Susannah in a mouth-organ—an old man with his chin on his old fiddle, comforted—the artist in the golden hall with the hushed thousands before and above and around him. Musicians do not cramp their ideas in words or paint or stone; and they can hear and project what is too fast for the eye to see and too fragile for the fingers to handle. They are the Seers of the profundities. See-ers! They press on timelessly in absorbed ambition and returning courage alongside mountain climbers and pioneer priests.

"What I mean is," he tamed himself down, "that if Jessy keeps going on in music as she has begun, it will do her a lot of good. And I especially want her to play that sonata."

The hours at the piano were otherwise productive. Not much was said but a great deal could be expressed and interpreted: beauty jointly produced in a sort of music-marriage; hours of contented abeyance when the lesson drifted on into twilight and chatting and living silences.

He had sense enough and finesse and selflessness enough to spend considerably less time with Jessy. Lyddy noticed it, but also that Jessy was in good spirits and full of initiative.

# CHAPTER TWENTY-TWO

Jessy drove her lively horse homeward over the firm smooth roads, Bingo trotting evenly alongside. At times he still loped off in a semi-circle through woods or pasture and waited ahead to fall into step again. All three had had a good day: a long drive across the causeway, following coast-wise roads toward the blue mountain, never reaching the blue mountain but rewarded by glimpses of it across sparkling water or, inexplicably swung around forty-five degrees, beyond a series of wooded hills folded below and around it. There was no objective in the journey and no turning back. The afternoon trip was completing a circle. She never had had such a day, though the roads were familiar and autumn in the woods and on the shore long loved.

After lunch for all three, from nose-bag and basket, Jessy had lain on the spruce needles of a sunny spot and watched the radiations of the branches till the hush of noonday and of autumn drew her into sleep. Bingo slept, too, his nose on his paws. When he woke her up, they walked through the thinning woods, russet and green, lighted up in one shielded spot by tardy yellow birch leaves. It was a long and absorbing walk.

October was closing on a day full of the beat of the months. It had dreamy brilliance: a sense of cessation and the feel of advancing change. ... The present was living and breathing and growing into Time. Berries and seed-pods would drop to thicken next year's ground-cover.

Creaking wheels and a high old voice were coming nearer, and she pulled into a turn-out place. Slowly, a cart was drawn around the bend—drawn by yearling oxen, an old man walking beside them.

"Good afternoon, Mr. Tewkesbury," she called.

In a few moments he paused companionably beside her.

"Don't be afraid," he said. "They're gentle."

They were indeed gentle animals—small creatures who still had the baby appeal of calves. They looked frail before the high-piled hay in the cart—sad patience come early into their soft eyes. Their driver was watching her, for after a time, he said, "They're all I've got to haul my hay."

The words circled in Jessy's mind, in and out, as the slow miles unrolled, "They're all I've got to haul my hay"—in the beat of human striving. In a grown-over clearing, a valiant chimney with a field-stone fireplace still firm at its base stood in the sweet fern—an angle of wall beside it.

The horse trotted smartly toward the home crossroad. Bingo's circling had run him many more miles than they had driven; he snoozed, compactly curled on the seat, only his hard tail responsive to an occasional touch of Jessy's hand. She liked a big strong dog nowadays. And she liked laughing by herself as she did presently; it was bracing and relaxing. Nailed to a dooryard tree was a home-made sign, dimmed by the rains and snows and dust of many seasons: Free Kittens... Jessy laughed again and again. Kittens... kittens... kittens frolicking through the years and mousing through the centuries. Sabre-tooth kittens... kittens by the Pyramids. The laughter quieted down. Endlessly kittens—kittens when the year 2999 swings into a new millennium.

She paused once again at the foot of her own road, the horse looking around reproachfully. The reins in her hand, she stood up on the curving floor boards. Early evening light lay over the scene she knew so well. Of a sudden she saw a rocky point of land and the water that washed against it as though new colors had been that moment splashed over it—singing colors. She swung from west to east, and her breath shut off in a sharp gasp.

Four red pines thrust their clustered boles upward—strong in roundness, sweepingly straight and parallel, silver-pink in the light sunset mist. Her father and her grandfather and perhaps her great-grandmother had loved those trees. They were landmarks—notable on that spruce-lined shore. Jessy had known them all her life.

"I'll go with you as far as the pines," she used to say to an occasional visiting little girl. ...

Her Uncle Eugene was standing with Sinbad at the curve of the drive just below the terrace. A level ray of sunlight pointed up his checked suit, Jessy was amused to observe as she stopped to greet him.

"All those larches ought to come out," he turned back to Sinbad to say. "They're shutting us in again. The view from the terrace and from all the windows on this side is blocked. Ought to get all that birch stuff out. Clean out the alder around those big spruces. Might as well make a wide, irregular corridor down that way. Those experts know how to do it."

"Big job," commented Sinbad. "Several weeks' work for the crew after the designer gets through."

"Well, it's worth the money."

Surprisingly, he turned back to Jessy to say, "Don't you think so, Jessy?"

She agreed, of course, and said so. She did not say, however, that the new corridor would lead happily to Stephen's outdoor studio.

"All right. Then we'll go ahead. I'll write tomorrow."

Bingo and the horse went hopefully off with Sinbad.

"Yes, it's worth it," Eugene went on expansively as he walked into the house with Jessy. "Pays to do things right. You paid a good deal for that horse and dog, but you enjoy them, I see."

He had bought the horse and dog himself, before she came home from college, Jessy remembered, but she did not bother to correct him. An evening breeze brought the tang of autumn odors through open windows; and a lingering bluebird was singing his late song. He reminded her of something lovely which she could not re-capture. However, she heard Eugene inquire whether he could borrow the dog for November shooting and she assented—chiefly to give Bingo a good time. Her uncle was not very important somehow. His clothes and the double chin on the back of his head seemed rather pathetic, and so did his shallow pomposity as he discoursed on "conditions in Europe," observed on a four months' tour. A polite query had started him off, she supposed.

He would not stay to dinner, he thanked her; but he went on talking about the Balkan situation and the drawbacks of European food. She wondered why he was staying.

Rhythm, Stephen had said; she remembered when Eugene lighted a cigar with a breezily perfunctory, "If I may." Stephen was right. Her uncle's rhythms were not like hers, but she did not care. She planned telling Stephen about her rhythms and Uncle Eugene's.

Eugene's conversation finally landed in New York at a Waldorf dinner table and reviewed in detail his first American meal. Bingo, weary but pleased in an after-supper way, ambled into the room toward Jessy's feet and his favorite rug.

"Get out of here," Eugene's voice was rough and loud, but Bingo was only surprised.

"He can stay, Uncle Eugene," Jessy said with decision. "He is a well-behaved dog. He comes in for a while every evening. Charge, Bingo!"

Bingo charged. Eugene was halted and he did not like the feeling.

"What about this young man I hear so much talk about?"

She did not answer his question: it was no question.

"What is he hanging around here so much for? You can't afford to get any gossip started. You ought to know that."

Jessy rose before she spoke. She did not know she was acting; in reality she was not, but her manner and posture were tinged by a forgotten memory of Rose Coghlan in The Lion and the Mouse—Rose as she stood intrepid before the bulky entrepreneur who, having previously spumed her as a daughter-in-law, was now condescending to accept her. But Rose was white-hot and Jessy was not, but she spoke with dignity.

"I cannot permit you to speak like that of Stephen, Uncle Eugene. I have found him a delightful and helpful friend."

Her prim sentences made an effect but not the kind she intended. He grasped nothing for gazing at her body—a woman's body of grace and fire and ripeness.

"God!" he said under his breath.

Then he spoke to her. "Sure! A pretty young lady who owns a big house and has her own income! Fiddler, I hear."

Her sense of timing was good. She made no corrections and no retort. He still sat in his chair, his gazing at her almost gaping.

"Well, never mind." He spoke with laborious jocularity. "Come and give your uncle a nice kiss. He's not so old!"

Then Jessy really did go Rose Coghlan.

"No, I thank you, Uncle Eugene. No, I thank you."

She made a superb exit and enjoyed it.

Eugene was annoyed.

Jessy sailed from the room without a destination in mind, intent only on sailing. The stairs were before her and her impetus swept her upward and into her dressing room and to the pier glass set between the windows. She suddenly wanted to see how she had looked during her big scene.

"I look strong." She though it in actual words of declaration like a creed. "And alive. And grown up. And pretty!"

But she also looked tousled as to hair and dusty as to shoes and the tail of her red blouse was pulling out of her belt. She dressed for dinner with absorbed attention in an elegant—too elegant—dress which Genevieve had persuaded her to buy. It was satin of peacock blue with velvet shoulder straps and glittering trimming of colored beads, and a train. She had never felt at ease in it, and Lyddy's taste had not approved. But tonight before the mirror it made her feel as she did in the gown of the princess, swaying the great fan of golden feathers. Tonight was real. She put on Isabel's wide topaz bracelets, but they felt heavy and tight and Stephen did not like them. Her arms were pretty, Stephen had said more than once. She thought so, too, and lifted them as she had the night of the play when the prince had embraced her. Stephen liked the Janice Meredith curl on her bare shoulder, too.

She walked down the broad stairs with state and grace, one hand on the balustrade. So sumptuous she looked on the gold damask couch that the substitute maid did not finish the sentence Lyddy had carefully coached her to say. She said only, "Dinner is—" and fled. In a few minutes Sinbad entered—smart in livery but a little blown.

"Are there to be guests, Miss Jessy?"

"No. Oh, no. It's been such a wonderful day! An evening to dress up. The whole world is dressed up, Sinbad."

"Yes, indeed." Sinbad was again imperturbable. "Just a moment and dinner will be served."

He thought they must be engaged, he managed a minute to say to Lyddy. Lyddy thought not. They had not seen each other for several days because Stephen was home with a slightly sprained ankle. Tom Greenleaf had been at Mrs. Spencer's to bandage it.

"Whatever has happened, it's good!" Sinbad insisted. "I will serve her myself."

The crystal candelabra were on the table when Jessy entered—fourteen candles lighted and Sinbad behind her chair, very correct. He served a plain dinner of two courses with high decorum for a lady beautiful in the candlelight. Jessy ate with appetite. It occurred to her in the middle of dinner that she had forgotten her uncle from the moment she left him; she felt a twinge of mannerly remorse at the thought of him, trying to pick up the pieces of his pompous dignity on the way to the door. Not much of a twinge, however, for she was still enjoying the verve of her clear indignation.

At the end of the meal, Sinbad, to her amusement, ceremonially placed a wine-glass and decanter of port before her, loyally and blindly celebrating what she was celebrating. She was touched, too, in a misty way. She remembered the decanter on the table long ago, the stemmed glass turning in her silent father's fingers.

Sinbad held open the door—the embodiment of etiquette—and Jessy was swept past him as she knew he wanted her to do. It was fun and it was real besides.

She played the gold piano—herself her own zestful audience at first, with Tom Greenleaf added later. He brought a message from Stephen.

"How is his ankle?"

Tom was carefully honest.

"Why, I think his—ankle is all right. He can be out tomorrow, probably. He would like to come to see you in the evening if you wish. I can bring him up."

"I do wish," said Jessy.

He liked the kind of music she was playing when he entered the house, he said. Would she go on?

The music and eyes shining as hers were and color so brilliant and the flamboyant dress were all and each symptoms. ... She was riding high. But she was not nervously exhilarated. This was vitality—new vitality—a late spring.

"She's got to do it without you," he had said to Stephen.

Tom was pleased but sober as he listened and watched for another half hour. As he left, he took something out of his pocket.

"Stephen sent you this—to keep," he said.

He held out his hand and dropped the big copper penny into hers. She held it tight as she went up the stairs. She could not quite remember.

Her sitting-room was pleasant with open fire and lighted lamps, the chintz chair placed just right. Stephen had pollished up the penny; it gleamed in the fire-light on her blue satin lap—pinky-brown copper … from the copper country!

It brings you luck. He had said that on Ordination Rock.

"What kind of luck?"

"Luck in living!"

Stephen's father's penny. Stephen's father who has a knack for living. And Stephen, beloved Stephen, had somehow known to send it to her this very night. She could keep it—the sight and feel of it for remembrance—a sacrament. The eagerness of her afternoon's defense of him rushed up from the place where it was hidden in warm and intimate memories. She brought them out: the length of his body tall against hers; the power of his arms around her; and the stirrings. She could feel it even now in her breathing, in the beating of her heart—intolerably disturbing but ineffably living motion, springing fertility. … A knack for living—a curious but meaningful way of putting it. She could never forget it now.

She did not light the lamp in the bedroom where she undressed; it was pleasant to move about in the darkness-putting away the dress in its place, brushing her hair in the ritual motion, laying the multiple other garments in order on a chair, stockings hung on the back. Before she put her night-gown on she stood a few minutes, the air cool on her flesh—cool as water in the cove at high tide. But Lyddy had taught her always to put a garment on at once. She and her roommate had writhed out of their underwear beneath a night-gown already partly on and writhed into underwear in the morning. So she put it on—long and full and fussily high-necked and long-sleeved. Then she opened the window and knelt before it.

The moon was dropping down behind the ridge with a swiftness that almost had in it the rhythm of the saw-tooth horizon line. The wind had the same movement in sound. It was the rotation of the earth, she thought, the beat of time.

She unbuttoned the night-gown and pushed it off her shoulders, and felt the cold wind sweep down over her bare breast, saw the last gleam of the moonlight on its whiteness.

"I've swung into the Eternal," she thought.

# CHAPTER TWENTY-THREE

She was still on the crest of the wave for the new day. It was a day to match her mood—stretching out enticingly from breakfast to evening, and Sinbad was sailing to Rat Island in the sloop on an errand, Lyddy said. Would Jessy like to go? Yes, she would and she had a new blue sailor suit to wear. She would be down in a few minutes.

The telephone—the only one in Bold Water—rang while Jessy was upstairs. Its sudden noise always annoyed Lyddy. The house arrangements were so smoothly settled that rarely was there occasion to connect with the other end of that wire—the quarry office. There was always some one to send. She never used it.

Sinbad answered it.

"Yes, sir. . . . I'll see, sir."

"Mr. Sparks wants to speak to Miss Jessy," he reported to Lyddy.

"Well, tell her," she snapped.

He did, his ceremoniousness of the evening before still in ascendancy and Jessy played up.

"Tell him to leave a message," she said grandly.

"I will make a note of it, Madam."

They both laughed.

Aboard the new sloop he was the old Sinbad who had taught her all she knew about boats and sailing. The water was dancing blue and the air was lively with puffs of clouds—on top of the up-drafts, Sinbad explained. More going on in those pretty little puffs than you might think, he said, and sure enough, the lovely beauty of the day was climaxed by a gorgeous storm that drove them home exhilarated by the feeling of danger.

"I love it!" Jessy yelled to Sinbad. He could not hear the words, but he saw a great surprise. She had been both scared and sick in certain other storms, he remembered.

She dressed carefully for the evening but not in the blue satin. She carried downstairs her father's flute; she had just had it put in order. The library, though a large room, had a sheltered snugness. The deep couch was drawn before the fire and crimson curtains over windows that must be black and streaming with rain. There was no clock and the couch was comfortable. Stephen was grateful. He did not need to put his ankle up, he said. ... Isabel's taste was good. There were no bibelots as in her room, and the mantel was not a fussy one with little piazzas full of ornaments. The furniture was all big and handsome. In a pool of mahogany light the flute lay on the desk. Jessy had a notion she would like to learn to play it. Of course, she could, he said, a nice thing to do.

Isabel's handsome books lined the walls. In one section a small niche was formed in the middle of the books where a white statuette of Shakespeare stood, his elbow resting on a pile of books piled on a pedestal.

"His works are around him, you see," Jessy pointed out. "But there is something funny about his legs. They aren't long enough or else he's about to sit down on nothing. It's the statue in the Abbey, though, mama told me. ... I love him."

"I bet you loved to climb up that little ladder to get the books."

"And some of the top ones I never have reached."

"Why haven't we sat here before?"

"It's a winter room, I guess. A little wing like the music room. Both of them are places to be quiet and busy and happy."

Pleasant silences fell between them on the couch. She thought of what he had said about one of his twig and cone fires—a fire is a means of communication. It was true. The lamplight was dimmed—an undertone to the flames.

By and by, she told him about her day's drive and sailing ahead of the storm, and about her rhythm and Uncle Eugene's.

"I don't like his—any of them, but somehow I didn't care. He smoked a cigar and I hate cigar smoke, and he's smarty and stupid and—kind of nasty. But I didn't care. My rhythm was stronger and higher than his, like a wind that sweeps along above the smells and noise of an unpleasant town—up where the big birds soar."

Stephen listened with the grave attention which she loved and valued.

"I think I've found out how to do. I could call my soul my own."

"Better than running away," he commented. "And much better than being drowned out.... How well you think things out, darling." He had a particular little accent on that last word.

She did not mention the moments with Eugene when she had become most dominant. That part she had forgotten about—almost. She did tell him about the telephone call, however.

"Why he didn't say what he had to say the night before I don't know. We never use that thing. I don't know what he put it in for. If he lived here it would be different, I suppose. All he wanted to say was that it was time for our annual business conversation and would I come to his office next Tuesday morning at ten o'clock."

Stephen's attention had a different quality, which she did not observe.

"He talks and I listen. That's about all. Lyddy really manages, you know. She sends him bills to pay. I sign things."

Stephen had a suggestion. "Why don't you have him come to your house at ten o'clock?"

"Why?"

"You can hold your rhythm better in your own place." He said it lightly, but Jessy picked up the suggestion at once.

"I'll have Sinbad telephone him."

The fire had died down and the room was cooling. He put on another log and put Jessy's fleecy white shawl around her shoulders. As he did so, his arm under the shawl drew her nearer to him, and his hand, its alert carefulness off duty for a few seconds, curved itself around her breast.

She tore from his arm and leaped up. The shawl dropped in a white pool on the crimson velvet.

"Don't touch me! Go away!" Her voice had a quality he had never heard before, and she stuttered on the *d* and the *t*. "No, I thank you! No, I thank you."

He could hear her sobbing breath behind him in the shadowy part of the room. He did not rise nor turn his head.

"I am sorry I frightened you, Jessy. I did not mean to and I won't again. Won't you sit down beside me for a while longer?" He could make colorless words very winning.

She did not move or speak. Neither did he—externally.

The soundlessness was beneficent. She walked back to the couch and sat down. He still said nothing. He could hear her quick breathing quiet down.

When the moment seemed right, he said.

"Did some fellow frighten or disgust you, Jessy, sometime?"

"Yes." The word was forced out miserably like a child's who is headed off from any escape but confession.

Neither spoke again for a time. The foghorn had begun to bray down at the point. Ships were making their difficult way—safely, he hoped.

"Was he anything like me?"

"No!"

Stephen slid down a little and rested his head against the high back. He began to talk easily and pleasantly.

"We were living in the Deep Place before and when you sprang up, weren't we? And I guess we still are. That's all to the good. . . . " He went on again. "Sometimes something gets in down in there that works against you. The bad can flourish there as well as the good." A movement warned him off. "Fear is bad, you know. ... This fellow now, who frightened you—what shall I call him?" He spoke the last words incisively.

"The boy from Yale."

"Well, this boy from Yale wasn't really very important, was he?"

She drew her breath and let it out in a sort of sigh.

"Why ... no. I don't believe he ... was."

"And, you see, he got himself into an important place, and he made you afraid of living. You should have hoisted him out with the crank of common sense. You'd better get him out now."

There was a silence—a questioning one.

"Because just now when I touched you with my hands that want only to worship you, his dirty and sacrilegious hands tore you away from mine."

She said nothing but he felt her attentiveness.

"There's too much power in that lamp to let the wrong thing in. ... Shrug him off. He's not important. I am!"

She made a little sound of amusement.

"I'll be glad to be rid of him."

"You are!" Stephen declared brassily. "Just like that. I have crowded him out. Forever."

The swift and inexplicable storm was over—as inexplicable to her as to him for different reasons. Given all the data he could have charted it; freed from twisted emotion she could have seen it coming.

When she spoke it was with a sharp meditativeness.

"The slave of the lamp can be too powerful sometimes, perhaps."

She was working out something for herself—not talking to him. So he did not listen, and companionable thinking continued when the talking lapsed. Stephen was tired.

"I'm not poison ivy any more. And that fact is more important to my darling than it is to me, even though a moment of supreme satisfaction is coming in a few moments."

Fanciful Jessy was realistic. "I feel as I did when the tooth was really out."

At the right time—he was sure—he crossed to the beautiful big desk and picked up the flute. He experimented with it for a while and then began to play—not too expertly. But he played music that had in it a golden thread that came in and out—gay and sweet and more than bewitching. He played it again—better—and then laid the flute down.

Jessy moved toward him.

"There's a kiss in it, Stephen," she said.

"And here is a program note," he responded gravely.

He picked up the fleecy white shawl and put it around her shoulders. As he did so, his arm under the shawl drew her nearer to him, his hand on her side. And the hand this time curved itself in comfort. His cheek dropped to the top of her curly head and rested there until he felt it moving upward and backward.

"And thus he was made immortal by a kiss," the sentence soared into consciousness from a forgotten book, his mother reading.

"It runs all through the sonata to the end," he said. His voice almost broke.

# CHAPTER TWENTY-FOUR

Jessy could not bear to take her Uncle Eugene into the library now nor into the music room: he would be a sacrilege. Nor into her sitting-room: he would be an intruder. And nobody could sit in the parlor and keep the right rhythm for business though she had never thought of it before. So she led him to her father's third floor study. After all, she was Miss Smithpeters, the head of the family now. She must take her father's place.

Lyddy went along to see that the room was in order, she said. It wasn't dusted every day, and she had planned to get out the winter bedding in the store-room that very morning, anyway, and might as well do it at once. She flung up windows on two sides for a few moments and lighted the fire already laid.

"That's one thing I insist upon," she said sociably. "Every fireplace ready to go." She was doing a little stagy dusting.

"Good thing," mumbled Eugene. He was again annoyed at the high hand Jessy was taking, though the telephoning and stair-climbing were only a last-minute impetus. His real drive was of long standing. It originated in this very room the last time he was in it. He experienced an ugly satisfaction when, somewhat slow-wittedly, he remembered. He'd fix the three of them. He'd said fifteen years ago he would.

Jessy sat with dignity in her father's red leather swiveled chair—not altogether at home, more little Jessy than Miss Smithpeters, looking at the globe on the desk where it had always stood, and the plain, crowded bookshelves with the bust on top.

"Who was Go-eeth?" she had asked.

That day her father started teaching her German.

"Kann nicht lernen das Ah, Bay, Tsay," she had learned to sing.

Eugene began, as usual, smoothly and pleasantly.

"Well, Jessy, I guess we'd better get things straightened out. It's run on long enough."

She had no reply to these obscure remarks.

"You can't go on spending money like this."

The obscurity became only puzzlement, but there was something new to take hold of.

"There must be some misunderstanding, Uncle Eugene," she said easily. "I am not spending too much. I keep accounts, so I know. I've been saving money. I want to go to Italy."

"Do you have any idea how much it costs to run this place?" He did not pause for reply. "How much it costs to paint the buildings, for instance? Repair and replace the furnishings annually? How much those granite slabs on the new terrace came to? What the wages amount to for your staff of high-class servants? Three women and a house-man. Two regular men outside besides experts like those tree men you O.K.'d day before yesterday. How much it costs to feed all these people that work for you—buy uniforms for some of 'em? Fuel? Light? Insurance costs money. Taxes come in regularly. To say nothing of the interest you are paying."

He was getting hot too soon. He was a fumbler but determined.

"Well, I can tell you. It all costs just about six times the whole income my sister so kindly left you. So you see."

Jessy did not reply sharply to what, in spite of his rising truculence, still seemed to her stupid confusion. She explained gently and carefully as one speaks to the very old or the deaf.

"I have nothing to do with house expenses, Uncle Eugene. Lyddy manages all that. She used to give my father a report, I remember. All those things come out of the House Fund."

"There is no House Fund!" First triumph snapped the words out like the retort of a quarreling boy.

"But my father—"

"Sure, he had one. That was his plan."

"But I am his heir."

"Sure you are, but you're no heiress. He had nothing to leave you but the house and its contents. His income was his for life only. And he didn't leave any will, either—too hifalutin' for business horse-sense. You've got a big house and a cottage income. Champagne taste and lager-beer pocket-book."

It was the jocularity of the brutality with which he spoke, even more than the content, that stirred the fear. She watched him extract a cigar from a leather case, cut off the end with the knife on his watch-chain, and walk over to the mantel for a match. He lit the cigar and stood with his back to the fire as he smoked. It was a long cigar. She would have to smell it a long time.

These observations did not connect with her mind's urgent searching, nor did his silly attention to the smoke curling above him.

Her idea came into focus.

"I have been home two and one-half years, Uncle Eugene, and the house has been operating as usual. What money have we been using?"

He laughed indulgently.

"Why, my dear little girl! You don't know much about business, do you? It's lucky you've got a good honest uncle to look out for you. That's what you borrowed the money for, of course, till you could see your way clear."

Bewilderment was receding and indignation was rising to augment and to steady her fear.

"I have never borrowed any money."

"Yes, you have." He was taking a long flat wallet from an inside pocket as he spoke. "Here are the notes you signed-three of them." He spread them out on the desk before her. "Aren't those your signatures?"

She did not leave the working of her mind longer than to glance at them. A hard silence pressed down.... She broke it.

"Why are you so prompt with proof if I am supposed to know all about it?"

She had shut him off temporarily.

"When did I sign the first one?"

He picked up one of the notes and mentioned its date and had no chance for comment.

"That was before I came home from college. Not long after my father's death. You took advantage of my grief and confusion. I was signing other papers then. You slipped in this first note. I didn't try to understand. I trusted you. And you tricked me."

"You can't prove it." Again he made an error.

She held her attack, however.

"It was deliberate. Your explanations were always hurried and vague. I could have comprehended. I have that kind of mind. I am good in mathematics."

"So I understood." Eugene was smooth again. "I thought you knew your own business—surprised that you signed the second and third notes. You've borrowed about all the house will stand."

"And I remember asking if the business was done, and you said 'just about.' Maybe one more little paper or two—next year.... I remember it clearly.... You planned it all out."

He could not utilize the pause that followed.

Suddenly, she burst out again, "The house is mine, you say."

He was ready for that. "Yes, but you owe me money. Lots of money. You have eaten up the house."

So there it was—the heroine and the villain who foreclosed the mortgage on her ancestral home—in a preposterous actuality. But she had come in late and missed acts one and two which had piled up this weight of hatred against her.

She demanded figures. It cost, Eugene figured, about one-third of the present value of the house to run it for a year.

"And, of course, you've been running it for about two and a half years—and more—ever since your father's death—and you've spent a good deal extra."

"*I* have spent a good deal? Many of these things were bought before I ever came home! The sloop and the phaeton! The new horses and the dog! I see now why you bought an imported one! And all the extra work on the grounds—more than had ever been done since mama died—much more lawn and the trails in the woods."

"Your manager O.K.'d every plan," he broke in.

"Lyddy? I don't believe you. Or else she didn't know about the notes. Did she?"

"That matter was out of her jurisdiction."

"Then she didn't," she said loftily. "And that silly telephone! How many miles is it to the quarry?"

Her voice was so demanding he had to answer, "Four."

"Four miles of wire and poles and labor! *I* have spent a good deal!"

Not many minutes had elapsed since she sat down in the red chair, but in that time she had become Miss Smithpeters, the head of the house, with all the responsibilities of its uunhappy history upon her shoulders. But she had kept her rhythm. Its beat mercifully held her back from realization.

It had also driven Eugene, and his triumph was impaired. Nothing more needed to be said or done, but his stupid revenge-fulness piled irrelevant insult upon effective injury.

"Your young man won't trouble us now. The rich and beautiful young lady isn't rich any more. Still beautiful, though. Maybe you can catch him the way your mother got your father. He stays all night already, I hear … "

It was a new form of a childhood horror: she was standing in the doorway of a woods cabin. From the track on which the door had slid open a long thick snake was swinging, his tail writhing close to her shoulder.

"Maybe he'll fall for your twenty-five hundred a year. And you'll have a little cash when the notes are paid off. You can have a sale of the stuff in the house. It's yours. You could support him all right."

He had much more to say. The years had been fertile.

"Your mother was a gay one. Used to do a swell dance without any clothes on! I knew her pretty darned well myself." He went on with spurious geniality. "Maybe you never knew your father was engaged to my sister. Not that she loved him so much. Then this little gutter-snipe turned up. Of course, we had to get rid of her. Wouldn't do to let her get away with it. Isabel always got what she wanted and she wanted that little slut to clear out. And she fixed things so that she had to! Your father had made an honest woman of her and that was enough. … Then Isabel and little Eugene died … "

His chatter ceased. His voice rose into rough and threatening loudness and his flat fist pounded the desk as he ended, "I told him I'd get even if it took the rest of my life!"

There were voices, she remembered, but she could not hear the words though unclear strife was real and disgrace intensified. It was the day little Eugene was buried. Now, today, when she was twenty-two years old, hard clarity had come. … She whirled in the red chair as she had recoiled from the thick snake.

He had never noticed her back before nor how pink her little ears were. It'd be a pretty back in a decolleté gown. Or no gown. His wrath faded in an inaudible snicker. Then he went around the desk, between it and the chair, and bent over, his mouth close as he spoke softly. … He wouldn't live here, of course, but he could keep both houses going for a while. Nobody would know.

"Only, the young man would have to go," he was whispering when Lyddy, carefully quiet Lyddy, let go the heavy lid of the blanket chest and, a moment later, the store-room door. He passed her on his way out.

Miss Smithpeters did not leave the red chair—in the lag between the blow and the pain. She felt that she must stay there. It was a matter between the three of them—her father, her mother, herself—like the day she "found out" on the day of the party. Her father had sat in the chair and she in his lap, his head bent over her. She had felt him kiss her curls. She belonged there and so did her mother. Lovely she was and gay, he had said. She loved pretty colors and good times. ... There was something he would not tell her! And now Uncle Eugene had told her with his dirty tongue. ... Pretty and gay, her father had said. And *good!* He had said it particularly. Stephen would understand about her mother and how the lamp could flare up if the wick were not tended. Uncle Eugene's hands made filthy whatever he touched. But he said he knew her well, and what was it he implied about his own sister?

The pain came: the hot shame for her mother and the fear of it—rolling over her again. ... The insult to Stephen, the pure in heart, whose hands upon her were like a priest's in blessing. ... Disgust and fright at the advances of Eugene, stupid and gross. The boy from Yale grown up. Stephen had cast him out but he had come back; the Gadarene swine did not want him. ... The gracious and elegant lady of the portrait and fifteen years of memory had of a sudden become ruthless. Like the wicked queen in the story, her pretty rooms were fouled with serpents and under her rich clothing was hideousness. ...

If it were all true.

She could not go to Lyddy now any more than she ever could, nor to Mr. Blake. Nor to Stephen yet, if ever. She must find her strength within herself and wisdom in her own rhythms as he would want her to do. She pushed back the red chair and stood up.

The phaeton would be ready at the door, she remembered; Sinbad never forgot her plans. She would want it, she had said, as soon as her business with her uncle was completed. It was not completed, but she would drive down the street just the same. She drew the screen before the still active fire and stood still a moment before she left the room—her eyes following the lines of books, resting on Go-eeth and the globe, and on the far and brilliant vista of late autumn trees and water with the cone of the blue mountain floating above. The moment was an island as real as Rat Island out there cutting the horizon with its long tail.

She stopped on the second floor for her outdoor things, adjusting the hat with care behind the pompadour and drawing on her new dogskin gloves—still carefully fitting their smartness to her hands as she walked down the broad steps where Bingo was awaiting her below one of the lions. He leaped into the carriage as usual when she snapped open the hasp and dropped the halter to hang on the stone post, and sat upright on his side of the seat. They went briskly down the smooth curves of the drive through the landscaped woods and clattered along the cobbles of the "street" where the surprised horse was pulled up at a new spot. Jessy took the hitching weight from the floor and attached its long strap to the bit. Bingo remained on duty also.

The main window of the little building between the bank and the drugstore announced in impressive letters of gold that this was the law office of Josiah P. Atwood. She had been there two or three times before. So she knew it was all right to say only good morning to the clerk and walk right through to knock on the inner door. Mr. Atwood opened it himself as she knew he liked to do.

With his old-fashioned bow he ushered her into his office, mellow with calf-bound books and the worn clients' chair tucked in beside the big pigeon-holed desk. It was a new desk he told her as he hung up her coat, and asked her how many drawers she could see, and when she fell short on the number made her hunt for the hidden ones and complimented her acuteness when she pulled out two pieces of apparently decorative woodwork to reveal shallow troughs which might possibly contain small articles.

"A few postage stamps, anyway," he chuckled.

"Or some dimes—not too many," she returned and wasted no more time.

"Did you know my mother, Mr. Atwood? My real mother, I mean."

He did not temporize.

"Yes, I saw her several times, and I talked with her once privately. You look exactly like her. She was very pretty and very charming if I may say so."

She considered that first sentence before she spoke:

"Thank you. Would it be all right to ask what you talked with her about?"

He paused at that for a moment.

"Yes. You were my client at the time, in a way, I now realize. You have a right to know."

But he found it hard to begin. He did a little introductory explaining.

"You know—or maybe you don't know—unless you've read about it in some novel—that sometimes a young man gets entangled with a young woman whom his family regard as undesirable, and they try to dissuade her if they can't do anything with him. Lawyers have to handle such cases at times—family lawyers."

"You mean a bad girl? One you could buy off?"

"Sometimes. But not in this case! Not in this case!"

She drew a long breath and let it escape. He noticed and reiterated flatly.

"She was a *good* girl. You can rely on that."

She waited in a cleared area of relief. He went on again.

"It was this way as I understood it: your father was planning to go into the ministry at that time, and it was thought that she would not be a very good helpmeet—as they used to say when your grandfather was young." He broke off suddenly to say, "Have you ever read *David Copperfield?* Of course you have. David made a mistake in marrying Dora, didn't he? Nice little thing she was, too, but childish and impractical. That silly Jip!" He stopped to smile about Jip. "He knew it later when he married Agnes. Not that your mother was like Dora. She wasn't at all. She had native wisdom as well as grace and charm. But she didn't seem much like a parson's wife in a staid little town like this. That was one point."

Again she waited so palpably that he struck off again with an unusual sense of being cross-examined.

"Sometimes, too, parents honestly think that such a relation is a passing fancy—that the marriage will not be happy for either party. Better to break off. However, opposition is likely to strengthen resolution. I knew a wise mother who asked a chorus girl her son had fallen in love with to spend the summer at their place. He did not marry her," he concluded dryly.

"Perhaps a long stay might have worked otherwise for my mother," she commented.

"I am inclined to think it would," he replied. "I liked her. She had not had the advantages you have had, but she had her own wisdom. She might have worked out a happy life for all of you. Later I was sorry I had taken the part that I did in the matter, though she didn't pay much attention."

"But they were married anyway."

"Yes, your grandfather suddenly insisted upon the marriage. There was—"

She finished it for him, "An urgency. I know about that."

"Then I should tell you that if you had known her, you would not have blamed her very much. She was a—child of nature. You can think of her with interest and pride and love. You come of good stock on both sides of the house."

The area of relief was only a partial one, but in its limits were tidings of comfort and joy. They would make a wonderful motif in the sonata. She wished she could tell Mr. Atwood so.

"May I ask one thing?" he inquired. "How did this matter come up just now?"

She would have to think of a way to answer. In a moment, she said, "Something my—stepmother's brother said to me."

He timed it exactly right and then laughed just the right laugh.

"My dear girl, let me tell you something about that gentleman who is no relation to you: he has never gotten over his sophomore delight in his vices or his supposed or dreamed-of vices. Don't pay any attention to anything of that kind he says—about himself or anybody else! Laugh him off for a little boy smoking cornsilk behind the barn!"

He said it so infectiously that she did laugh and remembered about her rhythm that overcame Uncle Eugene's.

"He's a mean enemy, though." It was such a swift parenthesis that Jessy did not know she had noticed its warning.

"I'd like to know something else. How did you happen to be concerned in my father's and mother's marriage?"

"I was the attorney for the Sparks family," he said slowly. "Miss Isabel was concerned in the matter, but I could not accomplish what she desired."

"So what her brother said about her was true? She drove my mother away."

"I cannot give you any evidence on that phase of it. Gossip said she did. I would not put it past her. She wasn't one to take a slight." After a moment, he concluded, "I can say this: after her death your father broke with the Sparks family. She died while he was in Germany for the first time. … I have no evidence, but I believe she did it and he knew it. Lyddy Sanders probably knows more about it than anybody."

"I have never talked to Lyddy about them," she said irrelevantly to her thought. She was trying to balance her emotional books. Two of the losses were written off. She told him so—in a way—as she thanked him and said goodbye.

But a new one was entered—a dead loss of which she did not speak. The place was devastated—the house and all the things in it, except in her father's study—and the grounds and the shore and even the stables where Bingo and the horses lived. It was catastrophe reaching back to the first Smithpeters in the first manse and forward like circles in a pond. She had swung the hitching weight into the phaeton and headed for home before she remembered about the money.

# CHAPTER TWENTY-FIVE

Lyddy would have to know. It was in panicky alarm that she told her.

Lyddy's concern was instantaneous, but she could not believe what she heard. Jessy must have misunderstood. The house was running as it always had, she explained. She and Sinbad had always done the purchasing and the employing, verified all the bills, turned in a cash account quarterly, made an annual report to Mr. Edward and now to Mr. Sparks, of all expenditures. The only difference was that they now no longer signed checks on the house fund. Mr. Sparks did it now.

Her own last sentence pulled her up short and Jessy's insistence rushed in again. There was no house fund; she had been eating up the house, he had said. He had the notes. ... Had she examined them carefully? No, she had not, but she saw her signature.

Sinbad and David Blake were skeptical in their turn. David would seek clarification and later advice, if necessary.

He found Eugene suavely regretful. He had thought that of course she knew her father's income died with him, he said.

"She was only six or seven when her stepmother died," David said with his slow carefulness. "She wouldn't know much about a will."

"Her father should have explained when she went away to college at the latest. She lived on her own responsibility there." Eugene spoke with tolerant but tart firmness.

David considered that statement.

"Yes, he should. But his administrator should have gone over everything again as a safeguard for so young and inexperienced an heir. Did Mr. Atwood handle the matter for you?"

Eugene explained. No, he did not. The business was a simple one. He had seen to it himself—had been rather leisurely in the press of other matters. He reported to the court in the end—everything in order.

"The expenses went on, of course," David remarked.

"Yes, Jessy paid her college expenses out of her income. What I lent her supported the house."

"I doubt if she knew she had an income. Money was available all her life, you must remember. You expected a good deal."

"She ought to know what a note is! It's in the arithmetic."

David presumed that she would if the matter were presented properly. "She thinks you slipped the first one in when she was at a disadvantage from grief and confusion."

"I know she does. Poor little girl. She didn't understand as much as I thought. She's smart, though. But she certainly signed. I don't really see how I can shoulder—"

David stopped him. Would Eugene give him the amounts of each of the notes? He certainly would. He wanted everything to be open and aboveboard.

"And the dates?" David jotted them down also. He needed to know exactly where she stood, because he wanted to help.

Eugene was glad of that. "She needs advice, but doubtless would not listen to me. Regrettably."

"Her father was my best friend," David said.

" 'David and Jonathan' we Sunday-school boys used to call you." Eugene shook hands with his caller.

David was appalled. He should have been suspicious, he told Lyddy and Sinbad, when Eugene got the court to appoint him administrator.

"I was only disappointed," he went on. "I wanted to do it for him. But it seemed kind of natural for Eugene to go ahead since

Isabel's interest was involved in the settlement. ... I never did know about her will. That was the year I went out west."

"I knew. Everybody did. The provisions were published." Sinbad felt blameworthy too. "I guess nobody thought much about it when she came home and went to housekeeping as usual. If they wondered, it wasn't their business. I thought maybe Mr. Edward had big insurance for her with her income and took care of her himself."

"When did that income begin?"

"Right away after Miss Isabel's death." Lyddy knew that.

"You didn't spend it all when she was a little girl, did you?"

"No, just for clothes and other little-girl expenses—dentist, doctor. The pony. Her school bills were not big. She was only a day scholar."

"Then what was done with the remainder?"

Lyddy did not know. "My accounts and checks were only for purchases I made. Maybe he did do something like what Sinbad said." Her voice was straining with oncoming tears. "When she was in college she had her own check book."

"Seems as if he put it away for her somewhere." David would try to find out about that also, but he did not want to have any more dealings with Eugene.

Lyddy wept when David had left, and Sinbad had no comfort to give.

"It's getting worse with every meal we eat and every stroke of work done on the place!"


"I want to report on my business affairs," Jessy said to Stephen, because she was thinking, "He is my helpmeet." There was content in the old word. She had led the way somewhat formally into the library and seated herself in a corner of the big couch, and he with matching dignity turned the high-backed chair from the desk kneehole and sat down to face her. He was alert to grasp what he had already sensed.

She told him only what she had told Lyddy, speaking in factual detail coolly—too coolly, he thought, as he got the drift. He listened gravely without interrupting questions. Silence fell across the space between them for a ticking moment.

"It's like a meller-drammer—in a tent. I don't suppose you have ever seen any, though," he remarked casually and was surprised to hear that she had—East Lynne and The Denver Express—but not in a tent. In a ten-twenty-thirty.

"No train wreck, though," he went on, "and no tubercular little boy angels. No Relentless Rudolph pursuing the beautiful and pure heroine to besmirch her honor."

She made no reply, but a flicker of peculiar recognition without any fright in it modified her eyes for a few seconds, lower lids drawn slightly upward.

"She's handled that alone." His silent praise was warm, but her reticence was pious like a child's first braveness.

"Maybe the foreclosed mortgage is in the next chapter, however," he went on conversationally. "I am not surprised but I had not anticipated such a move."

"I wouldn't put it past him." She liked Mr. Atwood's phrase but she hated its coupling of Isabel with Eugene.

The casualness had gone far enough.

"What are you going to do, darling?"

"I don't know, Stephen. I don't know." As she said it she began to cry. With a sudden twist she flung herself on the couch face down, and the crying grew into sobbing as a storm that has been a long time filling up the sky grows in momentum.

Stephen stood by the couch until the sobs grew farther apart. Then he sat down in the space beyond her feet. ... Waited until half-gasps were followed by sniffing and a hand reached into a pocket for a handkerchief. After a little, he picked up her feet and laid them on his knees, heels up, pulled down her skirt decorously, and held the ankles companionably.

Suddenly, they were jerked out of his hand and swung around. Without leaving the couch, she wriggled into his lap and hid her unhappy and unbeautiful face on his left shoulder and one arm held on around his neck. She fitted in comfortably. His right arm knew what to do and his face felt happy against part of a wet cheek and tumbled hair, but the moment had in it no love release. He felt the tension and solemnity of the minutes before he took the steps across the platform to the piano. Not stage fright. Responsibility for the good, the beautiful, and the true: held in his hands.

Weeping at last ended in a final sounding sigh.

"Stephen," she said into his collar, "do you remember the time I lost my mother's ring?" The sentence whimpered at the end.

He would never forget it, he said in clear truth.

"This is like that—only now it's hundreds, thousands of rings! Every place—every room—the attic—Eugene's baby-carriage—my mother's spoons and her furry boots—"

"You wouldn't need the baby-carriage. It's probably out of date," he suggested mildly. "And all your mother's things are yours by your father's gift, aren't they?"

She sat up quickly.

"All the things are mine! I forgot to tell you that."

"Well, then?"

Her tone rose to tearless wailing.

"But I will have to take them away! They wouldn't be the same! The land! Land where my fathers died! And Uncle Eugene will level off the cemetery where the captain and my mother and my brother are!"

"He can't," Stephen said succinctly. "The law forbids it."

There was stabilization in his voice.

"But, Stephen," she went on less plaintively, "all these things are in the Deep Place. To take them out—"

Stephen put both arms around her and drew her against him again. He spoke authoritatively.

"And there is something else very important in the Deep Place, and you have found it out, my dear. It is suffering."

She wept again, quietly this time.

"It has grandeur, though—the grandeur of reality."

There was no reply. She was thinking of a clear tenor voice singing again and again, "These are they, these are they—." "They" had come out of great tribulation.

"And washed their robes and made them white," she said to Stephen.

"Yes, they did. Nice and white." He kept his voice as matter-of-fact as he could. This stabilization was deeper and steadier. But not steady enough to control the irrelevance of disaster.

"I don't want any of the things but my mother's and my father's! I never want to touch that gold piano again and I don't want you to! I'll smash that short-legged Shakespeare and burn up her books and slit her portrait with a knife! I hate them all because I loved them so much!"

She had sprung up with her first sentence and stood blazing before him. His astonishment prevented any further moralizing, but he rejoiced in that rage: it was healthy and real.

So he said only, "I guess there is something you haven't told me about."

"I didn't mean to tell you that part, but I will." Her wrath-warmed vigor was still operating.

She told the story of what Isabel had done, clearly, cutting neatly away from it details about her mother.

"Her own brother—her twin-brother—said she did. And it was not love but pride that made her do it," she concluded. "Lyddy knows. Mr. Atwood—"

She apparently did not want to say anything more about Mr. Atwood. Stephen did not inquire.

"Then actually you don't want to stay, do you? She bought most of the things. And they have become venomous, haven't they?"

"I don't want to stay but I cannot bear to give it all up," she burst out. "I am like a vine with thousands of tendrils on this house. Tendrils of memory." It was theatrical but genuine. "If I have to be torn off I'll die!"

"Vines have roots," Stephen observed, "good strong ones. Cut back they grow out again."

He had her attention and seized his opportunity.

"I don't know that you'll go on feeling about your stepmother as you do now, anyway—cruel though she was and fantastically self-centered. She was good to you always in her way, wasn't she? You loved her for those six or seven years. And always since."

Jessy nodded, tears again in her eyes.

"And when she made her will—and will-making is a major action for such a person—she took care of you for the rest of her life. That little income for fifty or sixty years was a pretty nice present which she did not need to give you. Your father could have taken care of you and she knew it."

"Maybe it was just a part of her pride," Jessy cut in.

"Maybe, and maybe it came from a guilt hidden from even her to ease the sense of fairness she had outraged. Lots of actions have mixed motives, you know."

She was listening sharply. He went right on.

"There's a silly line in a silly song, 'When my love has turned to hate.' I don't believe that happens much. Love and hate get wound up together, though. ... If you run a knife down that canvas, both love and hate will make you do it. You said as much yourself. ... I feel rather sorry for her. We all walk a lonely way. I wonder what she was like when she was a little girl and a young girl—where that drive of hers came from."

He hoped she was wondering, too. He did not hurry her on. ...

"It's like mountains. Somewhere in the center of the earth was great pressure—earthquake pressure. And the mountains reared up. They couldn't help themselves. They had to be mountains."

She was ready to reply.

"I would rather feel sorry for her. Lyddy says it is better to be sorry for people than to be mad at them or afraid."

It was time for brevity. Stephen approved of Lyddy's philosophy and added only, "This business you are in now is cruel enough without any extras."

He was trying to be careful to say *you* and not *we*—not always successfully. How easily and happily he could have comforted her and himself by saying the good old sentimental words, "Whatever happens we will meet it together. No loss will be too great if we have each other." The good old pregnant words.

But she must not think about a joint life (and he did not think she had done so—not so much as most girls would). He could say the good old words maybe when she had weathered this crisis without too much help—help on actual procedure, that is. ... That Mr. Atwood slip was a good sign-independence in it.

# CHAPTER TWENTY-SIX

Stephen's principle of not-too-much-sitting-around called for strict practice right then. Sinbad's discreet knock and entrance was opportune. Mr. Blake would like to talk to Miss Jessy for a few minutes. Should he bring tea? Coffee for the gentlemen? He saw no reason for discontinuing the amenities, and Jessy's unusual appearance he considered as very appropriate.

The social interlude was good for Jessy, though Mr. Blake had to conceal anxious impatience. Stephen obliged him by a prompt withdrawal—coffee-cup in hand.

David wasted no time either.

"It's my business only because I think your father would be glad for me to take a hand, Jessy, but I'm no lawyer. I know you must be very much disturbed."

"I am. And I am ashamed. I did something very stupid."

"You had not been trained to suspicion."

David's kind voice went on. "Can you remember anything about it?"

"I can almost remember. I saw the signature—very black. I remember his handing me a pen several times."

"He said to me once, 'You will need some ready money, I suppose,' and he gave me some cash. I remember because I never had a hundred-dollar bill in my purse before."

"I don't know why you would need ready money. Your income was paid into your checking account, I understand. It had nothing to do with the matters in hand."

"I told him that I didn't need it, but he said I had better take it. Maybe he said that on the note days and I didn't understand."

"Do you remember anything about the interviews on these dates?" He mentioned the first one.

"I told him about that one! You know just when that was. I paid no attention to anything he said that day. I couldn't. I just did what he said."

She remembered nothing about the second. The third may have been the date of one of the last meetings when there was a good deal of business—the deed and all that. Insurance, she remembered. Taxes. She remembered because she had been provided with a safety box to put her papers in. And she had looked at the abstract. It began with a King George and carried on down to Jessy Smithpeters, spinster.

David had a primary report to give. He had figured the debt—the original sums and interest—compound interest he was sorry to say it would have to be. He had gone over Lyddy's and Sinbad's accounts with them. The totals corresponded pretty well with the amounts Eugene had advanced. And he had secured a fairly reliable estimate on the value of the place. Eugene was right; the three years had eaten a big hole.

"So then, he is financially honest—in a way," Jessy concluded. "And he could be honest in what he says about the notes."

"That's about the size of it."

"I don't believe he was, though. I think it was deliberate. I told him so."

He asked if she knew what had been done with the money that must have remained from her childhood income. She had no idea. Mr. Atwood might know. She would ask him. David's anxious depression was lifted slightly by the surprise of her initiative.

Mr. Atwood did know—the very person for her to ask, he said. But he did not give her the information at once. He circled in leisure back to the beginning.

"Do you know where your money comes from?"

"Not exactly. It began coming in the mail when I went to college and still does."

He nodded, but she went on, wanting to seem at ease.

"Before that Lyddy used to give me an allowance—twenty-five cents a week it was at first."

"She didn't want you to be a spendthrift, I see, but you are better off now."

He was smiling, but he changed to a formal manner and tone as he went on. His hands looked a lawyer's hands in a play, she thought—fingers paired separately in a skeleton dome. This call was different from the last one.

"The money came and is coming this way: Lyddy drew for you and you are now drawing on a Trust Fund. Your stepmother established it for you—to continue for your lifetime. It is in the custody of our bank legally acting as a trust company. I am an officer. Under the provisions of the will we send you checks monthly which amount to twenty-five hundred dollars a year. Your fund is known as the Sparks Fund for Jessy Smithpeters. There was a similar larger fund for your father; it has reverted to his wife's estate. Is that all clear?"

It was. He could not improve on Eugene's clarity. He must know she knew all that.

"And you own a house in the village which came from your Smithpeters grandparents. The Trust sees to that also and collects the income it brings. Now to your specific question. What was not drawn out is waiting for you now. It must be a nice little sum unless your father invested some of the surplus of your childhood elsewhere. You were not a very expensive little girl in Bold Water, I suppose. He would have had a right to do so. Any such investments would have earned more for you, of course. If he did, there would have been such papers among those you saw when he died—stocks, bonds, or maybe insurance."

She tried to recall the documents of that first interview with Uncle Eugene, while Mr. Atwood continued.

"I suppose you drew the full amount when you went to college. When was it, Jessy?"

"It must have been in March or April, 1905. He was drowned in February."

"I don't mean that. When did you go to college—begin drawing the whole amount? How old were you then?"

"I was eighteen—almost nineteen. My birthday is in December. It was 1903."

"And you were about six when your stepmother died? So there must be several years of accumulation." He would go over to the bank and find out exactly.

But he did not start. She must not think too ill of her stepmother, he began again. There was nothing mean about her in the literal sense of the word. He had originally suggested that she provide up to twenty-five hundred dollars in any one year, any money undrawn to revert to the state. But she wouldn't hear of that. He hoped Jessy would not condemn her in spite of all that had passed.

Jessy said that she would not and added, "We all walk a lonely way."

Stephen's sentence did not seem to mean much to Mr. Atwood, however. He went on. "And you stayed two years at college? I suppose you spent all your money then?"

"Yes, I liked buying and paying. And I kept accounts. Lyddy taught me to and how to."

"You do still?"

Jessy said she did. She wished he would go over to the bank, but he had more to say.

"Miss Jessy, you seem like a girl with an acute mind—a mind that takes to business though you have done so little. I guess you had a good arithmetic teacher in the eighth grade.... May I ask you a pointed question? It is none of my concern. I am an attorney retained by the Sparks family and the Sparks interests, and Mr. Sparks has told me about your recent crisis. But I feel a little responsibility for you personally.... How did you happen to do so stupid a thing as to sign papers you had not read nor understood?"

She looked straight into the keen blue of Mr. Atwood's eyes.

"It was stupidity," she said, "compounded of grief and carelessness and trustfulness."

"That is a clear and significant reply," he commented. "Now I will step over to the bank for that statement."

While he was gone, her mind went back again to those first financial dealings with Uncle Eugene. Mr. Atwood had apparently done so likewise, for after he had presented and expounded the statement, he said again, "What did you say was the date of your father's death?"

She told him again—mechanically—in her astonishment at what she saw on the paper.

The astonishment did not bring ultimate relief, however. David Blake went through a similar cycle—a more rapid one than hers when she handed him the sheet of paper at a "family" conference. She had called it—David, Lyddy, Sinbad. Not Stephen.

"This is a pleasant surprise," David said slowly, his eyes still on the typed figures. "You must have been very economical with Jessy's money, Lyddy, and apparently her father drew nothing for her benefit. But—" he took a notebook from his pocket and compared the statement to a page of his own figures for a few careful moment—"I guess Eugene still wins. I don't believe his main object was to make money for himself or to impoverish Jessy."

The situation came clear in the inexpert but careful discussion though nobody summed up. The accumulation in the Trust Fund was a sum adequate to pay off two of the notes with the interest—as Eugene must have known, Lyddy pointed out, and David agreed.

She would still have her income and a nest-egg of a size depending on what the house would bring—less the amount of the remaining note.

"She won't be poor, but—"

Jessy stood up like a chairman bringing a meeting to a close. "I can't go on living here in any case. I think you are right, Mr. Blake. Uncle Eugene has accomplished what he wanted to do. Stupidly. I would have had to go anyway and he knew it. He got the plan from some paper-backed novel. He needn't have taken all that trouble, but he wanted to dramatize his venom. And his treachery. He started being kind to me for the first time in my life in those first business interviews—"

She paused sharply, interrupted, it seemed to her by Mr. Atwood, and sat down in her corner of the couch, no longer the chairman. Her voice had a hesitant and childish quality when she spoke again.

"What was the date of that first note, Mr. Blake?"

"April 5, 1905."

"And how old was I then, Lyddy?"

Lyddy glanced at each of the men and then back at Jessy.

"Why, you know how old you were, dearie." She spoke as to one in the confusion of illness. "You were twenty, of course. Twenty-one the next December."

"Then—" her voice still childish and hypnotically commanding, Jessy gave neither man a chance to speak—not even to interrupt—"I won't have to pay that one, will I, unless I want to?"

Sinbad slapped his thigh with his meaty palm.

"By God you won't—not in this state!"

To Lyddy his oath was affirmation of faith.

But as the little meeting was adjourning, Jessy said, "I may pay just the same."

# CHAPTER TWENTY-SEVEN

Stephen was playing the piano when Sinbad opened the library door after the conference—he had just begun, Jessy noticed.

"That's a good lively piece," said Sinbad.

"It's about a man climbing a mountain, a high and icy one," Jessy told him. "Sometimes he slips and falls, but he always gets up again—climbs on."

She thanked David for his careful concern, as they stood there, arranged to see him again, and said goodbye. Sinbad was still listening to the music; she saw him at the far end of the wide hall with Mr. Blake's raincoat in his hand.

Stephen did not stop playing when she went in and she did not speak. The climber was still climbing.

"That's what you have to say to me, isn't it?" He was still playing as she spoke. "David can help me decide about the money. ... I hope you will make a little prelude for me as you did for the second movement."

He still did not stop playing. "This is it. Those sheets on top of the cabinet. And underneath the steamboat one for the third."

She was standing behind him now.

"There's a lot about water in this sonata—fresh springs—hidden brook—steamboat. Will the fourth movement have any?"

Stephen's hands wandered into smooth improvising, and he did not answer at once.

"Yes," he said and he played a little of the golden thread, "a river in it—deep river. Best of all, I hope. It is not written yet."

Then he played a river—placid in August ... then a river in sullen flood ... finally a wide deep river—formidable, majestic, commanding.

"I've been working on the river. Perhaps I'm getting something. Write that down for me, Jessy, will you—that last?"

He played the single notes while she set them down on the scored pad. Then he turned around to say, "We have the direction now. We know what we have to work toward."

"I haven't my direction, Stephen."

"Yes, you have. You and I must go the direction of the sonata always. That's a doctrine."

"But, Stephen—"

"You said it yourself a few minutes ago—about what David can do and the music does."

"But I shall have to decide—"

"Of course you will, darling. I am not so impractical as I sound. Let's go into the library. We've got to think."

But they sat side by side before what was in Stephen's mind rose to expression.

"Jessy, what would you have done if you had known two or three years ago what you know now: that you have an income only big enough to live on in a simple way and a big place that you could not possibly support?"

She considered the question like a problem in school—if a man had a hundred acres of land—

"I know the arithmetic answers. I should have sold the place and invested the money and lived somewhere else. But the real answer—I couldn't have borne it, Stephen. I couldn't. I couldn't."

"The arithmetic would have told you that you were losing a great deal of money. You would have had to put mortgages on the house—lose it in the end."

"I could have stood that. The two and a half years would have been worth it."

He let her make the obvious comment. "And that is still true. I am precisely in that position now."

"Except—" he must not spare her—"that you know some unpleasant truths—have been disillusioned about certain persons."

"Only one! And I am glad to know about them all. There is no use hiding. I can love them all just the same. Reality is better than a prettified picture."

Stephen wished he were playing the piano again. No words were handy for this triumph—come so easily—not too easily, he hoped.

"And as for Uncle Eugene," she concluded mildly. "I never did like him. And what he has done to me, I should have had to do to myself if he had been honest with me. I can get rid of him—push him out like the boy from Yale. . . . I don't owe him as much as he thinks I do, either."

Stephen, like Sinbad, smote his thigh and ejaculated profanely when she explained.

"And you thought of it before anybody else caught it?"

"Not really thought of it, I guess. It just came to me like a forgotten name. From my unconscious mind." She spoke casually. "I read a book about that in college. The professor said it was a modern organization of what men have always known. You ought to read that book, Stephen. He said it concerned the seat of all living."

"I will."

"The professor said we would hear more of it."

She looked at him with a sudden brilliant blankness.

"Why, Stephen, what a half-wit I am! I have been hearing of it all summer and fall. From you."

She did not stop for reply but swept along in the vigor of her concept. "It's an example of what we were taught. The unconscious mind is a great combiner, he said. You put something into it and, much later, perhaps, it hooks up with other things, and you get a new something."

"That is the way it is in composing."

She paid no attention to his remark.

"Maybe it made a plan for me when my father died. I didn't stop to think. I just went on. And now I think it was the plan I wanted all the time anyway."

She stopped for Selah, he thought, but not for long.

"Religious people call it guidance. A girl I knew at college was a Friend. She used to talk about the inner light. It is a guidance you don't know about until you get there."

"We are religious people," Stephen said with incisiveness and rather loudly. He wanted her to hear that. "We can call it guidance too. My mother's favorite hymn was 'Jesus Savior, Pilot Me.' Her voice was a strong contralto. 'Unknown waves before me roll,' she'd sing."

"And I used to say, 'All this day thy handeth led me.' I had to ask Lyddy what handeth meant."

She went right back to the Friend.

"But sometimes you know about the inner light. You have to wait for it with a sense of waiting that invites it. You must wait," she repeated as one emphasizes road directions. "And maybe when a decision comes in a flash it has been forming for you don't know how long."

She was so absorbed in the easy clarity of her thinking that she did not recognize the climax in those swift moments, but she repeated, "He said it was the seat of living."

If his mouth was not hanging open it ought to be, he thought. He was glad when she was summoned from the room to receive callers—glad for a half-hour to recover from the deflation that both chagrined and delighted him. He thought of the ideas he had so ingenuously yearned to expound for her benefit—those he had expounded. He recalled his fussy little schemes for reminders—souvenirs of high moments—all he had given so far an English copper and a bottle of perfume. No trinket was needed to perpetuate these last few minutes. That list of rides together! How he had contrived—he who did not believe in contriving!

He thought of the bridegroom who fell into the crevasse—in a grisly old story. In fifty years, a scientist told the bride, the glacier would have carried his body to the moraine. And, sure enough, the well-iced remains were on hand to greet the bride of seventy. His elaborate scheme had something of the same idea.

That phonograph he had bought so that she could hear him play the sonata for fifty years! He gave up that plan as soon as he heard the snarling and scratching that came from the big horn—hard to separate from even the golden tones of Farrar and Caruso. Still she would have the thing and would see the improvements come. Some day she might hear his music recorded by a master for a master machine. He liked to think of that. No glacier corpse in that idea.

And he was not sorry he had put the books and the music into his little trunk. She would like the ideas they would bring—the heavy black line down the O, the wild joy of living passage in his mother's Browning. (A lecture on reading had been teeming within him: she seemed to carry herself *into* books instead of bringing pleasure and power and wisdom *from* books, he had ponderously though it out.)

He was right, too, but he did not need to tell her now. She could and would see the implications and make the applications.

He remembered when he had carefully given directions for skiing to a new blond friend who listened respectfully and, after saying modestly, "I think I can do it," took off down the steep hill and into the air from the bluff in perfect Norwegian form.

He felt flatter then than now. She didn't really *know*... until this afternoon. Textbook and teacher might never come to life without the summer's experience. He couldn't simply have assigned lessons in that book. He had not been altogether wrong in the way he went at it. In fact, he had been right. By the grace of God. But the most was accomplished when he pushed least.

"She seems like a different girl and in all this new trouble," he had heard Lyddy say to Mrs. Blake outside his innocently opened door, and Mrs. Blake reply, "It is the power of love." That was what he had been afraid of; it was not enough.

When Jessy returned to the room, she said at once as though the conversation had not been interrupted, "I have decided not to decide for a while yet just what I shall do."

In this situation time for decision would cost something. She would still be living in the big house. Jessy was somewhat blank on that point but Lyddy was fluent with suggestions. It was lucky that that landscaping job had been delayed. And as far as that was concerned, nothing much needed to be done on the grounds except to cover for winter. In fact, The Boy could do what had to be done.

"You can see to your garden yourself, Jessy with him to do the heavy part. He gets three dollars a week and keep."

Sinbad struck in.

"Would you mind driving old Nibs in the phaeton?" If not, he could sell the new horse for her. A man over at Deep Haven was looking for one ... rich man. That horse and rig cost a lot of money.

Jessy would not mind giving up the horse, but she spoke a little anxiously about Bingo. Sinbad reassured her. There wasn't so much money tied up in a dog and anyway Bingo was a member of the family.

"There are lots of things in the house we can sell," Jessy volunteered.

Lyddy was prompt in agreement. "We'll think that out when we know where we are going and what we will need there."

Where we are going! The briskness of Lyddy and Sinbad was an acknowledgment of inevitability.

"We needn't make much change in the house now. We can close some rooms you seldom go into. That would keep down heating costs and wages." Lyddy, as always, was sharp-eyed and kind.

She did not believe in using capital unless you had to. She had a notion they could live on Jessy's income with other retrenchments she had in mind—the three of them. "Lots of families of five or six live nicely on that amount."

"Taxes," Sinbad said warningly.

Jessy surprised them and herself.

"Would the horse money pay them?"

"Sinbad said it would help anyway for this year—due in January. The place was in apple-pie order. There wouldn't be any big bills for painting or repairs before—"

"We will have time," said Lyddy comfortably interrupting, "to make up our minds gradually. We won't suffer and we won't have to set a date."

David Blake felt as they did except in one particular. He wanted to cut off that compound interest with promptness. He would consult an officer of the Trust Company about transferring her funds to her checking account, and about the first note.

Jessy eventually wrote a big check—ceremoniously—with four persons looking on like a president signing a treaty, she said. It disposed of the second and third notes. The payment of the first one would not be pressed, David reported. It was hoped, Mr. Atwood had said further, that the matter would not become a matter of general knowledge. Jessy was grateful for that proviso and so, no doubt, was her Uncle Eugene.

All three notes were returned, but Jessy destroyed only the last two.

# CHAPTER TWENTY-EIGHT

One decision came before Christmas easily in spite of, perhaps because of, Lyddy's carefully nurtured air of leisure—on Jessy's birthday. It was the day of the first big snow, too—snow that filled even the crevices of bark and cones. It spread evenly and deeply over terrace and lawn—like icing on a birthday cake, nice and thick, she had said almost every year; and every birthday or Christmas she had gone to the front door to see if the lions were snow lions and they usually were.

Sinbad drove out after breakfast standing on the triangular snow plow, its sharp angle of timber cutting into the whiteness like a boat through water and piling up frothily along the sides of the lengthening path. The woolly old horse wore the first string of bells of the season and stepped high in an elderly manner. The plow pushed all the way through the woods and down the hill to the road which the village cleared in due time and then turned for home, widening the path to a road.

Later—but not much later—Sinbad set out again in the cutter and brought Stephen up to the side entrance. Stephen was grateful. He had forgotten about winter and what it would do to the routine of his plans.

"People are pretty well holed up here in winter," Sinbad marked cheerfully. However, he'd be going to the village for one reason or another every morning and could just as well take Stephen back and forth. No trouble at all. He'd take him home tonight after the party whenever he was ready.

The party was Stephen for dinner.

"We wouldn't want to have twenty-three little girls, would we?" Jessy pointed out and Lyddy agreed delightedly.

The shut-in day was pleasant—with various little busynesses to see to; pleasant to think of Stephen at work on her piano in her house, eating lunch from her dishes on her tray; pleasant with a new rush of happiness—recent bitterness and anxiety gone like clouds from a sunny hill on a breezy day.

Sinbad came in to replenish the fire, laughing with the gayety of a cold day at what he had seen down street. He always told his stories well. Jessy and Lyddy enjoyed laughing with him, especially at his picture of Eugene's two Dalmatian dogs up to their hips in snow—their sharp black dots leaping in the white.

Jessy got out her hem-stitching for the afternoon—a task that was getting to be a joke—a long table-cloth she had undertaken some years before to hem-stitch "double hemstitching." Napkins still lay ahead. It was placid work—gathering the six threads, pulling the little slip-noose and securing it with a fine firm stitch through the hem—moving slowly down a three-yard length, eventually, she hoped, coming back; and it was pleasant in Lyddy's sitting-room (where they sat a good deal nowadays) in the warmth of a Franklin stove and the snow-sunlight pouring in the windows.

"We're two women now," Jessy thought. "It's nice to be a woman."

Woman conversation moved on slowly—with long pauses and gentle agreement.

"In our new house," Jessy said idly, "we won't need such long tablecloths, I suppose. But what would I do without my hemstitching?"

Lyddy laughed. Then she said easily, "Do you know that you own another house right now, Jessy?"

"Why, yes, I guess I heard it mentioned with the other property. Why?"

"I've been thinking about that house these last few days. ... It is the house where your father and mother set up housekeeping. You were born there twenty-three years ago today."

"Here? In Bold Water? Why haven't I known about it?" Jessy's thimbled hand was poised in the air over a stitch just drawn tight.

Lyddy thought out her reply before she spoke.

"Your father couldn't speak of that time to you, I suspect. Nor you to him. And everybody else was an outsider."

Jessy gathered the table-cloth in her arms and dropped on her knees by Lyddy's chair.

"That was just the way it was, Lyddy! Just the way! I couldn't talk even to you! Even in that desolation on my tenth birthday. ... But that wasn't my birthday! It was in the summer!"

She sat back on her heels.

"I thought you needed a party, but it brought disaster." Lyddy's face was twisted with the old distress. "I guess you had to know sometime, but there could have been an easier way."

Jessy's eagerness pushed the sadness behind her again and put her back in her chair with the linen at her feet.

"Where is the house?"

"Do you know where Mr. Sands lives?"

"The drugstore man?"

"Yes. That is the house."

"Right on the harbor with a captain's walk! They have a nice veranda over the water with a box of geraniums on the railing!"

"It's just about as it was in your father and mother's time there. Except that he made some improvements and enlarged a little when the Sandses took it—just about as it was in his grandmother Smithpeters' day for that matter. He said that some old shipbuilder had built it and that shipbuilders built good houses, big or little. He kept it up well, though he never went there any more than he had to, I suppose."

"When was it built?"

"I don't know just when, but it was a Smithpeters who built it. Your father inherited it from his father."

Jessy's face was set in concentration. Facts had come fast.

"Do you mean to tell me that my great-grandfather—the one who went to sea lived in that house?"

"Yes, she did until her husband inherited the old house on this land."

"Well, my goodness," said Jessy. "Why don't we live there then? It's mine. I would love it with every cell and fiber of me. If I had to buy it, I'd trade this house even for it."

Lyddy went on to say that the Sandses were going to give it up—were just now completing a bigger house for their growing family. She had thought a little how it could be made more spacious—perhaps a wing extending along the shore for a living-room, as people were beginning to call it—with the piano in it and furnishings to make it pretty and comfortable. Above it a pleasant bedroom or two and a bathroom. ... It would be nice if she could always have a Smithpeters house to come back to no matter where life took her, Lyddy concluded philosophically.

"There would be room for you and Sinbad, wouldn't there?"

They could use the little old house at the other end, Lyddy thought, if she wanted them there. They still owned their little village house in case she needed the whole house for her own use—in years to come, she added hastily.

"That's the real part, though," Jessy demurred, "where they lived. Maybe I'd want it."

They would "see," Lyddy temporized. The planning and building would be slow work.

"But delightful," Jessy added. "Just wait until I tell Stephen. What a birthday present!"

The winter was a steady one with regular and heavy snow-falls and the tempered cold of island weather. Living was vigorous and centered and intent. Jessy was zealous about the harbor house though David Blake pointed out that no building could begin until spring. But the house was soon vacated and the keys were in Jessy's hands. She visited it frequently—with Lyddy and Sinbad—with Stephen...with all of them at once, apparently undismayed by its simplicity and crudity. David thought it would pay her to employ an architect. A local man would build well, but he couldn't plan, he said. He knew a young fellow in a town not too far away who could do a good job.

"After all," he said, "this will always be your home and you want it right." Then he smiled his rare gentle smile and added, "A nice house will be an honor to your parents."

She studied and discussed the sketches and plans with the glow of that remark upon her; and in that glow heard only casually his later announcement that the big house was now on the market and that the agent had a client who would like to see it with a view of buying some of the furnishings also. She suggested pleasantly that Lyddy would see to it. Stephen kept her steadily on her music schedule—regular lessons and conscientious practice—not only on the sonata but on a modestly widening repertoire. She developed an enthusiasm for snow-shoeing and practiced on her lawn until she was able to go through the woods path to the village with invitations to a snow-shoe party—an affair of warm stocking caps and mittens, flying scarfs and oyster stew. Parties led to other parties and to a sleigh-ride in a deep hay-cart set on runners when the boys joked a good deal about keeping the girls warm all right. Stephen did as they did and wrapped a robe around Jessy and himself, each holding an edge around the other in an intricate but satisfactory manner, and everybody sang the song while the bells actually did jingle all the way.

The high school principal and the teacher of English, both just out of college, had an idea. Its success all depended upon Jessy, they said. She must not—and did not want to—refuse. So she plunged into six weeks of work as producer and director of She Stoops to Conquer, the first high school play in Bold Water.

She was busy—seriously busy—with the casting, the rehearsals, the seats, the costumes, the tickets, the ushering, the programs with youthful committees to supervise. She read industriously to make her production authentic. She knew all the parts before rehearsals had gone very far and worked on them analytically with Stephen as audience. With a sweeping cap on and her taffeta skirt tucked up as panniers over her ruffled petticoat, she did the saucy eighteenth century maid with an easy distinction that surprised him.

"Maybe you'd better be an actress yet," he said. "You're good. There's a woman out in Detroit you ought to work with. She'd make you, for you'd give her something to work with."

"La! sir," she dipped a curtsey, "I am building myself a little home by the sea."

"Well, actresses all have homes, don't they? Only most of them have to earn them first."

The play was a success, and Jessy took her bow with the cast, dragged out by two of her devotees. She felt again the high assurance that glorified the night her father saw her act, and as then the golden coach did not become the pumpkin at twelve o'clock. The coach was more real than the pumpkin.

Stephen's intentness was even deeper. Sooner or later he had to meet—the word shocked him slightly—a deadline, but he wanted to meet it with fullness of life—gay and forward-looking, quietly and leisurely; rich in plans and companionship as though "until death do us part" were no more credible than to meet most young lovers. He cut his music-room schedule to five days a week, five hours a day, and momentum of approaching completion made him sharp in the endless cuttings, re-arrangings, taming-downs, emphasizings, and in-sertings—in the later hours of the working day.

For the fourth movement he must indoctrinate himself in an unknowable theme. He must pause in each present to savor the delight of all things visible and invisible. He must throw off the tyranny of time, the millenniums and the eons, the year 1907 in which he and Jessy were set, and face outward to an apocalypse. He must be alert to concepts for which there could be no words nor intellectual form.

"Thank God I am writing music," he thought.

There must be no funeral march—no willow—no terror. Solemnity, yes, and grandeur. Ten thousand times ten thousand harpers harping on their harps the triumph of life. Hereafter. Here.

He did not push. The quiet winter weeks gave an ampleness. Waking or sleeping or on the rim he fostered his sensitivity to concept and pattern. In the clear morning hours he worked and waited—sometimes in despairing fruitlessness—again in vague but certain creativeness.

Deep River. ... There were times when he wanted to tell Jessy everything—when the appalling loneliness recurred. His visits to Tom's office gave no chance to talk freely. Tom was trying to hold him back, but he was going ahead—and would have to step alone. He remembered what his mother had "said."

Her stock of words had been locked up by the same blast that stilled her right side. Her thinking, her remembering were as incisive and vigorous as ever but she could command only two Welsh place-names for speech. With those two words and intonation and pantomime—increasingly ingenious—she expressed her thoughts and her feelings, asked for information and gave it with endless and agonizing determination.

Victoria could not bear it and could not understand her mother. Stephen and his father learned a patience of interpretation, following clues, asking questions, waiting for illumination. Nearly always it came, sometimes without apparent means. Sometimes they failed and she was furious in frustration.

"Mother," Stephen would say, "I don't follow your line of thought. We'd better drop the subject. Don't you want me to play the piano with all the doors open?"

She "told" him one thing unmistakably, however. An imperceptive visitor had just left saying, "You are certainly getting better every day."

Picking up her inert right hand she laid it over her breast and crossed the left one over it. Then she straightened out stiffly and closed her eyes.

They snapped open again at once, however, and locked inquiringly at Stephen.

"Caernarvon?" she said.

"Yes," he said evenly and quietly, "I know exactly what you mean."

In a moment she was sitting up, her strong back erect.

"Llangollen! Llangollen!" Her voice was loud and strange. "Llangollen!" She flung her left arm upward and swung it, reaching, in wide arcs.

"Llangollen! Llangollen!" she called again in that strange voice, and it was as if the low dull ceiling had opened to opening skies.

Then she "said" more quietly that she wanted no weeping.

"Why, no, mother, I will rejoice with you."

She smiled and sighed comfortably. She had wanted him to know with her, he now knew.

That was his only experience with death. He wished Jessy could have learned that way. She knew too much—cruel deaths of the young, embittered sorrow with no glory and no solace. ... He could not tell her in advance—saturate the days with dread.

Finally there came a day when, in a mood of delicate suspension, he put the music together at one long sitting. He worked freely and lightly. And when he had finished, he laid himself down on the music-room divan.

"I bet I feel like a woman that's had a baby—forgotten what she's been through and pleased with what she has achieved," he thought. "And pretty tired."

Deep River needed revision. Cool reading on another day pointed it out, but not too much, he decided; and when it was done, the whole big job was done. Two complete copies were ready: one neat and beautiful which he had kept going, copying and re-copying as changes were made—official. The original with the interlinings, the crossed spots, the guiding arrows was to be the special Jessy edition.

On a Sunday morning he laid it on the writing table before him, his hands flat on the surface, thinking of the day she would receive it. So he took a clean sheet of music paper and in his clear manuscript printing—large here—wrote in the middle of the page: *This is a special delivery letter from Stephen. Please read it in the music-room as soon as Tom brings it.*

On a second page, he wrote: *Jessy, darling, I wish you would play your three little preludes right now—at least All My Fresh Springs and The Hidden Brook. Perhaps Young Man With His Girl on a Steamboat wouldn't be so good except that it has a lot of the golden thread in it, and you said, "It has a kiss in it." It runs all the way to the end and beyond, you know.*

Maybe that would be all right whether the time came in the morning or the afternoon, but he must not be rigid. He wrote a little more.

*Your prelude for the fourth is ready for you now: Deep River. Leave that for another day perhaps.... Here it is,* the next sheet was headed. *Play it more than once before you go on reading, please. I hope you will like it.*

He wrought that little piece with special intent on that Sunday morning. It would be new to her. Later in the week he made some entries between bars on following pages.

*Jessy, once I heard the famous Negro singers sing Deep River, and they called it Swing Low Sweet Chariot and Nobody Knows the Trouble I've Seen, jubilees. Glory Hallelujah in the middle of rich wild sorrow. My mother died like that. Jubilee.*

*I hope you will study this prelude before the—he* groped for a gentler word but any other sounded mawkish and the fact would be before her—*before the burial. I knew, but I could not tell you during these happy—it* might be years or months or weeks. So he wrote—*happy days. I can tell you better this way; your sensitive fingers will listen; and your mind—that deep passion-mind of yours—will interpret what neither of us could put into language.*

*Once you asked about my mother's grave. I didn't go there somehow after the first. Headstones are all right for the little time they stand or last. But where her strong bones are dissolving is not important. Nor the gold ear-rings she gave me for my bride. (They are in the little trunk.) Your mother left you more than her furred boots and the thin spoons. Everything that makes a woman a woman and beautiful. Everything that fulfills life: the power to see and to love; to bear children. To enjoy to the end of her days. Your days, beloved. To hold the hope of eternal growth.*

He re-read those last lines, wondering if they sounded preachery. They came naturally, though ... like an organ in church. She would be facing the ultimate.

He could write more about how the hidden brook went through every movement and more about the springs that fed the brook—springs of deep, strong, unobserved activity. But the music had said it all and she would know where her great-grandmother belonged in the sonata and her mother and even old Savonarola with his St. Francis eyes. "And she would find herself and me all along the way," he thought with a quick sweet comfort.

So on another day, he added only a few more lines.

*Hans Christian Andersen was a wise man. That's why children love him, for they are the wisest of all. The Bible says so, doesn't it? He knew and the children do too (until their wisdom is dimmed) that enchantment is calamity. The eleven swans and the swineherd must become princes again. ... He knew that the hampered must be freed and the condemned redeemed. I think he would like Bold Water.*

*You were a wise little girl when you pored over that book, Jessy, and so was your gay little mother. And there was redemption for the dancer in the red shoes.*

He hoped he had said enough and not too much.

The Jessy edition, neatly hinged, followed, the Jessy titles lettered in red ink.

Tom would bring her the official copy later—using his judgment as to when she was ready. Stephen wrote out his directions:

"This is my will, I guess, Jessy dear, and with it all my property—*Sonata for Piano in B major.* I hope it has both musical and financial value.

"I want you to be the executrix of my estate as well as my heir. It will be your duty to arrange for and superintend publication with critical advice from others and to receive the royalties. To sit in a box at the premiere!

"Take it to old Wolfgang (full name and address herewith affixed). *Take it,* notice. Not right away necessarily. Wait for the Inner Light. Please say to him 'I am Mrs. Stephen Geddes.' That will be true whatever happens. I think he will kiss you and I hope he does. He will probably ask you to play the piano and he will play. That is his way of carrying on a conversation. He may give you a lesson on the spot.

"Tell him about the sonata and my hope that he will edit it. There will be rough spots if I am pressed for time. He will realize that you can be of real value when he hears you play your preludes. Let him deal with the publishers.

"Tell him about your acting. He knows that Miss What's-her-name whose coaching I told you about. Tell him about the big house and that first note if those matters are still pending ... whatever problems come up. His advice is always wise and kind.

"This will is getting out of hand. So I shall say *hereunto* and *affix* again and close with a big gold kiss, strictly legal, with two little blue ribbons. (I got it from Mr. Atwood.) P.S. Some day if the piece proves to be good and phonographs grow up have a recording made by a concert pianist. Love. S."

# CHAPTER TWENTY-NINE

They never could decide afterward just when it was they became engaged—late February or early March.

"Because we've been engaged to be engaged for so long," Jessy said.

And she could not remember how it came about. After a few words—words lost like a strain of music heard only once and far away—Stephen was putting his mother's ring on her finger as they stood almost formally side by side before the library fire; the lighted candles and the moment made the mantel an altar—the clock and the ornaments blotted out. His left arm was around her and his head was bent above her as he reached across with the ring to her extended hand. As it slipped on, he swung her around close to him in both arms—murmuring brokenly into her hair the platitudes he had longed to say—nothing can ever separate—no matter what happens—belong together. . . .

She could feel the quick beating of his heart and the power of his arms; and then a relaxation drew them apart.

"I am alive," she said suddenly and clearly. "I have begun to live at last. There's a deep strong peace in me. Not a passive resting peace. There is something moving strongly, quietly."

Stephen said nothing for a moment. He stood motionless—his eyes looking over her head at the candle-flames—before he said, "I know. I know. Darling, I know."

"You've known all the time, haven't you? All your life. And you have been waiting for me to find out. . . . You are a prophet. You know that deliverance will come to the captive. Or is it a priest—a priest who brings one to God? You must be. ... You are like Jesus to me. All the things the gospels say he did for people you do for me. And you do it in the same way—by your presence—even by the thought of your presence. Words sometimes. Your hands. ... He laid his hands on them. Your arms—the strength of your body. Do you suppose he ever held a girl in his arms—in a strong quiet peace? ... Is that blasphemous? He took up the little children. He talked about the abundant life."

He sensed no worded meanings—only the rush of her adoration and the music he could hear—the Alleluias, the Glorias, the Nunc Dimittis.

The wedding was on a May morning, late enough that the birches carried little lacy leaves and the spruces wore bright green boutonnieres on their dark suits. Everybody went to the church to see them married. A smaller company came to the wedding breakfast—enough to fill the long table at its longest—silver and white with the tiered cake in the center.

"Just like the one I made for your mother," Lyddy whispered in an odd moment. "And you look just like her in your wedding dress."

It was a friendly and mannerly party with a quality that made the matrons misty-eyed and the girls somewhat subdued.

"Everything was so lovely and they were so perfect together," Louisa said almost tearfully after Jessy had gone up to change her dress.

The little company gathered outside the front door, both its leaves opened wide. Stephen handed Jessy down the broad shallow steps and into the car; Sinbad tucked a plaid rug around her knees and put in a little hamper with their first luncheon in it. There was a big white bow on the handle. They were ready to start.

The girls, gayer now, were singing, "Come with me, Lucile, In my merry Oldsmobile. ... Down the road of life we'll fly. ... On an automobile honeymoon."

Sinbad stayed his hand on the crank until they should finish. Lyddy's swimming eyes were memorizing the picture she saw: the red and brass car brilliantly polished; Jessy's smile under her smart wide hat as she leaned forward from the other side; Stephen's clear features—his wise and quiet eyes—the hat he never wore aloft for a flourish.

It was never flourished. Suddenly, it dropped from his fingers; his hand wandered down to his head, clung there a moment and then fell. His head dropped limply forward on his breast. He was gone before he was lifted from the car, Tom said.

Only once in the hour that followed did Jessy break a dreadful silence. It was when someone trying to be helpful put a hand on the little hamper to begin unpacking the car. She flung up a window and shrieked.

"Don't touch it! Don't touch it! Never touch anything in that car! Leave it as he left it! Always! Stop the clocks! Stop the clocks!"

Tom came back later in the afternoon. He guessed he had better see Jessy now, he said.

"I don't know," Lyddy said. "I don't know. She doesn't answer—doesn't hear. Just sits in her chair."

"Which room?"

"I got her upstairs but she won't lie down."

She took him to Jessy's door. Without knocking he went in.

"Jessy," he said. There was no movement in her body and no flicker in her face.

"Stephen—" he began, again.

She moaned a little.

He spoke again—authoritatively. "Look, Jessy!" He held out the pile of music sheets with Stephen's handwriting before her eyes.

He saw her eyes focus on the little note in the middle of the page—saw her spasmed body relax in a long quiver. Then he left the room.

He stood quietly for a few minutes with Lyddy in the hall. She clung to his hand as she wept—wept for Jessy and for Stephen.

"I wish she could go with him," she said.

He did not answer but he held tighter to her hand.

Jessy was coming down the stairs with the packet held close to her side. She passed them without notice and down the hall to the music-room.

Lyddy sat down on a tall straight chair and covered her contorted face in her hands, her vigorous back bowed in an arc of grief. Tom still waited by fhe door.

She raised her head a little, listening, her hands still in the position of support.

"She's playing the piano," she whispered loudly.

"Yes," said Tom. "It's his piece."

The music grew surer and stronger.

"It's kind of comforting," said Lyddy.

"Yes," Tom replied. "It'll help her a lot. First, she can do some crying. Don't try to stop her."

Jessy woke early in the morning. There was something she wanted to do for Stephen. As she went down the stairs, she wondered if she had ever told him about the locust she and little Eugene had watched as his wings came out like fans and opened in iridescence. She hoped she had.

She wanted to find Sinbad and did in the library. As she opened the door, he waited for her to enter before he left.

"Not now, Sinbad. Come outdoors with me."

The car was standing at the foot of the steps as she had directed. She could see the white bow on the basket handle.

"Please help me carry in these things, Sinbad."

He let her load up with coats, the rug, the basket, the smaller bags—make two or three trips. He took in the heavier pieces afterwards.

She waited for him outside.

"Now if you will crank her up, I'll back her into the carriage-house."

The roar of the motor brought Lyddy to her window. Jessy was backing the car more expertly than Stephen's lessons had ever seen her do. Lyddy's tears flowed again—different tears this time, though.

Jessy walked quietly up the steps.

"You didn't stop the clocks, did you, Sinbad?"

"No, I didn't guess you really wanted them stopped."

"No, I didn't really."

It was Sunday at six in the morning. The bell was ringing across the bold water. Jessy listened acutely as long as it rang.

DAVIDA MCCASLIN